The
IMPOSSIBLE
SHORE

A Story Cycle

Marc Porter Zasada

Upper Story Press
www.upperstorypress.com

Book Website: www.impossibleshore.com
Publicity: Screenfire Media LLC, info@screenfiremedia.com

ISBN: 978-0-578-88585-8 (pbk)

Upper Story Press is a Division of Upper Story Arts

First Upper Story Press Edition: June 2021

eBook Available on Kindle Books
Distributors: trade paperback available through KDP
Cover and interior design by Rafael Andres

In memory of my father, Arthur S. Zasada,
who taught me to read Thoreau
and to believe in the infinite expectation of the dawn.

Acknowledgements & Notes

*A Story Cycle progresses in much the same way
as a novel: it's important to read the tales in order.*

Thanks to my mother, Yvette L. Zasada, for her sanity, her love, and her sense of adventure.

To my wife, Martine Porter Zasada, for her steadfast love and her ceaseless desire to see more deeply.

To David Charles Deller, for a conversation on the seawall at Saint-Malo in 1978, in which he explained that things matter.

To my children, Max, Sofi, Pace, and Leo for teaching me that things matter even more.

To Reb Mimi Feigelson, for her friendship, and for the principal ideas in "The Freedom of the Dead."

To my readers and editors, Shannon Lee Clair, Tom Lane, Linda Hepner, and Martine Porter Zasada for their invaluable feedback.

To the Storm Weather Shanty Choir, who sing "A Hundred Years."

To Christian Williams, sailor and author, for inspiration, and for some of the ideas expressed by sailors in "The Birth of Noah - Part II."

To Josh Silvera, for adding music to "Stop Asking" and helping refine the lyrics.

To the Moody Blues, for a fleeting glimpse.

An earlier version of "The Birth of Noah - Part I" first appeared in *The Antioch Review* as "Letters to America." "The Bright Forest" first appeared in *Aquifer*, the *Florida Review online*. "The Productions of Time" first appeared in *Big Fiction*.

CONTENTS

PROLOGUE

We like to think of each moment in our lives as a kind of birth canal, taking us kicking and screaming from the past into the future.

But it's not true.

We do not leave the past to move into the future. It's more like past and future stand ever side by side, fighting and embracing like lovers. We are the child caught unhappily between, siding sometimes with the one parent, and sometimes with the other. Torn as they pull us back and forth with terrifying violence, moment to moment, hour to hour.

The future, of course, seeks total victory. It attacks all previous assumptions, all stated reasons, and everything it considers childhood—which covers pretty much everything we have ever done.

Although its victory is never assured, the future does, of course, usually win. That's because the past suffers from an enormous burden. No matter how much it fears the future, chastises the future, or tries to bully the future—the past knows that the future represents the very purpose of its own existence. The past knows it must ever try to seduce, and even to love the future; while the future knows it need never try to love the past at all.

Day by day, century by century, the past cries out to the future: "Do not set aside my beauty, my desires, and my carefully constructed truths, even as you try to take my precious child to some impossible shore."

VISIONS

The TREMENDOUS MOUNTAIN
Part I

As the hand held before the eye conceals the greatest mountain, so the little earthly life hides from the glance the enormous lights and mysteries of which the earth is full—and he who can draw it away from before his eyes, as one draws away a hand, beholds the great shining of the inner worlds.

—Nachman of Breslov

Unlikely as it seemed for a man like Mickey Kohl to be granted a vision, one nevertheless came to him on a pleasant Tuesday afternoon. Mickey himself immediately recognized it as more than a dream. After all, he was sitting wide awake on a bench in Central Park on a perfectly clear April day, and had just moments before polished off a turkey and pastrami club. The only warning came when a lively breeze played in from the east, and the leaves on the elms fluttered a brilliant spring green.

At thirty-one, Mickey Kohl was working for his brother Karl, who owned three delis: two Midtown and a fancier one on Amsterdam above Eightieth. He had never considered himself the religious type and he had completed only two years of City College. Unlike most people granted visions, he was neither a great man nor a simple peasant. He wasn't at war or in a passionate romance, though he had an on-again/off-again thing with a woman named Frances. Besides the job with his brother, the only slightly interesting fact about Mickey was that he owned an apartment in Brooklyn with a limited view of the East River. He didn't even hate his brother. Well, didn't hate him much.

At 3:16 pm on this particular Tuesday, Mickey crumpled the bag that had held the club sandwich and tossed it neatly into a nearby bin. He hadn't bought a newspaper, and he'd forgotten his phone, so at 3:17 he glanced at his watch, decided he still had a few minutes, and began just staring across the mowed grass, and up through the elms toward the upper floors of The Dakota.

At that moment, the wind picked up, the leaves began to flash, and suddenly, the world broke into pinpricks of color, like a pointillist painting. For a moment Mickey worried that something had happened to his eyes. And then suddenly he was staring not across a Central Park lawn, but across a broad, sunny meadow in some vast and unknown place. The only consistent object was the bench, which had apparently come along for the ride.

Immediately he noticed that the new landscape was dominated by a tremendous snow-capped mountain, which had taken the place of The Dakota. At the feet of this mountain appeared a rushing river which used to be Central Park West. Both mountain and river were strangely close by, in an unreal sort of way. So close that he could see the detailed crags and escarpments way up at the peak. He could pinpoint the passes where a high and unheard wind blew snow horizontally off into space. If he wanted, he could have counted the little trees clinging to the black and nearly vertical cliffs. The mountain was exciting and terrifying, improbably alone and unclouded: just exquisitely there.

"Gee," said Mickey. For the mountain seemed strangely familiar. Perhaps from a documentary or a dream.

The river was also familiar, and perhaps derived from a drawing in some children's book he'd read, way back when. Or maybe a video game. Or a movie—certainly it didn't seem quite real. Mickey did not startle or move from the bench when the vision appeared. He just let his eyes travel up into the mountain in a leisurely way, drawn to its beauty. And then down to the banks of the river, roaring loudly through the meadow like traffic.

Just to be clear, Mickey was still aware that he sat in Central Park. He knew that if he looked away and back again quickly or blinked rapidly, the vision would disappear, and he would again see the big granite boulders rising from the lawns and The Dakota peeking through the elms. If he moved, the river would disappear behind the trees and become again Central Park West. The vision simply filled his mind like an overlay: like a spectacular, if transparent projection across mere reality.

"Well," he thought. "What does this mean?"

When he could tear his eyes away from the glorious heights of the mountain, he could see that the meadow at his feet was not in fact empty. In the distance, just off to his right, three white horses ran in a wild and angry circle, as if on a track. If he concentrated, he could catch the sounds of these horses snorting and crying out.

It was odd how the angry horses ran in a circle, he thought, round and round, oblivious to the rest of the beautiful meadow, the river, or the mountain. Then, just as this thought crossed his mind, one of the horses broke away from the other two and galloped magnificent-ly across the long grass, stopping suddenly right up at his bench. It snorted madly. And yet more angrily, it bucked. He could see its flar-ing nostrils and its straining, maddened eyeballs. The horse looked from him to The Tremendous Mountain (as Mickey began to call it), and he saw at once the desperate longing in its eyes, and he knew that the horse wished to cross the river, reach the mountain, and climb it. And just when he realized all this, the great beast turned and ran headlong and helter-skelter toward the roaring river.

"No!" he wanted to cry. But before he could say or do anything, the horse, with one swift motion, launched itself into the river and was swept away. He saw it struggle only briefly in the powerful current as it was taken downstream, lost forever.

The other two white horses continued in their circle, chasing one another's tails yet angrily and ceaselessly, and for a time Mickey watched them in terror, worried that they would break away and follow the first.

"Good Lord," he said aloud. "What kind of vision is this?"

And then, the vision was gone. Poof, just like that, the Tremendous Mountain, the meadow, the horses, and the river dissolved. The elms and the Dakota returned. He tried to conjure the vision anew, but soon our hero was forced to acknowledge the more solid truth of Central Park: Strolling workers. Bicyclists. Tourists. Light breeze. He reached up and wiped his neck and found himself sweating. Then he gathered his strangely weak legs into some kind of motion and headed back to work.

When he arrived at the office, situated above the Original Kohl's Delicatessen on Fortieth just off Lexington, Mickey's brother Karl knew immediately that something was wrong.

"You look like yesterday's laundry," said Karl. It was a phrase he'd used before. Maybe he'd even coined it.

In a normal mood, Mickey would have ignored the comment, but he was not in a normal mood. The vision of the Mountain had a terrifying effect, and the death of the horse shook him deeply. He felt not elated by having a vision, but saddened, and he thought carefully about the tone of Karl's voice. He recognized it as the familiar, patronizing, older-brother tone of voice which implied that Mickey was not entirely reliable, not sufficiently ambitious, and not completely committed to the deli business. All of which Mickey knew to be true.

For a couple hours Mickey threw himself into reconciling a series of shipment errors from a supplier, and he composed a tersely worded email, along with a spreadsheet clearly demonstrating three blatant mistakes in the invoice. He ran out to the drugstore to get nail clippers. He called his sometime girlfriend Frances to make small talk and confirm their date for the following Saturday night. He called a plumber about a persistent problem in his apartment and argued with the co-op president about who should pay for it. Still, for the rest of the afternoon, the sad mood clung, and he could not get the vision out of his head. In memory, his eyes roamed the forbidding passes of the snowy peak. Its vast ledges of stone. Its dark ravines. From time to time, his ears recalled the cries of the white beasts.

Surely the vision had an obvious and brutal meaning.

That night, alone, Mickey drank tequila from a shot glass and sat by a window, looking out at the sleepless street below his apartment. He felt all wrong—just all wrong. As if he had been doing something naughty and had been caught out. A few vintage Beatles posters graced his walls. His season tickets to the Yankees sat on his dresser. Beyond these accomplishments, he recalled the two great moments in his life: At fourteen his middle school art teacher had praised his sketches, mostly of animals, in front of the whole class—and he'd dreamt briefly, foolishly of becoming an artist. At twenty-four, during his brief career in the military, he and a bunch of buddies had been arrested for a magnificent night of disorderly conduct in Prague, and he had cursed out the military policeman at dawn beside the Vltava. Beyond those two events, and a few forgettable girls, he could claim only the daily joys and tribulations of the city. As often happens to modern people, he realized that nothing really mattered to him.

The next morning, Mickey was distracted and unproductive until about 11:30, when the necessities of his work began to reassert themselves. He went out to lunch by himself and had a couple of drinks and more or less forgot about the vision. In the afternoon he had an argument with the temperamental Georges (possibly not the man's real name), who ran the brothers' fancier deli, "Kohls of Amsterdam" on the Upper West Side. The argument concerned mayonnaise. Karl was drawn into the argument, which was not a good thing. As usual, it turned out to have been Mickey's fault all along. Then he had dry cleaning to pick up, his accountant to call, a problem with sales taxes. Then a dozen even more trivial details came to drive the massive vision back into the secret folds of his soul.

By evening the simple pleasures of life began to return: movies, sports news, alcohol. Two weeks later, he bought a dog. The dog had to be housebroken. It had to go to the vet. It had to be taken for walks. Four weeks later, he had sex with Frances twice in one day, which was an exceptional occurrence. All this was, for a time, enough.

Then, three months later, Mickey went out with Frances—a woman with brown bangs in the dated style of the actress Marlo Thomas—for an evening in the Village. A warm breeze blew, and they held hands. After dinner they wandered down Third Street looking for live music, and chose a place more or less at random: a packed little bar one flight underground that offered a Stygian darkness lit mostly by a few table candles and the green lights of amplifiers. Five musicians had been jammed onto a tiny stage. The lead singer was a young man who wore dark eyeliner and sang stripped to the waist. His long blond hair swung stringy and wild. His skin gleamed sweaty and white in the half-light. He wore extravagant tattoos. Two raucous guitars, a bass, and a drum set backed him up, though they could hardly be seen.

When Mickey and Frances entered, the band was in the middle of a frenetic rendition of the classic "Whole Lotta Love," and the singer was in the deep throes of the song, his eyes flashing. Mickey had the strange sensation of having forgotten something. He and Frances sat at the bar and she felt his soul move far away from her.

We'll talk about Frances another time. Despite the awful bangs, she was actually an impressive woman.

"It's too loud," said Frances. But Mickey's soul was already so distant that he did not hear her say it. Then, when the singer flung himself into a passionate scream and leapt to one side, our hero was suddenly back in the vision.

The Tremendous Mountain again dominated the landscape, but this time Mickey was walking toward the remaining two horses across the meadow. What he would do when he got there, he had no idea. As he drew close, he saw they had worn a circular track in the grass, full of mud and droppings. Here the horse smell arrived strangely like the sweat and stale beer smell of a bar. In the same way, the wild motions of the two angry white creatures resembled the wild motions of the lead singer and the bassist. Mickey wondered if he should wonder if he were losing his mind, but he tried to concentrate on the horses. How could he possibly get one of them to follow him? Or allow him to ride? How could he get them both safely across the river, as of course he must? It was even less probable that he and a horse could find a path up the mountain. Just as he was contemplating this impossibility, one of the beasts looked at him in panic, even horror, stopped running in circles, and reared up tall on its hind legs.

"No, no, it's okay," Mickey wanted to shout, but did not, because after all, he knew he actually still sat in a bar. He could see the lather on the horse's neck, and the foam on its mouth, and the terrible red flare of its nostrils and its eyes. Panicked.

Then this second angry horse turned from him and like its brother weeks earlier, ran with huge and thundering strides toward the mountain, oblivious to the river. Oblivious! It stumbled right in, straight out into the current. This time he could hear its screams above the rapids as it was swept away forever. "I gotta whole lotta love, oh!" cried the lead singer. Now there circled only one angry horse. Circling, circling alone.

"What happens when the last one dies?" Mickey wondered, terrified.

"It's too damn loud in here," yelled Frances, bringing him back.

Mickey looked at her, and the vision evaporated. He said nothing, but gulped the rest of his beer and smiled. When Frances made him leave, he walked beside her silently to the subway—afraid he might say something ridiculous. He remembered to kiss her at the turnstile, but did not invite her onto his train. If she was annoyed, he did not notice.

The beers and the music still roared in Mickey Kohl's head as he got back to his apartment in Brooklyn near the Jews. He ran to his closet and pulled out old boxes until he found some of the drawings he had made back in middle school, and could never bring himself to throw out. Here were the faces of his mother, his father. Several trees and birds. A leopard. A dog. He was disappointed to find them all much more stiff and amateurish than he had remembered. Truly, you had to say, nothing but childish and unpromising. Though maybe, if you looked very closely, something angry did come through. Something angry in the line and color. And he remembered the feeling of that anger, from long ago. Indeed, that teenage anger constituted the only truly great and passionate thing he could remember in his life, apart from Prague. Something there, perhaps. He knew from the movies that only a few things could cause God to send a vision of such magnitude. If not art, then what? Religion? Politics? It couldn't be about his relationship with Frances, for that was no great thing. Neither was the deli business. So he sat at the desk by his apartment window with its distant, partially blocked view of the river, and found a pencil. He was too scared to sketch a horse, so he turned to a clean page in the yellowed, twenty-year-old sketchbook and tried to sketch his new dog, a young retriever, sleeping by the door.

He felt himself in a Hollywood movie: maybe he was about to experience that kind of moment of realization. But the sketch immediately took on an unsatisfyingly cartoonish shape. Childish. He plugged headphones into loud music and pulled out a bottle of tequila and used it to help him focus.

Anger, he thought. *Anger is a tremendous thing.*

The next day Mickey rolled into work a full two hours late, haggard and hung over. He had missed an important call with the state tax board. They would not reschedule the call for six weeks, which would cause a problem at the bank. Worse, the temperamental manager, the supposed *Georges*, had left a message on the office phone saying that he had quit the deli on Amsterdam. Karl had been trying to reach both Georges and Mickey unsuccessfully. Mickey would have to cover for Georges, said Karl. In fact, Mickey would have to get his ass right over there. Mickey seemed to have a hard time following all this. At one point, Karl said, "What gives, Mick? You awake?"

Mickey finally got his ass over to Amsterdam, where the staff seemed to be standing around waiting for instructions. "What instructions?" he yelled. "Open up! Open up! You know what to do." And he began rattling at the cash register, which he did not entirely know how to operate. The lead stock boy, Mateo, twenty-two, was uncovering the salads from yesterday, but he wasn't sure if they were fresh—Georges had always told him which were fresh and which should be thrown out. Mickey told Mateo to throw them all out and start over, which made Mateo angry. This was stupid. A huge amount of unnecessary work and expense. Mateo swore in Spanish.

Through all this Mickey tried to hold on to the image of the sleeping dog and work it in his head. He had twelve drafts of the drawing in the sketchbook he had thrown into a backpack, now slung carelessly atop a pile of torn boxes behind the counter at the deli. The drafts had started out mawkish and clumsy, but had become progressively more abstract as the night had worn on. Still clumsy, but less mawkish, he thought: such is the advantage of an abstract. Were they really "abstract" or just "muddy"? How could he tell? He knew fucking nothing about art. It was ridiculous to think that could just, well— Fuck! Even so, the dog looked angrier and angrier in its sleep. "If it's not dangerous, it's not art," his teacher had said, way back when he was fourteen. "If it's not dangerous, it's not art," he repeated under his breath, and tried to make the dog look dangerous.

Around 1:30 in the afternoon, Mickey left the cash register and dragged the sketchbook into the stockroom and redrew the dog's eyes with a pencil. Now they were tightly shut, not so much in sleep as in concentration. The dog dreamt a fierce dream. The light here was bad, so he went and sat in a far corner, behind a big stack of boxes, mostly canned tomatoes, where he could see his work in a dusty glow from a window. What was there of wild horse, and of wild-eyed lead singer, in a sleeping dog? When the dog awoke, what would it do? Bite someone?

He let his hatred of his brother grow, and for a moment, he was happy.

Indeed, at that very moment, Karl tried calling him. But Mickey had left his mobile on the counter back out front. He was always leaving it somewhere. Mateo picked up the phone, saw that Karl was calling, and went looking for Mickey, first in the office, and then down the hall to the stockroom.

Ring, ring, ring.

And lo, it came to pass that the rest of Mickey's life hung on this brief search in the back of a deli. If Mateo walked into the stock room and actually found him behind the stacked boxes, mostly of canned tomatoes, within the next seven seconds; and if Mateo managed to hand Mickey the phone before it stopped ringing; then Mickey would be distracted by Karl's harsh words, and he would never be able to answer the question about the sleeping dog, or entirely recall what the question had been. The last wild horse would run into the river, the meadow would be empty, his life would continue more or less the same, and he would die a cheerless bachelor.

If, on the other hand, Mateo failed to find him before the phone stopped ringing, Mickey would spend the next nine years of his life trying to lead that last metaphorical wild horse through the river. He would try to ride it to the top of the Tremendous Mountain. And in that effort, his life as he now knew it would be lost.

Ring, ring, went the phone. Search, search, went an irritated Mateo.

The PRODUCTIONS
of TIME

The road of excess leads to the palace of wisdom.

Drive your cart and your plough
  over the bones of the dead.
Prudence is a rich ugly old maid
  courted by Incapacity.
He who desires but acts not, breeds pestilence.

The cut worm forgives the plough.

The hours of folly are measured by the clock,
  but of wisdom no clock can measure.
If the fool would persist in his folly
  he would become wise.

Eternity is in love with the productions of time.

—Proverbs of Hell, from
"The Marriage of Heaven and Hell,"
William Blake, 1790

When he was twelve, he was already Red Peters, but he was a boy soprano. Gentle of face and freckle, he had a soft glow in his scarlet hair, or so it seemed, wherever he went. Red was the darling of Miss Tomlinson, choir director at the East Lawrence Middle School in the Bronx. Miss Tomlinson, who had ambitions, tended to choose works a little too hard for her troupe of seventh and eighth graders, especially as she had them for only two years, best case. Often her ambitions proved an embarrassment at recitals, when an otherwise perfectly good Bach was slaughtered as a sacrifice to high culture. But Red! He would get the solo bits and sing like a messenger from Heaven, holding the sopranos together as he looked Miss Tomlinson straight in the eye, his face intelligent with concentration, his voice spot-on. And if the sopranos held, the other parts didn't matter all that much really. Naturally, in later years Miss Tomlinson spoke frequently of her time with Red, and stood one of his publicity stills, lovingly framed, on her mantelpiece—even if he had not responded when she had tried to contact him, no less than five times.

Red did, of course, remember Miss Tomlinson, even when he became *the* Red Peters. He had received her messages through his agent. But he had avoided her along with everyone from his past, because *the only fucking thing* he cared to recall from those years, and remember often, was that one concert, near to Christmas, when Miss Tomlinson's little choir stood on the steps of the Metropolitan Museum of Art to unleash sixteeenth century madrigals on unsuspecting passersby.

You see, forty seconds of that afternoon had changed everything.

East Lawrence was last on the program, the kids were tired and antsy, and in general, their performance was worse than usual. But during "Shepherds Awake," right after the first repeat, all four parts came miraculously into both tune and synchronization. As genuine music arose from the ragged choir, time seemed to stand still. In this magical suspension, Red saw how the pillars of the great museum stood forth in regular majesty above their heads, how the great shadows marched down Fifth Avenue as they moved toward evening, how the sun chose this tree and ignored that, how the traffic could be seen to move in dance—and for a few forever minutes, Red was filled with wonder at the universal order of all things.

It was an order which spread out from the museum as a complex, but comprehensible map. He saw how the madrigal both expressed that order and existed within its confines.

And then he saw how it was within his power to *break free* of both the madrigal and the order. "This," he thought, "would be greater yet." And for forty seconds, he allowed himself to soar entirely unrestrained. In his head he heard a higher counter-melody, not written into the score, and his strong little soprano improvised like a great bird taking flight. A dark bird, that is, in a startlingly related, but minor key, full of jagged blue notes. This dark bird soared laughingly, mockingly over the madrigal, over the museum steps, over the spectators, over Fifth Avenue and over the city itself. People turned in alarm, as the world did not sound like Christmas any more.

During this strange but musically brilliant rebellion, Red broke eye contact with Miss Tomlinson and looked inward. Indeed, he allowed himself to grow unaware even of the *existence* of Miss Tomlinson, who did not, after all, fit within the suddenly discovered universe of his own making. At the tender age of twelve, Red Peters saw how easy it *was to win the game. As in completely win the whole fucking game.* And when the piece finally ended, and Miss Tomlinson caught his eye with a look of blank incomprehension, he gave her what can only be described as a mean little smile.

After that, of course, Red dropped choir entirely so he could perfect his guitar work and focus exclusively on a specialized form of contemporary song called "heavy metal." By fifteen he had lost his virginity in his girlfriend's parents' bedroom as *Paranoid* by Black Sabbath played in the background.

At sixteen Red left home with a forty-year-old who had a tattoo of a scorpion on her left breast. With this move he felt, perhaps correctly, that he was embracing chaos wholeheartedly. He felt *unbound.* The next two decades exploded. And by his thirty-fifth birthday, anyone would agree that Red Peters was one of the world's leading representatives of chaos. It was his job. When he stood at a microphone, clothed in sweat and ragged glitter, lifted his Stratocaster and stated his worst intentions, chaos was not just celebrated, it was *conjured*. It was brought into the world *bitching and screaming*. Or so believed the 20,000 fans in his average crowd as they lifted their glowing phones for a shot of Red unbound.

Indeed, Red Unbound was the title of the present tour, though of course, it offered only the illusion of chaos. In truth, each show in each city was a carefully controlled event. Before Red's arrival in Chicago, for example, a dozen unionized workers had been toiling five days to construct the stage, perfect the sound system, tune the lighting. Vendors had carefully laid out the Bitching & Screaming t-shirts, stocked up the beverages, hosed down the snack pavilions. Contracts bound Mr. Peters, his touring band, the promoters, the people who wrote his backing tracks, cut his famous hair, and arranged his lodging. Two lawyers tracked everyone's deliverables, three accountants tracked expenses. Security was, of course, exquisitely tight. Much as a ride in an amusement park offers the safe illusion of danger, so did Red Peters offer the safe specter of chaos. When he cried out:

> *Up to it, up to it, get on up to the start,*
> *Lay yourself on the steeple top,*
> *Stop asking for the devil man,*
> *It's me gonna shoot a hole in your punkshit heart...*

... he meant it only metaphorically.

Tonight, after the last encore of a three-night Soldier Field run, and now leaping from the stage wet, hoarse, and briefly happy, Red looked for release. The adrenaline had to drain. The coke had to run out. Now was the time, as he said, *to fall apart*. This too was part of his job: to rest the chaos generator for the next show, a week hence in Atlanta. He would go fall apart, probably gracelessly, even as the stage hands moved into the still-lit stadium to gather up the enormous equipment, the sets, and the spent pyrotechnics; even as the crowd, having fulfilled its own mission of release, filtered into the wee hours of the city.

Out in the big world, other workers slept while preparing for their jobs as bakers, bankers, brokers, or limo drivers. And often the whole system worked beautifully: Generally, all men and women were *bound.* But briefly, all men and women could believe themselves *un-bound.* And often, instead of actually killing one another, or raping one another, or screaming down midnight streets, the fire of chaos within each human heart could be wonderfully torched to life; all the Miss Tomlinsons of the world could be overcome in one fatal blow; each man or woman's flame could be found to burn still brightly; and then that flame could be ignored once again so that the world might continue.

A great deal, however, depended on Red—and he knew it. Always, when the drugs and adrenaline wore off, fear moved in. What if one night, the fire failed to catch? What if one night, the crowd just stood and stared? This vision haunted him, woke him at three a.m. It was the reason he usually had to get plastered before he went on, or tried to write a new song. Or lately, even to rehearse. During such times, he had to *not care* whether or not he succeeded as a demon. When he was plastered, he could *just be* the fucking demon, as he liked to say. Sometimes it helped if there were people around to worship him. To tell him he was a genius. To let him take them to bed. To limit his drug and alcohol intake. But sometimes it didn't help, for sometimes he found himself loathing these people, and sometimes trying to live up to their expectations, and sometimes having just really too much sex with them, and sometimes not believing a word they said. Worst of all, Red Peters often felt he was faking it: *just pretending* to be Red Peters and to represent chaos. That it was *all an act.* That he was now *just imitating* the younger Red Peters of five or six years earlier, who would soon be forgotten. Worse, he knew that when it came *right fucking down to it,* he was alone in the world: when it came right fucking down to it, *he couldn't trust anyone's punkshit heart.*

And so it happened that come 1:10 a.m., after running around manically backstage hugging the band, kissing the bald spot on the head of his manager, pulling down the blouse and kissing the (surprisingly untattooed) breasts of a woman who might be his current girlfriend; after eating a huge roast beef sandwich and drinking champagne and pissing grandly out the window of his dressing room onto the parking lot below, Red Peters became depressed and locked the door. The crowd had seemed perceptibly older. He had not written a song in five months. His manager had been an ass earlier in the evening, chewing him out for taking too many bennies before a show, causing him to forget whole verses. The tantrum was no doubt a ruse to hide the way the manager was ripping Red off. Not to mention that Red's back hurt even worse than the night before. Two fingers on his left hand were bleeding. He was pretty sure the coke had been spiked with something nasty. His mother was dying of some autoimmune disease he'd forgotten the name of, but she wouldn't speak to him. He'd had a weird red welt on his neck for a week that he hadn't told anyone about. The list went on and on until he remembered, gratefully, that it was *time to fall apart. Time to shut 'er down for the night. Time to 'ave a drink and get some sleep, mate,* he told himself in that fake English accent he used when he needed to remind himself that he was a fucking rock star. And lo, there appeared a bottle of English gin, as if by magic, in his left hand. He took it to the couch in the dressing room, where he collapsed all sweaty in his ragged, yet skin-tight stage glitter, tearing a couple of seams in the process. This was, at first, a sleep without dreams. His manager had to get the janitor to unlock the door, and two stagehands to carry *the famous scarlet idiot* down to the limo, and then two grunts from the Hyatt Hotel to haul Red into a back entrance and up a service elevator to his room, where his manager and the woman who might be his current girlfriend got him undressed and into bed. It was too much to ask the two of them to haul the hairy and naked singer into the shower, even though he stank like Hell.

The manager, whose name was Alan Cork (leading to many ribald jokes from Red), wasn't sure whether he should let the girlfriend sleep there, even though she claimed that Red had begged her to. Cork hadn't known her long enough to decide if she was one of the safe ones, and in the end, he decided no.

This proved to be a mistake, for Red Peters was left alone. And lo again, the Representative of Chaos, bobbing like a wayward dinghy on a mix of drugs, lying filthy between the clean sheets of the Executive Suite, his body drained by the wicking of tremendous energies from thousands of desperate citizens, did begin to dream.

He dreamt first of Heaven and then of Hell.

Heaven looked a good deal like Tuolumne Meadows, high up in Yosemite, which he had once visited while on tour. He was standing by a river, much like the North Fork of the Tuolumne as it tumbles gently through wide grasses beneath great mountains. It was a sweet summer afternoon. Men in tuxedos sat at baby grand pianos spaced gracefully along the banks of the gentle river, far into the distance. They were playing Mozart. Indeed, they were playing Mozart with a sense of joyful inevitability. As sometimes happened in his dreams, Red himself was again twelve years old, with his sense of wonder still intact. "Mozart," he reflected, with all the happiness of revelation, "represents eternity: ever occurring anew, yet ever the same." For what seemed a forever, he wandered along the river, smiling shyly at the pianists.

After 20 minutes, however, it was time to dream of Hell.

Tuolumne Meadows disappeared, and Hell proved to be not a *place* at all, as a *place* would be far too safe and predictable for the most terrible fate of humankind. No, Hell began with three women talking at the same time, shouting and gesturing about things unsettling or perhaps annoying. They might have been from a film by Almodóvar, but Red could not make out a word. And then something else, he wasn't sure what, began with a dirty snowstorm or perhaps a fall of ash, but just when he was almost sure it was something he should understand, a big organ came in, pipes quite loud—or maybe it was an organ of the body, possibly the pancreas, wrapped in a dull newspaper from an organization which told him something which many persons agreed with, persons who might have been Swedish. Or not. In any case, due to the noise, he couldn't get a thought together, *any thought*, much less a tune, and certainly not Mozart, put together. Not considering that his left hand was handicapped by the cane he had to walk with, or perhaps the caning he was receiving— or maybe he was actually in Cuba, stripped to the waist in a terrible summer sun, harvesting sugar cane with a hundred other sad men, singing a work song to which he could not remember the words.

Did that make sense? Like chaos itself, no doubt not.

In his bed he sweated and clutched the pillow. In his dream, he was only certain of one thing: he should *ask someone who knew,* but then he wasn't certain that would be the right move at all—as suppose maybe he was just supposed to listen. And then it was night and he was horribly not alone on Hollywood Boulevard, as he had wished to be, but followed by a gang of youth or perhaps police with nightsticks—but he could not see properly. It was, at least, *a place*. And they drove him at last, with some relief, into another actual place, a store called "Aunt May's Antiques."

Aunt May's was the kind of musty little antiques shop you find in small towns in the South—and like the Tardis, which he normally worshipped, but not this time, bigger on the inside than the outside, a space packed floor-to-ceiling with a confusion of bric-a-brac and the entire lost effort of humankind: lamps in the shape of the Eiffel Tower, light switches in the form of Mickey Mouse, serving bowls shaped like artichokes, elaborate signs for cigar shops, tin fire engines for children, old guns for old men, old hats for old women, serving platters shaped like loaves-and-fishes and ears of corn, along with hideous watercolors of the Grand Canyon.

The great noise of Hell did not abate. The cheap objects seemed somehow *made* of the noise. And Red, who did manage *one goddam thought in Hades,* thought only of how all the people who had made all that cheesy crap were lucky to be dead.

Unlike, say, himself.

After twenty minutes of Hell, Red awoke, terrified. It was mostly dark, with just a sliver of light from somewhere. He felt that an enormous amount of time had passed, but the glowing clock on the nightstand read just 2:42. The clock was a clue that he was, as so often happened, in a hotel room, and now he saw with relief that the sliver of light was coming from a partly open bathroom door. No doubt Corky had left the light on in the bathroom so he could find it. This much, at least, was as it should be. He roused himself out of the bed, stumbled toward the light as toward a revelation, and began to shout when the shower came out cold.

Unfortunately, however, even though he was pretty sure he was awake, Red could not remember Heaven, and could not shake the memory of Hell. *Could not shake the fucking memory of Hell.* It haunted him with its many voices, far too many of which, he was almost certain, were familiar. A haunting mediocrity of voices. Of fucking everyone faking honest emotion to produce rapidly antiqued kitsch.

"Oh. My. God." he said aloud.

He wondered if he were having a drug event of some kind, and found that a bit of a comfort. A drug event, after all, was something familiar. When it came down to it, however, the only thought which could now fully form in his head was his oldest and most familiar thought of suicide.

Suicide was a thought which had been with him since he could remember. You might even say that Old Joe Suicide was his only truly reliable friend, a buddy to whom he felt especially close when booze or coke were wearing off and bringing on a PDD: a Post-Drug Depression. As usual, he pictured a headline in the music press like, "Red Peters Slits Wrists After Amazing Concert: Obviously Wanted to Go Out at His Peak." Nobody carried razors around anymore, and the windows on the 10th floor of the Hyatt were sealed, but fortunately, room service had never cleared the dinner tray. He grabbed a steak knife and went to wash it off in the sink—it wouldn't do to use a dirty knife. Should he write a suicide note? Not so easy, as it turned out: nothing but a cutesy pad of paper in the fucking drawer and a ballpoint that didn't function. In his luggage, he found only a thick black marking pen he'd used to scribble on his shipping boxes.

The note would be awkward, at best.

You will be shocked to learn that the woman who might be Red's current girlfriend had the name of Crystal, was twenty-two or thirty-two, possessed large breasts, wore trampy clothing, and was not considered bright by others. She had dyed her hair a streaky and uncertain green, she wore three silver rings in her left nostril, and six in her left earlobe. When Alan Cork made her leave Red alone at two a.m., Crystal was steamed, but she dutifully followed the manager down to the lobby, where the band, now in civvies, was having its usual chill-down. There she made a show of joking with the drummer, who was careful not to overstep his bounds. Sometimes he drummed his hands on the bar to keep them occupied.

It was nearly three before Crystal could slip away and head back upstairs.

In the hallway she was lucky to run into Tom Donkins, a young room service guy she'd seen earlier in the night, way, way back before the concert, when she was coming out of Red's door.

"Is that Ed Brown's room?" he'd asked, coyly. "Ed Brown" was Red's usual hotel pseudonym.

"That's right," she had smiled coyly. "I'm Ed's boring wife."

"In town for a convention?" pursued Tom, who was charmingly blond.

"That's right," smirked Crystal, liking this Tom, who was cute in a dorky way. "The Unconventional Convention."

"Right," said Tom, "I hear it'll be cool."

And lo, here he was again in the dead of night, pushing a cart to pick up trays left on the floor outside of doors.

"Oh look, it's Ed Brown's boring wife!" he greeted her.

"Tom, sweetie pie, I left my little door-cardy-thing in the room. Could you be a darling and let me back in?"

"I'm not really supposed to do that if you're not registered to the room, Mrs. Brown."

"Do you want me to start banging on the door and wake Ed, along with half the floor? I'm sure your boss would love that."

And so she was in.

The room was dark, but somehow, instantly, she sensed that something in the universe had shifted. (People were wrong to say that Crystal wasn't bright. She'd just never had the opportunity to use her smarts properly.)

"Red, baby, you in here?" she ventured, but stayed in the entryway of the dark room.

"Who's that?" came a suspicious voice from the bathroom, which was open, but out of sight around a corner.

"It's Crystal," she said loudly, but did not venture forward. "You wanted me to stay, remember?"

There was a pause. "Give me a minute, will you? Or actually, just leave, darling. I want to be alone. Yes, as it turns out, I want to be alone." Red was drifting into his fake English accent again.

"Sure, baby." But she did not move. Instead she watched his wavering shadow, cast into the room.

"I didn't hear you leave."

"No."

"I thought you said you'd leave."

"I will when I see that you're okay."

"I'm okay. I just want to be alone. Like I'm pretty sure *I just said.*"

"What are you doing in the bathroom?"

"What do you mean, what am I doing in the bathroom? What the fuck does that mean? Maybe I'm taking a crap."

"Or maybe not," she said boldly, for she knew something in the universe had shifted.

"Jesus H. Christ."

"Just come out and show me you're okay. Then I'll leave."

"Why don't you think I'm okay?"

"Just show me."

"You've known me what, two weeks?"

"Three, actually. Since Boston."

"I'll call the fucking desk and have you bodily removed. Did Corky send you up here?"

"Red, just show me you're okay."

And with that he stepped out of the bathroom, buck naked, both hands up. His wiry, hairy-but-pink body was covered, head to foot, in the lyrics of *Punkshit Heart,* scrawled wildly with the black marking pen. On his right cheek was the word *Stop* and on his left the word *Asking.* Written backwards. Crystal recognized the lyrics instantly—and knew they were a pathetic choice for a self-abusive statement, given that the song was nearly ten years old. The steak knife was in his right hand. His left hand was open as if in a gesture of surrender. He was, however, apparently not yet harmed.

"See? I'm fine."

"A naked man holding a steak knife is not fine."

"Oh, the knife?"

"Yeah, the knife."

In a show of yet-youthful defiance, Red Peters improvised. He brought both hands together, raised the steak knife above his head, and leapt straight up in a stage move, ready to plunge the weapon down into his belly like a samurai. But in her heightened state, Crystal was too fast for him. She took three rapid strides and leapt forward, catching Red in midair, and causing the two of them to fall heavily to the well-padded carpeting of the Executive Suite.

As they fell, Red let go of the knife, which flew away with a sharp slap against the wall. Red did not, however, rise to retrieve the knife, or struggle, or even shout. Instead, like Crystal, he just lay back on the comfortable carpet, full length, naked, marked with nearly-ten-year-old lyrics, and breathing heavily. At last he said:

"I had a dream about Hell."

"No kidding?"

"Seriously. It was terrifying."

"Was it like, a cavern with fire?"

"No. I'm not sure I'd remember, though. Something like an antiques shop."

"With, like, spooky porcelain dolls?" asked Crystal. "I always get freaked out by those old-fashioned porcelain dolls."

"I don't remember any dolls. There were a lot of other things though, and people talking. I wanted to shut them all up so I could think. But I could not."

He said it with such seriousness that she felt compelled to reply, "It does sound like Hell. Maybe you were really there."

"It's not a 'there,' that's part of the problem." He paused briefly, unable to explain this remark. "I'm afraid to die, Crystal." he said finally. "But just think how quiet it would be."

"Everyone's afraid to die, baby. It's like....reasonable. And *everyone* thinks how wonderfully quiet it could be. That's not unusual at all."

"Really?"

"Yes. Absolutely reasonable. And normal to want to die for the peace and quiet. I mean, if it *is* quiet. It's fucked if it's not."

"You're not treating me like an idiot," noted Red.

"Are you an idiot?" asked Crystal.

"No," said Red. "I'm really not. I'm actually quite bright. Did you know that I started out singing classical?"

"Like, Mozart?"

He looked at her quizzically. And then she became the first person he ever told the story about Miss Tomlinson and the madrigal on the steps of the Met. With all the hundreds of interviews he'd done, he'd never said a word about that afternoon. He'd kept that one single thing to himself. Because unlike, say, his first sexual encounter listening to *Paranoid,* which he had related many, many times, his afternoon on the steps on the Met was personal. He and Miss Tomlinson were the only ones who knew. The other kids were too young or stupid to remember. Crystal did not interrupt, but when he was finished, he wasn't sure he'd done the right thing telling her until she said, "Ah," and asked no further questions.

This made him somewhat interested in her.

"Is that your real name, Crystal?"

"No. Is Red Peters your real name?"

"It is, actually. Well, Richard. But even my mother called me Red. Though I'm no longer sure that I *am* Red Peters. Maybe he died, like, a few years ago, and now I'm just filling in for him."

His angst was tedious, even stereotypical. And at that moment, she could have said many things. She could have called him a poser and gotten thrown out. Or she could have said the things everyone said: *Oh don't talk like that, Red. You're just tired. I'm sure you'll feel better in the morning. Everyone loves you, Red.* But instead she said:

"Why is *that* unusual? Nobody's really the name they use in public. That's just, you know...standard."

"Really?"

"Of course. You're not that different from anybody else."

This made him smile. "Are you sure?"

"Absolutely certain," she replied, matter-of-factly. "You play Red Peters to make a living. Duh. Five afternoons a week, I play a cashier at the Walmart, all the way until closing. Seriously, I wear, like a uniform. Mostly, I play Crystal, and I'm not ashamed to admit it. Otherwise, how would *anything* work? I mean, we'd all just be completely *helpless.*"

Then she yawned. When she got tired, her speech patterns generally declined. "If I fall asleep, do you promise you won't try to kill yourself again until sometime, like, after two p.m.? I mean, like, after you talk to your manager or someone? Otherwise, I'll have to, like, call 911, and neither of us will get any goddam sleep."

"Okay, I promise," said Red. "Not till after two p.m."

"Good." And then some time passed in quiet until the sound of their breathing took over, and they slept side by side right there on the carpet: Red naked, but marked with his lyrics. Crystal marked by her trampy clothing.

R ed awoke first, and realized with some relief that he had not dreamt again. Sunlight entered in a sharp and menacing halo around the hotel blackout curtains. He saw Crystal, and the sight of her soothed him, and he recalled his promise about waiting until after 2 p.m. to commit suicide. He meant to honor the request, and needed to check the time. He even tried not to wake her as he stood.

When he saw the marking pen all over his naked body, it actually shocked him. Though he did have a vague memory of writing *something* all over himself, it was depressing as crap to see *Punkshit Heart* instead of some brilliant new lyric. The only cool part was the way the two words *Stop Asking* were written large, right across his face. It couldn't have been easy to make that come out the right direction, doing it by himself in front of a mirror. Or wait...it was only right when you saw it in a mirror. And he stood for a time in the bathroom, checking it out. Indeed, after he dressed in a long sleeve shirt and jeans to hide the rest of the lyrics, he found his phone, returned to the bathroom, shot a selfie in the big mirror, and posted the pic without explanation to social media for his fans. *Idiot,* he thought to himself, *I could have recorded a suicide note. Never mind a goddam pen.*

Momentarily inspired, he went to the bed and picked up an acoustic guitar and his little portable recording machine and tried to write a song. After a while, he gave up.

Then he took a couple of pills he thought were for hangover, and added a couple more. But he was right that the cocaine had been spiked with something nasty. The gin was still in his system. And the pills, alas, were not for hangover. So after he staggered back into the bedroom, took a pillow off the bed, and laid himself ever so gently back down beside the surprisingly sweet and intelligent Crystal, he fell into a coma that lasted six years.

Naturally, the selfie went viral.

Indeed, the phrase *Stop Asking* became not just a meme people used to label tens of thousands of creative images—placed as a caption above sports figures, works of art and pics of New York cabbies—but it appeared in graffiti throughout the world.

It appeared on overpasses. Abandoned buses. Subway walls.

Stop Asking became a symbol of repressed youth, of the desperate masses, of the terrors of modern life, of the timeless frustration of everyone with the hassle of everything and everyone else in the batshit age we live in. In casual conversation, *Stop Asking* came to mean, very roughly, "You are wasting my time and challenging my dignity as a human, and you *still keep asking for more. So now, fuck off.*" Ultimately, of course, like all the best memes, it was untranslatable—and ever associated with the famous look of infinitely exhausted, infinitely defiant disregard on the face of Red Peters as he stood gauntly in a long-sleeve black collarless shirt in a hotel bathroom— just minutes before he checked into the world's greatest-ever *fuck off* coma.

A few people noticed that the words "stop asking" appeared together in not just one, but *three* Red Peters songs, so they created many rabidly argued theories about Red's actual intentions: Alan Cork being enough of a showman not to spoil the meme by telling the world that the entire lyrics of *Punkshit Heart* had been written on Red's body. As noted earlier by Crystal, that would have been pathetic instead of heroic. Corky paid off a couple doctors and nurses to keep the secret. He tried to pay off Crystal, but she said she was insulted by the offer. Of course she wouldn't say a word.

Here's what happened during the six years of coma, aside from the usual depressing global events, which we will ignore.

In the first month or so, fans organized candlelight vigils outside the hospital in Chicago, and Red's catalog enjoyed a surge of interest. Corky had the doctors do inconclusive encephalograms to check on brain activity, and they replied: *Maybe he has periods of consciousness or perhaps he enters the dream state from time to time, but mostly there's not much going on.* By month four, the prognosis hadn't changed.

So Corky felt free to do whatever he wanted.

Part of what he wanted was to properly time the release of the song Red had composed and recorded on his little recording machine sitting with his guitar on his bed, that night in the hotel. The song only Corky knew about. He had it digitally enhanced to fix the out-of-key parts. He had the engineers add some repeats, and worked in a few subtle backgrounds while keeping the raw acoustic guitar and hoarse-throated essence.

Which is how it happened that in month six after Red Peters entered a coma, his song *Stop Asking* was released as a single to pandemonium in the music industry and headlines around the world. In month eight, it appeared as the last track on a new greatest hits album, *Stop Asking,* which went platinum, earning big bucks for the Red Peters estate, administered by Alan Cork.

The song was goddam depressing, but still...*so right.* It was in such contrast to Red's usual bitching and screaming, that it left everyone kind of breathless. *Stop Asking* clearly represented the end of a certain road, and the end of a certain function for Red Peters in the world. It went like this:

Stop Asking
by Red Peters

Stop asking the sky to be blue,
Stop asking for something new,
Stop asking me how it should be,
Stop asking me how to be free.

Stop asking the wind to blow,
Or asking me to know
And shout out your needs,
And shout out your needs.

Just keep flowing down to the sea,
You and the river and me.

Stop asking the bright lights to shine
Through every new verse and rhyme.
Stop asking for some new desire
That you can stoke into a fire.

Stop asking to be beautiful,
Stop asking to be musical,
Or sound a spectacular note,
Baby, in this land of smoke.

Just keep flowing down to the sea,
You and the river and me.

And hey, stop asking to be loud
Or cry out to the crowd
Riding your limousine cars
Down impossible boulevards

Just keep flowing down to the sea,
You and the river and me.

Stop asking the sky to be blue,
Stop asking for something new,
Stop asking me how it should be,
Stop asking me how to be free.

Despite all this drama, by the end of year two, the fact that Red Peters was still breathing in some secret nursing home somewhere had ceased to be a subject of great interest, even to his fans. (Actually, the nursing home was in the medium-sized town of Elizabeth, New Jersey. Corky had Red quietly moved close enough to his office in Manhattan that he could keep tabs, but far enough so he wouldn't feel guilty about not visiting so often.) Red's mother had died of complications related to lupus. Corky had stolen most of his money. By the end of year three, his Stratocaster was hung in the Grammy Museum above a sad plaque. Occasionally a talk show would host a round of "Should we pull the plug?"

As for Red himself? After the first year, his only steady visitor, aside from interested doctors and lawyers, was Katherine Louise McPherson, aka Crystal, who had moved to Jersey and found a part-time job in another Walmart.

When she heard that Red might or might not have periods of consciousness, and maybe or maybe not could sometimes hear people, Crystal decided she would personally try to keep him from going mad. So she made a routine of visiting as many as four times a week, sometimes staying for hours. She would chat for a while about anything that came into her head: concerts, albums, her childhood, bad recipes she had learned or invented, her life, whatever.

If Red was indeed listening, he would have learned not just about her part time work at Walmart, but how, back in Chicago, she had reluctantly slept with the dorky bellhop from the Hyatt, Tom Donkins—or as she called him, now that she loved him, "Tomkins." Red would have discovered that when she got pregnant, she actually married Tomkins, who had followed her to New Jersey and was presently working at a Hyatt in Newark. Already, they had a little girl, whom Crystal often brought with her to visit—at first nursing the child by his bedside, then letting her run wild in his nursing home room.

After these chats, Crystal would carefully place earbuds in Red's ears and work a portable media player. She played the great Red Peters anything and everything. Mostly head-banger stuff, of course, as she figured that's what he liked best, but also nearly everything else she knew: oldies, folk, country, news, sports, talk shows, speeches, comedy routines, radio dramas, whatever—the incessant song and chatter of millions for hours every day.

Her random audio hodgepodge may have seemed like a lot for an unconscious man to absorb, but the total input of song and chatter was probably not much more than average for a modern human. In fact, likely she provided no more than the same amount of song and chatter we all absorb every day.

Though, of course, Red could not fight back.

For Red, the first three years of his coma were literally Hell. What had been hinted in his terrible 20 minutes of dreaming after the concert now extended for 1,576,800 minutes. Hell is like that: always wanting more. The dream began where it had left off, in the overcrowded antiques shop: the repository of all the useless and unwanted effort of humankind. The stuff in the shop was discarded and ignored, *but still shouting for fucking attention all the time.* All our desperate, inspired efforts at art and beauty—which taken together, includes 99.999% crap, from kitsch to worse—were collected together to shout at poor Red, who in the past, was privileged to be *the guy doing the shouting.* But no more. Now Red's consciousness drifted darkly among a broken jukebox, a cracked chandelier, a porcelain pig with a smile, a worn and unsmiling Miles Davis record cover without the vinyl inside, a lit neon Pepsi sign looking cheerful, Abraham Lincoln's portrait mysteriously painted red and looking grim, a clock decorated green with towers like Oz, a clock decorated brown and stitched like a football, a clock decorated like a wedding cake; and a billion other objects in the infinite inner space of the antiques store, including rhinestone-decorated horseshoes, two sets. Then, thanks to the audio player and the earbuds provided by Crystal: CNN, CNBC, Fox, CSPAN, talking heads, shithead nasty political commentators, crying women, screaming refugees, dark predictions, dark productions, heralds of dark outcomes, and well, everything else dark and light, but mostly dark.

Somewhere in the back, and for years, the same three middle-aged women were speaking at the same time, and still incomprehensibly, possibly in Spanish, but probably not Almodóvar. Somewhere nearer by, perhaps from the dusty jukebox, several strains of music played ever simultaneously and with increasing volume, slowly rising over the three years of pure Hell: a mix of rock and country and world and Incan bells, not to mention oldies like "Tubular Bells." All that music and radio and talk and talk and talk allowed the terrifying "everything of everything"— yes, provided unwittingly by well-meaning

Crystal—to crash any last gates poor Red's unconscious mind could erect. He was helpless before the onslaught, as into his brain, unfiltered and unresisted, came rants of politics too broadly stated, lyrics of songs too well known, pointless speculation on topics too well discussed, unhinged claims about things too well promoted, bawdy jokes about body parts not well washed, along with the arguing and triviality of everything that jangled and buzzed from childhood to adulthood and into senility without the hope of death.

As a result, Red Peters served yet a new purpose in the world by becoming the unwitting repository of modern life. The world no longer *asked,* it *took* his mind as it pleased: just as it had always wanted to do to us all. The result was terrifying, and naturally in his dream state he began to run. At first he ran down crowded chasms of New York City, then down crowded chasms of Hong Kong, Dubai, Singapore, Adelaide, Houston, Downtown L.A., Chicago inside the Loop, London near the river, and the uglier parts of suburban Paris, mostly toward the north.

He had a lot of time to run.

Never once for three years did Red respond to any of Crystal's efforts, even when she massaged his sex—though sometimes this produced a cluster of spikes on the brainwave monitor. At such moments, she'd run and get the nurse, but the nurse would reliably smile at the foolish girl, and write the event in Red's chart, where it would be forgotten. Her sexual efforts to revive Red were duly reported to her husband, Tom Donkins, who did not mind in the least. After all, he was a big fan.

In fact, Donkins would sometimes come and stand beside the bed with her, and stare at the unmoving star, aware of the sound of both the patient's breath, and his own. Over the years, he came in better and better clothes, as he advanced from bellhop, to front desk, to shift manager. But it made him uncomfortable to see the iconic Red Peters reduced to this state, aging soundlessly before his eyes, and he did not come often.

Fortunately for Red, in year four of his coma, Crystal decided she needed help in her sanity campaign. Corky had long since stopped returning her calls, and the band had long ago dispersed to other gigs. She had friends who still listened to Red Peters, but they weren't people she particularly liked. Most of them were, like, hung up on *Stop Asking*, as if it said it all. Plenty of times she thought about telling them the truth about that phrase, but she honored her commitment.

At last, desperate for an ally, she decided to track down Red's old choir director, Miss Tomlinson.

Everyone else just seemed so useless.

It wasn't actually that hard to find the old lady. Crystal had remembered the name of the East Lawrence School from her fateful night at the Hyatt, and the school had no issue in giving her contact information for Crystal's "favorite old music teacher," the now retired but ever-wonderful Miss Tomlinson, "whose first name I can't say I ever knew, but who gave me my love of music."

Crystal decided not to call in advance, but just to show up at the woman's house one afternoon, a modest colonial out in Morristown. It seemed like fate that Miss Tomlinson had retired to Jersey, just like Red.

Miss Tomlinson (not Ms), now seventy-seven, answered skeptically. Before her stood a thin young woman of twenty-five or thirty-five with streaky green hair and eager eye, dressed like a streetwalker and leading a ragged three-year-old by the hand: boy or girl she couldn't be sure, as it had so much hair.

"Hi," said Crystal.

"Sorry, I am not going to give you anything," said the old lady, making to close the door.

"Are you Miss Tomlinson?

"Sorry?"

"Who used to teach choir?"

The door hesitated. "Why do you care to know?"

"Who was Red Peters' teacher?"

Long pause as the universe shifted again.

"What?"

"I'm Red's girlfriend...um, ex-girlfriend. Still friend, though."

Another moment passed. In fact, two moments passed.

"Sorry?" asked Miss Tomlinson.

At this point we must mention that Miss Tomlinson was not just an old lady, but a bitter old spinster. Her retirement, eight years earlier, had been forced. She had never progressed beyond middle school choir teacher at East Lawrence. She had never married. Once upon a time she'd been religious, but now she thought all religion was bullshit. Instead of reading Dickens and Trollope as she once did, going to the theatre, or listening to great music as was once her wont—she now watched a great deal of television. In fact, mostly stuff on the rerun channel from the golden age of TV. Out of sheer depression.

The framed but unsigned publicity photo of a much younger Red Peters, pounding his guitar and singing in full glitter beneath strong spotlights, stood on her mantel among the photos of her dearest relatives. It had stood there for many years. She also had a newspaper clipping with the *Stop Asking* selfie photo lying face up, but unframed on the mantel. Just a scrap of paper, really.

Twenty-eight years had passed since the great moment when young, promising Red had willfully violated a madrigal under her baton, and ten years had passed since the last time she had tried to contact him. Like Red, she often thought about those forty seconds on the steps of the Met. They had brought a vision from another realm: a place of dangerous meaning which she could not comprehend, but to which she could not help but be attracted. It was a place as out of a dream. She had followed Red's career closely. Though she hated his loud, trashy music, she nevertheless obsessed over it, marveling at its mysterious popularity. She wondered:

Why do people love darkness?

She had not wanted to contact Red merely as a form of self-aggrandizement or self-justification, but because she had wanted to talk. She had wanted to truly understand the meaning of those forty seconds at the Met. Not that she ever had any exact idea what she would say to the great and dangerous Red Peters if she actually tracked him down; only that the conversation somehow needed to occur. It frustrated her how he didn't know that they had *both* understood something important that afternoon. Yes, that was it: they needed to compare notes. Her life, too, had been changed, though not in a good way. Some of the joy had gone out of it in that fateful moment. Satisfaction had mysteriously departed. Over the years, however, Miss Tomlinson had come to accept an inevitable lack of closure. Just as she would never fulfill her dream of sex with a good man, a meaningful conversation with Red Peters would never occur.

But now, here stood this woman in her doorway. With a child.

"Come in dear," she said to Crystal. "Have a seat while I make some coffee."

Crystal sat on an overstuffed sofa and looked around the old-lady living room, noting the baby grand and the thirty or so group photos of kid choirs hung above it. Years and years of kid choirs. Of course, she also noted, on the mantel among the pictures of nieces and nephews and visits to cathedrals in Europe, an ancient publicity still of Red—probably from around the time of *Loud Animal*. Crystal pulled out a bag of blocks and scattered them on the floor for the child to play with.

"How is it possible you are here?" asked Tomlinson.

"Red told me about your choir. He had fond memories."

Miss Tomlinson let this sink in. Then she replied:

"Isn't Red Peters still alive in a coma somewhere?"

"Over four years in a coma. He told me...he told me about you right before he went under. In fact, just before. Like minutes, probably. Now he's in a home in Elizabeth, about a half-hour east of here. He's still out."

Miss Tomlinson stared at her. "I tried for years to contact Red Peters. He never replied."

"Maybe he never got the message."

"And you? What's your name?"

"Katherine," said Crystal, surprising herself. She hadn't used that name for years, but the old lady reminded of her mother, who totally hated the name Crystal.

"Okay, Katherine. I never read about you...and I've read pretty much everything about Red Peters."

"Yeah, somehow the reporters missed me. Or actually, I avoided them like the plague. The police helped. So you're still a fan of Red's?"

"I never liked his music. Not my style, but I—" The old woman hesitated. This sounded wrong.

Crystal raised her eyebrows. "I guess everyone has their own taste."

"I'm sure I just never understood it. I thought he might explain it to me. Or at least—you see when he was a boy, he loved everything classical. He listened to Haydn. Sang Bach beautifully. He had a sweet, wonderful voice as a boy."

"Wow. I guess he would have."

"I do have all his albums, though."

The two women sipped coffee as this sunk in.

"Listen," said Crystal. "I have a favor to ask."

Miss Tomlinson merely raised her eyebrows.

"It's kind of crazy, maybe," pursued Crystal.

The eyebrows went higher.

"Red is still in this stupid coma. The doctors say he doesn't really, you know, have *consciousness,* like, per se. But I don't believe it. I mean, he's basically asleep, right? And when you're asleep you're not entirely unaware. You can still hear things, right? So I think either he's bored or sad. And I—" She hesitated, then drove forward in a rush. "Well, I go to the nursing home and I play him stuff two or three times a week, when I can. To maybe keep him sane for when he wakes up. That is, if they don't, you know, pull the plug on him. They might, though there really isn't a *plug.* It's more like they'd stop feeding him. They've talked about it, for sure. I play him the news and music and everything. But I don't really *know* much about music, only like the current hits, and of course his stuff and other metal from the big years. I don't know anybody who has much taste." She paused to consider this last remark, then forged ahead. "But anyway, like I said, he remembered your name—and I thought you might, well, bring some classical stuff for him to listen to. Or other stuff too. Do you know like good jazz? You seem like an educated person. And maybe you have time. And it's only a half-hour drive." She looked the woman eye to eye. "I'm basically asking for help."

Only rarely is anyone offered the chance to grasp the lost thread of their life's meaning. Miss Tomlinson hesitated only long enough to save face.

"Of course. More coffee? I probably have some cookies for the child, too."

"Her name's Honor."

The girl turned at her name.

The Riviera Nursing Home was a squat, depressing, one-story af-fair, crowded between a gas station and a 7-11 on a busy boulevard in an uninteresting part of town. It was painted green and had a faux mansard roof, painted the same green. Miss Tomlinson arrived on a Tuesday at 1 p.m., just after lunch. Beside her on the passenger seat sat a battered NPR tote bag holding a large stack of old-fashioned CDs and a small, by-then antique CD player. Just parking in the lot and exiting the car proved a surreal experience. After all, *this place was less than thirty minutes from her house, and he had been lying right here for four years.*

Was she really about to see Red Peters?

Crystal had not yet arrived, and at the front desk, Miss Tomlin-son hesitated only a moment before asking if she could go in alone. Just knowing Crystal's name seemed to establish her *bona fides,* and besides, Red was no longer hassled by unstable fans. That had ended a good while ago.

A CNA took Miss Tomlinson down a hallway of old wood pan-eling painted over in chilly white. She could hear the traffic on the boulevard every time she passed a room, accompanied by the buzz of old florescent light fixtures and the babble of TVs.

The door to Room 17 was open, and *there he was,* lying alone on a narrow hospital bed. The window was up, the glare of summer en-tered freely, and like the other rooms, this one rattled with traffic. At first Miss Tomlinson wasn't sure the man on the bed even *was* Red. Then her eyes traced the familiar nose. The famous pointy chin. He appeared horribly thin and pale. The famous scarlet hair had been cut ugly and short. He was sleeping, but not peacefully. He looked older than his forty-three years and decidedly *bound against his will.* Not a rebellious child, but a prisoner. You could not say that any expression actually appeared on his face, yet his face showed a grim restlessness. A clear unhappiness.

Not surprising, since Red was still in Hell.

The CNA left, and Miss Tomlinson sat in a hard wooden chair next to the bed. It proved fortunate that she had time alone with Red Peters, for when she laid her hand on his, she became his new mother. Indeed, by the time Crystal arrived, and very much like a mother, Miss Tomlinson had saved Red from Hell. It wasn't that difficult: she had carefully placed headphones on his ears, and she was playing him Mozart's Piano Quartet in E-flat major, K. 493.

Four years after his first visit, Heaven still looked like Tuolumne meadows, high in Yosemite National Park, on a sweet and sunny afternoon. The air tasted fresh with altitude. Again Red Peters walked along the north fork of the Tuolumne River in the grassy field. Only now, in addition to the baby grand pianos placed at pleasant intervals along the banks and beneath great mountains, he found cellists and violinists, even the occasional violist or oboist in neat folding chairs, spaced into the vanishing distance. All the musicians played Mozart with the same sense of joyful inevitability he now recalled with mounting excitement. He himself was thirteen years old, with his sense of wonder just peaking.

"Mozart," he reflected, with all the happiness of revelation, "represents eternity itself: ever the same, yet ever occurring anew." He leapt atop the nearest piano, his boy-face shining in the sunlight, and began to sing along, *la, la la*. But then, remarkably, he improvised his own melody above the melody. His own lyrics. It was a counter-tune—chaotic, separate, but necessary. He caught the eye of the pianist and they played off one another, back and forth in sympathy and laughing syncopation. The music became visible, Disney-like, as if built of color or birds. And when at last the sun set and the meadow became dark, Red Peters climbed down into the long grasses of the warm night and curled up to look into the stars until he became twenty-one, and a woman appeared by his side, and she said she loved him.

Then it was the next afternoon at around the same time, and Mozart returned.

And Red was again allowed to create beauty.

And then again and again, the next and the next day.

And lo, within this rhythm he realized that *the only thing human beings truly desire is creation. To be fruitful and multiply.* "That's what it means that we are made in the image of God," he said, as if aloud. "It's just that simple. Like God, humans also wish, ceaselessly, to create. Not just children and art, but fields, food, houses, buildings, machines, moments, music, politics, emotional crises, you name it." He wanted to explain this to someone, so he said it to the beautiful, if nameless woman who appeared beside him: "Sometime go visit an antiques shop jammed with bric-a-brac from the ages, all of it created for some unknown purpose by some eager craftsman, and you too will understand spoons shaped like shepherds and lamps shaped like tubas, gorillas flying tin planes around model Empire State Buildings, artificial flowers painted like the flags of the nations. Humans will create anything and everything, just to build *something, anything* to be fruitful and multiply and fill the earth."

And here he paused a moment to complete coitus with the woman. Surely, he thought, there would be a song in coitus.

"My friends were all wrong to say that Heaven is dull," reflected Red afterwards. "Why, for Heaven's sake, would God allow Heaven to become dull?" He saw the full truth. He saw how all of history and all ideas and all creation wanted to re-enact itself through him, just because he was *alive.* To use him as their vehicle into the future. He saw that all information, all beauty, all music, all organisms, all microorganisms, even the inanimate wishes to persist. Bach, Haydn, Hendrix had their strategies. And even forgotten songs find a way to survive, through their echoes in later songs. "But to survive," he reminded the woman and everyone and everything that wanted to exist, "everything requires destruction and re-creation. By God or by man. Death and rebirth. That is to say, Hell and Heaven, Heaven and Hell, Hell and Heaven again. In riffing off Mozart atop grand piano after grand piano, his job was to destroy and to create Mozart, again.

And then he awoke.

When he opened his eyes, Red Peters saw two women watching him in surprise. He found them strangely familiar. Through a window, he heard the sound of traffic. Above his head, he heard the hum of cheap florescent lighting. The room was unfamiliar but very bright, and he blinked uncomfortably for a bit. Strangely, it did not seem to be a hotel room. He opened his mouth and tried to speak, but his throat hurt and would not make a sound.

Both the women's eyes opened wider. He tried again, and managed to form the word "who?" Though it came out more like "eew."

He knew that a great deal of time had passed.

"It's Crystal," said the younger of the two women, who was dressed in modest professional clothing. "And you are Red."

Both were strange words, and he wondered for a moment whether they came from Heaven or from Hell. Crystal was like Heaven. But "Red" came from Hell. He saw red flames, and his eyes began to close as he felt himself slipping back into the image-stream of his dream.

"You wanna wake up, Red? Red?"

The word "Red" kept sending him back to Hell, and he might have been lost forever if Crystal had not by chance changed her line of attack:

"Hey there, mister. Wake up for me. Wake up for me."

Better, she reached out and took his hand. For Red, it was the strangest sensation, this physical touch. It short-circuited the memes and the histories and the philosophies and the music and the art and pull of both Heaven and Hell.

"Eeew?"

Sitting on the other side of the bed, Miss Tomlinson felt very odd. For a moment, perhaps, she hoped he would not awake. These last two years had been very comfortable and fulfilling. She had been happy just coming to the nursing home for a couple hours three or four times a week as the sun declined along the boulevard. She had been happy to play Mozart and Haydn, Vivaldi and Handel for Red Peters—to what? To stem the tide? It was odd, but for some reason, she had never ventured past the eighteenth century. Something about the calm, the control of the neo-classics had seemed necessary. Rather than the Romantics. And never mind the twentieth or twenty-first centuries. Out of the question.

"That's Miss Tomlinson. Do you remember? She was your old choir teacher. Miss Tomlinson."

And lo again, to Red, it seemed the most natural thing in the world that Miss Tomlinson should be at his bedside, aged and wrinkled. Almost, but not quite, beyond recognition.

"Yes," he said, managing now to articulate the word quite clearly.

Crystal still held his right hand. Miss Tomlinson now took his left. Crystal was as close as he would ever get to a wife. Miss Tomlinson was as close as he would ever get to a mother. It was enough.

With the considerable logistical help of Tom Donkins, who moved through the world as a man of increasing competence, the two women brought Red to Miss Tomlinson's little house in Morristown. Or, to be more accurate, they brought him to her home after weeks of physical therapy, two lawsuits against Corky for malfeasance, a countersuit, a court order, global headlines, and general pandemonium. Not to mention renewed sales of Red's whole catalog and several days of *Stop Asking* demonstrations outside the nursing home (location leaked by the press), from people who thought that Red was being detained or exploited or woken up against his will.

In the end he had to leave the facility by secret midnight ambulance and police escort. Tom even flew to L.A. to pick up the Stratocaster from the Grammy Museum—a personal triumph.

For a time, a pleasant routine fell upon them all: Miss Tomlinson fussing about breakfast, a little annoyed when Red didn't rise 'til noon. Crystal coming by nearly every day with her child, and often staying over (chastely). By now she had become expert in handling the lawyers and the press through a variety of ruses to hide their new location.

Everyone fell into their proper roles and fulfilled their necessary jobs on Earth; except, not yet Red. Crystal began using the name Katherine full time. Her professional clothing grew increasingly expensive. Tom advanced to convention services manager at the Hyatt.

Honor grew.

And yes, finally one afternoon, out in the back yard under her large oak, Miss Tomlinson traded notes with Red Peters about that fateful afternoon on the steps of the Met, now thirty-one years before. Given everything at stake, it was a remarkably brief conversation.

"I did it because I *could,*" explained Red, who rightly thought this explanation enough.

"Of course," said the old lady, with a smile. "I see that now. And I could do nothing to stop you. None of us could. It's like that with all children. Why didn't I understand that before? *Exactly like all children.*"

He returned her old-lady smile with his by-now-famous mean little boy smile.

She said, "The cut worm forgives the plow."

"What?"

"Never mind, sweet Red. Now you have made me happy."

He looked up at the banal suburban sky and was, for a time, like his new mother, happy also.

It wasn't easy to play the guitar again: his fingers had become so soft and his arms so weak. But about six months after he awoke from his coma, Red wrote a new song. News of his location leaked to the press, so the first time he sang the new song, he took a folding chair out on the front lawn, just a few feet from the sidewalk.

A considerable crowd of fans and gawkers and media had gathered, leaning forward with phones and microphones and cameras. The crowd was held back by police standing just inside Miss Tomlinson's little white picket fence. Red played a few chords of intro, and then the song went like this:

The Productions of Time
by Red Peters

Baby, come close to me,
Hold me bucking and free,
Come ride this sweaty steed
Into the future.

Don't give a single damn
Who you are or what I am,

Let's the two of us scram
Into the future.

(Change-up to rapid rap rhythm)

We'll see DNA clocks and galaxy rocks,
Happy new juice and Superman socks,
Moebius news and laser cocks,
Pretty ghost planes and astral games,
Collapsing digital old man canes
Littering lost country lanes,
All the far fucking away
Into the future.

Kickin' an' screamin' babe
Kickin' an' screamin' babe
Into the future.

You and me babe, sweaty mare and steed,
Will buckin' together make a child who'll cry:
Please daddy, mommy, please,
Let me take you with me...

Kickin' an' screamin', hey!
Kickin' an' screamin' hey!
Into the future.

"Listen daddy," says our child,
"Listen mommy, wait just a while...

"I'll invent driverless stares,
Solid silhouette airs,
3D holographic gears,
Virtual fears, designer tears,
Hophead stocks and black hole walks
To rev my darlin's atomic box...

Mommy, daddy, just you wait,
'Cause it will never be too late,
It'll never ever be too late
Into the future.

(Back to opening rhythm)

Here on the sea of dreams,
Ain't no sweet whipped cream
Without you and me, babe
Ridin' a fierce riptide
Into the future.

Kickin' an' screamin' babe
Kickin' an' screamin' babe
Into the future.

Heaven applauds our kind,
Angels sing our longtailed vibe,
Ours not to wonder why,
Ours but to birth and die.

See how it has to be?
Got nowhere to flee,
Gotta buck till it rhymes,
Till it finally, finally friggin' rhymes, because...

Eternity's in love with the productions of time
Eternity's in love with the productions of time

(then slowly, almost spoken to the final chord)

Eternity is in love with the productions of time

The BIRTH of NOAH
Part I

*"When I was a child, I caught a fleeting glimpse
out of the corner of my eye. I turned to look, but
it was gone. I cannot put my finger on it now."*

–Pink Floyd, 1979

Once out into big cities and finding himself alone, the irrepressible Thomas Putnam took to writing letters home to his sister. From Chicago, high in a cheap hotel with the window open, he felt himself full of his youth and wrote: "Already it is summer here. The armies of the wounded move on the streets below me, their cheeks puff out with wind, their eyes fill with light. Our nights are ten miles high and Arabian. The lamps are moons. One is surprisingly aware of trees, how deep they are, the way they hold themselves aloof." And he sealed up the letter and dropped it in a mailbox the next day. From there it was delivered to Concord, Missouri.

The year was 1957.

His sister Ramona had dark eyes, of which the more said the better: "...dark as olives, and the secret pleasure of knowledge within those eyes. I have often asked her what she was thinking," the remarkable Thomas had once written to Avery Caldwell, the boy next door who loved Ramona. Now she opened the letter written high in the hotel room and took it out on the back porch where she could hear the dogs and the screen doors. Ramona was only fifteen and so, despite her brother's poetry, she could not be expected to understand more than that Thomas was happy and alive and apparently not yet out of money—though he had been to three cities and not found work. "Perhaps you could try fixing bicycles," wrote Ramona back in her ignorance, "you were always so good at that," and she posted the letter to the address he had included, though knowing it might not find him at all. She had always loved Thomas, but she always knew he would leave Missouri. When they were children, Thomas had played astronaut, and constructed spaceships out of bed sheets and folding chairs. He was always fated to be the traveler. Ramona had played house, and she had baked him cookies.

Avery was due that afternoon, and she now sat placidly waiting for him, not yet to that age when one prepares for the arrival of others.

Avery, all of seventeen, arrived in his jeans and felt shirt and that satisfied smile on his tight, blond face that Ramona found so complete. He stood above her silently as she finished her letter to Thomas.

"Tranquility has two Ls," he said after a time, and she crossed it off and miscorrected the word without even acknowledging Avery's presence; that's how familiar they were already. The tall boy sat beside her on the step and watched the sunlight settling among the willows and fences as day opened into eleven o'clock. "I am happy," he might have said aloud, for there was as yet nothing of yearning adolescence about Avery, none of that nervous "walking with the girl next door" that plagues youths of every nation and age. He was at that time confident and free and easy. "She loves me," he had written to Thomas only last week, and that was all he needed to say.

"Avery plans to be an engineer," wrote Ramona to her brother later. "He told me this afternoon that he wants to build bridges. I said fine, if that's what he wants to do. I don't understand men at all." She posted this letter dutifully to the address of the hotel where Thomas had been heard from last, but it had been some months since her increasingly legendary brother had replied specifically to one of her letters. It didn't seem to matter though, really. The things she wrote about she often forgot a week later, the issues so hotly discussed already seeming obscured in the short distances of youth.

In the same mail came a letter from Thomas himself: "I look into people's faces—they don't seem to mind. In the city, everyone lives for everyone else's entertainment. We turn down our collars and let the air into our shirts. Our necks therefore grow dirty. And oh yes, I'm working as a carpenter for a man with fat breasts and yellow eyes. He listens to country music, but seems to divine my innermost thoughts."

"It sounds dreadful," said Ramona next day as she sat with Avery in a hamburger shop and ate fries. "Imagine, a man like that; I suppose Thomas has to work day and night."

"That's because he hasn't an education," said Avery piously, and ordered a milkshake. "That's why I'm going to be an engineer. So I won't have to work that hard."

"All right, I'll marry you," said Ramona, with a laugh, and threw her sixteen-year-old arms around his neck. And Avery smiled too, even though she got ketchup all over his felt shirt and he would have to go home and change.

"Where are you, Thomas?" wrote Ramona only a little time later. "Some nights I wake up and say to myself, 'where is my brother?' I can't get it out of my head, and the next morning mother must comfort me or some such nonsense. I know perfectly well you're safe and somewhere in New York working on the docks, but still I worry. You're nearly twenty now and you really should start thinking of settling down. Avery says he wants to marry when he's twenty, which will make me eighteen and a woman."

But Thomas apparently hadn't received that letter, for just two weeks later, he was writing to Avery: "When I see great ships I feel them in my chest like a weight. My legs are driven into the earth and I am struck dumb. They are a terror and a joy. On the shore, the men and women are corrupt, stupid, far from God. But on ships! What a pure life must be led! Nothing but salt and ringing metal. Perhaps I should go to sea. Perhaps you should go to sea, Avery. Or build ships. Just as good building ships as sailing them, I suppose."

Avery said to Ramona that day, "Your brother wants to go to sea."

"No! Then how could we ever write!"

"I don't know, they have radios and perhaps planes or helicopters bring them mail."

"Perhaps." They were going to a horror movie to relieve the boredom of a Saturday afternoon. The movie mattered for a couple of hours. Then it did not.

A year or so passed. Avery was accepted into college. At college he wore khaki shorts and polyester shirts. He learned about large sheets of tracing paper. He owned a red sports car and drove over weekends to visit Ramona. She was taking a class to be a secretary because, "after all, everyone should have a profession." They still had secretarial schools in those days. Avery would drive up before the high cement walls of the school and see her sitting outside among the landscaped juniper bushes and practicing in a little notebook. And she would look up with her dark eyes as the sun caught the windshield of the car. And all the world would stop on that dime and wait for their eyes to meet through the sultry air. Nothing more could be said of this time but gossip and mere romance.

From Marseilles, where he sat among the potted palms of a café and like a sailor, let himself be tossed on the waves of the foreign conversations all around him, the ever-more-legendary Thomas began another letter to his beloved sister. The sister who no doubt still fished in the creek or played among the deep willows. Why did he write her such soulful letters? He had no one else, and he had something to explain. Desperately, even. He wrote:

"Surely, America is the great barbarian, come to sweep aside civilizations of the old and the weak. It makes me sad and full of tragic energy. What is an American but a housecat left to feast on the dinner scraps? We are the children on holiday, building empires like sandcastles. We don't know where we come from or where we're headed, don't have the least idea of war or peace, hunger or plenty. Meanwhile, surprise: the world learns from *us*. You can see it here, where American pinball machines are moved into the rotting cafés of the seaport, where the prostitutes take American clothes and American smiles. Me, I am intoxicated by the cigarette smoke, the sound of taxicabs. The air stinks of fish and tar and diesel; it is an incense and the great ships are moving cathedrals."

He wrote like that, like a man from a greater past. It was a far and away kind of writing.

The letter never reached Ramona until months later, for she and Avery had taken off to the mountains of Arizona for their honeymoon. It was his idea, not hers, but she bought rugs and maps. One night, alone in the open and thinking of lost pagan religions, Ramona was breathless with the scent of dirt and distant pine. It had its effect. She wrote to her brother: "I remembered tonight that God is large. Otherwise, things are fine. Avery sunburns easily and drinks beer, which I didn't know before. We make love with the lights on but the window closed, so making love has become hot and uncomfortable. We've packed the car full with rugs and maps. I may collect pottery. I wake up before my husband and go down to the coffee shop and drink coffee. I've begun drinking coffee, Thomas! Men stop at the coffee shop with trucks and look tired and also I see men who are up early to go hunting or whatever. I know because they're full of laughter. I am often the only woman at the coffee shop in the mornings, and I enjoy the rough conversation, the projects in their voices. Avery has no rough conversation; do you think that a lack? When we're married (okay, we are married, but not, you know, yet in an apartment with a television and a child), perhaps I won't work. I want to be beautiful."

Within months, Avery grew a mustache. He developed a taste for certain movies on Thursday nights which he did not, of course, discuss. He began to wear after-shave. Come June, he left school and went to work building bridges. He liked a good wristwatch and kept his car running well, even gave it a name which he had etched onto a small brass plate and screwed into the dashboard.

Ramona received a letter in the cold of February: "So you have married Avery! What news! I just got one of your letters on returning to Strasbourg. I am pleased. Avery is strong and determined. He has no giddiness about him, and no male vanity. He is handsome and will learn the ways of the world. You were always so dreamy, but perhaps he will take you out into that world."

She tried being beautiful for a while, but discovered it only made her husband and his friends treat her as a fool. Then she tried being a secretary as she had planned, but found it a bore and anyway, Avery made plenty of money for the two of them until they might have a child. They had a child. Ramona named him Noah, thinking of the Biblical tale and how he might save the world, but then was disappointed to find that Noah was among the most popular male names being given that year.

"You know, I wanted to please God with that name," wrote Ramona to Thomas. "Does that sound stupid? Everything sounds stupid these days. Everything I say seems to echo off a tinny plate and sounds foolish. I've been reading Dostoevsky, as you suggested, but I can't fathom it, except for the extreme sadness. Incidentally, my address has been changed this last year. If you're getting these letters, you should stop writing to me at home."

She got a letter from Thomas some weeks later, forwarded from their home address, which read: "They pray here five times a day; they have a man who sings to them in that rhyming language from a tower to call them to prayers. They keep themselves clean and walk these corrupt streets like so many millions of forgotten saints. I question them (for many speak English) and they treat me like a child. I am not a child any longer though, but a man with a thin neck and sunwashed blue eyes. I read their books, the books they have memorized, and I can make nothing out of them but a kind of big rhythm, like the tide. At the same time I dream of home, of the sun on the back porch. Tell me, Ramona, I figure you at twenty-five now, are you a woman? And do you live at home? Write me at the Kashmir Victory Hotel, Peshawar, Pakistan."

It was a place far away.

Ramona began taking night classes, learned how to cook Chinese, taught her child to sing. "Noah, Noah, sing me the one about the lamb." The boy had her dark eyes and looked nothing like his father. Avery, meanwhile, took up fishing, television, Sunday softball, exotic beers, mystery novels, laughing loudly in restaurants, sex manuals; he spoke of a trip to the coast of Mexico, but he was no longer free and easy.

"I don't want to go to Mexico," said Ramona, in her far-off way. She had become far off, or so Avery said to her, and he wondered again if they had married too young.

"But why don't you want to go to Mexico?" he persisted, drawing forth the inevitable travel brochures. They glared in the late afternoon light through the apartment window. "It's a great deal."

"I don't like Mexican music," she said, and walked off to the boy's room, where Noah, now five, was busy with toy boats.

Ramona began to think about things like crime and war, the dirt in the streets, the heavy air of their neighborhood, the way cars droned, the triviality of her religion, the nakedness of her emotions. She felt weak and did not want to feel weak. She went back to work when Noah entered school, and she took up the flute. One day she grew up completely, and discovered the adroit patience of adulthood. Now she began to scorn Avery, who worked all day and indulged in nonsense all night, and so had never grown up at all. She wrote to Thomas:

"I am trapped, but unafraid."

Thomas did not receive that letter. But some months later, he wrote: "How I miss America! The freedom! The honest ambitious male of the species. The female without illusions! The bustling innocence of the cities! I would like to take in a hamburger and a movie and fall in love with a nice girl. The old world is just that, old. And I, even at thirty, am an American, and so I am young."

Ramona dropped the flute, took up diaries, exercise, popular music, driving her child around in the afternoons. She used lipstick now, and applied eyeliner around her dark eyes to emphasize them. Nothing worked.

Noah was not an unusual child, but at ten, he began to romanticize his world-traveling uncle. He wrote a letter, which Ramona dutifully mailed to an address in Jakarta: "Dear Uncle. My name is Noah. Mom tells me you've been to Germany. Did you see any old tanks or bombers? I hope someday you'll visit us here in Missouri and tell me all about those things."

One night not long after, in late summer when the air was dank and full of thunder, Avery came home from work and found a letter from Thomas addressed to himself. He loosened his tie and went into the kitchen to drink milk straight from the carton and sat down at the table in a pool of light to read.

"... and now I dream about children and envy you. I imagine little Noah has model planes hanging from the ceiling and reads those boys' adventure books. I imagine you bringing him up to love running in the forests, to love the study of old books. For myself, I feel like a cloud in the mountains, rising up out of the green valley, gathering up moisture and floating away. How I envy you. Already, I find it's too late for me to come home. You and Ramona have taken the right road, and may grow old with dignity. I would have to go to a monastery in the Himalayas for dignity, would have to commune with some other people than my own. Too late for me now. I imagine you there, loving a woman and a child."

The next morning, news of the war grew to a crescendo. Avery was nearly too old to enlist, but not quite. He saw his last chance to escape, abandoned his job, and in a sense, his family.

He died within four months.

Ramona found she liked being a widow. She took Noah out of the public schools and put him with the Catholics, because religion seemed like an option, at least for her son. Then she learned to play tennis, joined the museum league, and at last left Missouri. She moved to San Francisco, of course. She took Noah up Mount Tamalpais and showed him the sweep of the coast. She wrote to her brother Thomas:

"It is not enough, as it has never been enough, but it is much more than it was. I can think, at least. I should have built rocket ships, too. Incidentally, America is dying." That last was a thing a lot of people said in those days. The rocket ships were personal to her and Thomas.

She took on the trappings of the age because what else was there to do? She put up Escher prints in her apartment, cultivated houseplants. Noah became a dreamy boy under her influence, and he was a dreamy boy throughout Catholic school, ignoring religion while reading magical books written for children that promised too much. He thought his mother was wonderful and only vaguely missed his father. He indulged moderately in pornography, avoided alcohol, and didn't care to associate with large groups.

At college, though, Noah's eyes opened. His mother seemed eccentric, foolish. He began to loathe her excessive makeup. He read her incessant letters hurriedly, and scoffed at her spiritualism. He fell in love, but after living with the young woman for a time, could not keep his attention sufficiently focused to stay in love. He floundered in school, losing interest in his studies. He began to drink more coffee and then, at last, alcohol. It was the 1970s.

When his mother died, Noah was on a playing field of the school, throwing a football casually. A man he'd never seen jogged up with an actual telegram—such things still happened then. Noah went to sit in the shade and tore it open. The grass at his feet suddenly appeared in all its individual greenness. The sounds of the field crowded in upon him. He began to cry.

Noah Caldwell, son of two sad Americans, drove all the way to San Francisco in one night, and woke up the apartment manager at six a.m. to open the door. Evidently, someone had been in to clean up. The scatter of books had been organized, the ridiculous weaving loom leaned against the wall and the yarn was not tangled everywhere. He began taking things apart, examining the titles of books, reading her overflowing boxes of correspondence. Those serious looks she had given him since he was very young had meant more than he imagined, and he wondered if she had committed suicide. He felt again awkward and young. It was a terror. At last he went out on the little balcony that overlooked the city and turned to the letters from his Uncle Thomas as the sun rose.

Reading the letters from far off lands, Noah felt that he grew five years in two hours. Light filled up the streets as he read, and the sounds of the city were for the first time truly in his ears. On a sheet of paper, he wrote: "Dear Uncle Thomas: They taught me to ask all the wrong questions," and hurried it into an envelope. At ten o'clock the postman came and Noah met him at the door. He did not hesitate to open one last letter from his Uncle, forwarded from Missouri, and addressed to Ramona:

"....Australia is young and blustery and very self-conscious about itself. I think of America in pioneer days, and wonder how much American Western films have influenced the Australian present. As for me, I find myself examining the mirror closely. Suddenly I antici-pate growing old with fear, as apparently everyone must. They say the old grow closer to God, like little children. The circle closes. Perhaps. That I am lost is no matter. I only ask for new beginnings; what else can an American demand? Always to be starting over, that is the se-cret. Australia is full of new beginnings. One more second chance. So you are unhappy, Ramona. Does that surprise you? There are so many other things besides happiness. To name them would be trite. I walk by the sea and watch the sailboats, of which I can see numbers beyond counting."

Noah put the letter down and walked to the door, where he caught a taxi for the airport.

He had to wait only six hours for a plane to Melbourne.

MORE

*"The future doesn't actually exist, right? I mean,
it's only something you imagine, because when
you get there, you only have the present."*

—Anonymous woman, overheard
in conversation on a New York subway

Like most people on earth—like Miss Tomlinson and Mickey and Ramona and Noah, and well, maybe everyone—Joseph Testa knew there was *more*. Joseph knew because one summer evening when he was a child of nine he got lost on a family camping trip in the Alleghenies. There he lay on his back for a full hour looking up through a small opening in a stand of tall straight pines as the sky became star-filled and infinite. For that hour he was without family or ideas, and he was conscious of the mountain beneath his body pressing toward a secret and jagged hole leading into a greater universe. It was a crisis in which he felt he knew everything and nothing. So clear and profound was this experience, that over the years, when he saw similar moments imitated in exquisite music, tearful plays, brilliant novels, extravagant films, spectacular photographs, abstract paintings, sincere prayers, meditative retreats, bold architecture, desperate drug experiences, and heartrending cries of ecstasy, he always knew there was still more.

Unlike most people on earth, however, Joseph Testa was given the opportunity to find out just how much more.

Joseph grew up as a single child who loved his mother more than his father. She was his anchor in the world. His father, Emile Testa, was merely a hard-working immigrant gone long hours running a small warehouse down at some New Jersey docks from which he could see, but not touch the Manhattan skyline. Both his parents, as they often reminded him, were born into poverty—a poverty which had made his mother practical, and his father taciturn. When Emile Testa came home he spoke little, or said things like, "I'm building my business so that, God willing, Joey, you should have a little more than I had." When he said this he would hold Joseph by the shoulders and look him directly in the eye—which Joseph did not enjoy. Meanwhile, Joseph's mother, Irene, raised on a small mid-western farm, kept a comfortable home and dreamt little. She had organized the camping trip only "so that Joseph should have the same experiences as his friends."

His mother was the one who, searching desperately, found him under the stand of tall pines that night. The boy had not answered her call and was at first unwilling to leave the spot beneath his jagged hole in the sky, even when she pulled him up for a hug. He had tried angrily to get her to look up through the trees at least *once* before they returned to the campsite, but she would not.

The Testa family never camped again. Indeed, other than that one large experience, Joseph led for a good long while a pretty sheltered lower-middle-class life. He and his parents lived in a cramped 2+1 ranch-style house they owned a mile from the docks, and he never received, for example, an expensive present or fancy party. Irene was brought up to believe that happiness was impossible without a solid sense of *enough,* and though every extra dime went into keeping the ever-precarious family business afloat, she succeeded in ensuring that her son never felt deprived. She accomplished this by telling him again and again how proud she was to have done better than her own parents, who had never owned anything, not even their own farm. She was proud when she put together money for movies or amusement parks. She was proud of young Joseph for every B he received in school, every positive report from a teacher. "We are doing just fine," she would say to friends, as she clipped coupons.

Joseph was handsome from age eighteen to age twenty-five. He graduated state college with a degree in political science, which of course he never used. He nearly broke his father's heart when, after graduation, he refused to enter the family business. The family business repelled him. He only visited Testa Transit Storage, just back of Dock 56, a few times, finding it depressingly silent and gloomy, filled with sad empty spaces, diesel fumes, damp metal, and choking dust. Anyway, everyone knew that given the new efficiencies of container ships, warehouses were rapidly becoming obsolete. Why his father hung on, he had no idea. Still, after Joseph graduated, he settled in the greater ports area, and he did okay on a management track at a large snack food company which had placed its HQ close to its supply chain. At twenty-four, just under the wire on his handsome phase, he married a pretty assistant manager in Accounting named Emmy Baker. She displayed a pleasant and competent air, and a few months later they had a little girl named Penny, short for Penelope, the name of Emmy's grandmother. Joseph's parents got over the fact that Emmy was Presbyterian, and she warmed when she saw them spoil Penny with candies and toys. After some years, his father seemed to get over Joseph not entering the family business. Indeed, every now and then Joseph and Emile shared a glass of Chianti out on the back porch of the 2+1—but as during his childhood, they spoke little. Instead, they just listened with manly amusement to Irene and Emmy chat about schools, recipes, and Penny.

His life was okay.

This was the stability and wealth most humans around the world only dream of realizing in their lifetimes. But it was not, of course, *more*. For a time, this was troubling. During those years, Joseph rarely became excited about work issues, often feeling numb. In the early years of their marriage, he felt sincere love for his wife, but then a certain depression set in, during which he developed a short fuse, saw a therapist, viewed pornography, listened to music in headphones, found despair in the glare of sunlight on the hoods of cars on freeways, resented the noise of modern life, complained about the tyranny of digital devices, encountered a great sadness in the hallways of airports during work trips, and became impatient during obligatory conversations—in other words, the usual.

Knowing about *more* from his childhood incident beneath the stars contributed to this depression, but he felt it kept him, at some level, human, and made his life in some way, important.

In his mid-thirties, Joseph pulled out of his depression. He accomplished some travel, and treasured his travel photos. He went to comic-book movies. He took up hobbies, and by the age of thirty-nine, he had largely and blessedly forgotten about the unanswered universal question of *more*—recalling the great fact only to sustain himself on long drives or at children's piano recitals. For without a great need, even the greatest question may be ignored.

Until the day of his dad's sixty-fifth birthday party, that is—a hot Sunday in July.

J oseph had been asked to come over early to help set up for an afternoon barbeque which would include the usual relations, plus a few of his dad's buddies from the docks: men who would open many beers and make many bad jokes. These barbeques were by nature uncomfortable, especially as his parents insisted on staging them on the patchy grass of their small and treeless backyard, where guests searched in vain for shade. Always, his father would produce a large and unappetizing mound of hamburgers. Penny would be asked to wave away the flies with a paper plate. Sometimes, but not always, a radio played.

On the big sixty-fifth, Joseph and his mother were setting up chairs when Emile appeared at the back door with an iced tea in his right hand and a set of car keys in his left. He seemed oddly alert.

"Joey," said Emile, "Maybe you're wondering why I asked you to come over so early." Only his father called him Joey. His mother had succeeded in making everyone else, including us, use "Joseph."

"It's okay, dad. Penny just has practice this morning. There's no game."

"I asked you so early because I wanted just the three of us to talk. Just the close family. Before anybody else gets here. Even Emmy." With that, he let the screen door slam with a decisive bang.

This opening made Joseph look closely at his father. The man was not aging well. Today he was more overweight than usual, with a big spare tire weighing down his leisure shorts. His face had tectonic folds. Two ugly warts. Clearly, it would be better if he shaved himself entirely bald than to continue combing badly-dyed hair over the empty spots. Emile was sweating seriously in the sun, but now he showed his wife and son a strange little smile. They stopped opening chairs.

"As you know, it's my sixty-fifth birthday."

"Yup, another big one," smiled Joseph. "I was thinking you should take a little time off—maybe you and mom should take a trip."

Emile Testa held up his iced tea in a gesture which asked for quiet. "I bought myself a present. It's the only thing for me. All the rest is for you two. Mostly for you, Joey, as my only son."

"What present?" asked Irene, rather more sharply than she might.

Emile's smile grew more strange. It became boyish. He was breathing rather harder now. "Maybe you saw it out front."

Joseph paused, then smiled too. "I saw a car under a cover out on the street—looked like a sports car. Did you get yourself a sports car?"

"Yes. It's a Lamborghini," said Emile, and now he dangled the keys before their eyes. "Red."

"Wow, cool dad. What, did someone steal it off a ship for you?"

"No, I bought it new, at a dealer in Brooklyn."

This took a second to sink in.

"Aren't those really expensive...a Lamborghini?" asked Irene, baffled.

"Really, really expensive," said Emile. "Outrageously expensive," he added.

Joseph stared. "Like *two hundred grand* expensive?"

"That's just the base. I got the *Avventura* package."

"What are you talking about?" asked Irene, bewildered.

It was then that Joseph's father pulled a hidden lever to tear another ragged hole in the sky, thirty years after the first. "I bought it because we're rich."

"What are you talking about?" repeated Irene.

"The three of us. Our little family—we're now officially rich. You, Joey, you can quit your job tomorrow."

"Dad—"

"I'm not kidding. We're rich, as in tens of millions rich. Maybe more. Definitely more. I'm not exactly sure."

"Dad—"

"It took me twenty years, Joey. Forty-five, if you go back to the beginning."

"What are you talking about?" demanded Irene for a third time.

"Twenty years ago I saw something nobody else saw, down at the docks. I will now explain the whole thing to you—it's finally time." He took a deep breath, as he'd rehearsed the following speech, during which he paced aggressively around the porch, and made much use of his hands:

"As you know, Joey, I was born in Italy. Down south. My father was a fisherman, did I tell you that? When I was a boy, I was a fisherman."

"Yeah, I know that, dad," replied Joseph. Irene just squinted.

"We never had anything. We were like subhuman, Joey. Fishermen. And there was no way to do any better, for me, at least. But everyone said a man could do better in America, and it was true."

"Emile," began Irene. "Are you—"

"Please, Irene," Emile stopped her.

"Long story short, okay, okay…In America, I found your mother. I managed to buy the warehouse, right?"

"Dad, look, we've—"

"Shhhh," said Emile, putting his fingers to his lips. "Don't worry, son, it's all okay now, all okay now." He steadied himself. The smile returned.

"As you know, we own a little warehouse. You've been there not so many times, Joey, right? That's okay. Just one of a dozen crappy warehouse operations between docks forty and seventy. It's a tough business, right? You were right to stay out of it, okay? Too much goddam competition, and commodity pricing killing us. All of us tried specializing—some in fresh food, me in machinery—but, as you know, once the whole industry went to containers, then refrigerated containers, and then to goddam digital routing, well the warehouse business went to hell, really just went to hell, right?"

Joseph and his mother exchanged glances. Emile had never used foul language. And in their memory, had probably never said more than three sentences in a row.

"One after another, guys went under—some warehouses just abandoned. It's been sad, Joey. You wouldn't know, okay? Thirty years of downhill. Down, down, down. You were right to stay away, because... because I wasn't ready to explain the bigger picture....but you were too young then," he added, obscurely. "Anyway, as you know, I only have three employees left... goddam fucking downhill." He took another big, agitated drink of iced tea. They could see he was getting off track from his prepared speech. Maybe the iced tea would help, so they didn't interrupt.

"But what did I see, twenty years ago, you may ask me?" He paused, but they did not ask. "I looked across the bay, and I saw those big ugly highrise condos marching down to the shore. Then right *along* the shore. Then I saw that even though nobody in their right mind would have wanted, back then, to live on our ugly dirthole side of the bay, I saw that it was inevitable, inevitable—I mean there's only so much shoreline, but ever so many rich people who want a view of a bay. If you're up high enough, it looks great and I guess you don't hardly notice the fumes and crap from the barges. Do you see now, Joey, where I'm going here? I realized that the warehouse business wasn't worth shit, but *the land under the warehouses?* I saw that someday that land would be gold. Do you see it now, Joey? Do you see?"

At this point, it dawned uncomfortably on Joey that this entire speech was addressed only to him.

"So every time I could, I bought up the old warehouses—sometimes just assuming the debt and letting 'em rot. One after another." Now his voice rose for a moment in pent-up anguish: "That's where all the money went all those years, Joey. Why I could never give you anything? Why we had to live in this crappy house? Okay, I'm sorry! I'm sorry! I'm sorry to you, too, Irene," he said, finally glancing at her for a moment, and then away. "But it was okay, right? I saw a better use for the money. I was looking *ahead.* For you, Joey. For Penny, for *Penny's children.* Right? What good would money be for us? For your dad and mom? I'm old—no seriously, really fucking old for sixty-five.

I'm older than my own father at eighty, I swear. I feel almost crapped out. Your mother's almost crapped out, too. Too much goddam pasta and red meat, not enough exercise. They were right, all those *health types*. Who knew? You kids are right to exercise, don't ever forget that."

He paused then, almost too worked up to go on. A little confused maybe. "Please, sit. I'm sorry. This isn't coming out right." And then he turned around several times to calm himself, and sat down on the porch steps. As he took another big gulp of iced tea, Irene silently pulled up a chair and folded her arms. Joseph chose to remain standing.

And now, here came what Emile had hoped to be the greatest moment of his life:

"Okay, okay: *But I was smarter even than all that. Your old man was smarter even than all that,* Joey. Never forget that. Not only did I keep the secret of the warehouse buys, but when it came down to it, *I didn't sell the land!* No, over the last three or four years, when everyone else started seeing the way it was going, and the values began to shoot up... You didn't even know, did you? You didn't want to have anything to do with it. Well, I didn't sell out to these shyster developers. No, I had them cut me in! Cut me in! Twenty-percent on this project, fifteen percent on that, forty-percent on the Eleventh Avenue parcel. That's where the rest of the money went, Irene," he said, again momentarily addressing her, even looking her in the eye. "Over the last few years, most of it went to fucking lawyers. I've had three fucking lawyers working, even while Testa Transit Storage went to hell. You need shysters to deal with shysters. But now it's all sealed in concrete! All protected! They're good deals! Solid deals with no bullcrap. And finally, after forty years....and sweet Jesus, the debt!" He paused a moment to think about the actual terror of the debt, and the hiding of it, before he brightened to his remarkable climax: "You see, don't you? Both of you? Over the last year, the money started rolling in. Rolling in! Today, we have a bank account with sixteen million dollars. Sixteen goddam million with only four point five million of debt! You've driven by the Bay 500 project? Three hundred seventy-five units, mixed-use? The units are all pre-purchased!

And the building almost finished. In five months, we should make another twenty million, easy." And he snapped the fingers on his free hand, laughing and raising both his arms in a strange and theatrical manner. "We're rich! It happened!"

His arms were open in expectation, but they still just stared at him.

"Well, what do you have to say? What? Look me in the eye so you can see I'm not lying."

Probably they were both about to speak, but at that moment, Cousin Louie poked his head around the corner of the house. He wore a loud shirt.

"Whatever Emile said, trust me, he's lying!"

"Louie!" cried Emile with huge and uncharacteristic élan, and ran to grab his hand.

"Hey, happy birthday Emile! You don't look a day over sixty-five! I thought I'd come early to help out."

"You betcha, Louie," said Emile, pumping a handshake.

All the guests said that Emile appeared more animated than he had in years—for once the life of his own party, arguing politics, making jokes and teasing his grandchild, the highly-thirteen Penny, now a shy girl who wore tiny sandals and a thin white camisole that showed her midriff. He hugged Emmy warmly, several times, so that she laughed aloud and brushed off her dress. He barbequed the usual mountain of hamburgers. The sun was, as usual, too hot. Shade proved, as usual, nearly nonexistent. He drank, perhaps, more than usual. A radio played, but Irene and Joseph seemed strangely subdued. Emmy noticed her husband's distraction, and prodded him at one point to show some cheerfulness for his father's big day. He tried to comply, but around two, he snuck out front in the blinding sun and peeked under the cover to see the car. The Lamborghini was real and fireball red. The finish was mirror bright. He saw that his father was mad, and that he, Joseph, had not ever actually reached adulthood, but had been living nearly four decades in a fantasy of the old man's creation.

Only after dark, when the three of them were again alone, did the future really start. Joseph had sent his wife and only child home to their little apartment, saying he had to help with the cleanup.

"Let's go over this again," said Joseph.

"What do you mean, 'mostly for Joey'?" interrupted Irene, shaking. Her face looked older, desperately etched into some kind of chalky stone.

"Well, he's got his whole future ahead of him," explained Emile, opening his hands, and again with the boyish smile. "But you and I, Irene, we're going to have the time of our lives with the years we have left! We'll go to Rome and Paris! San Francisco! Monte Carlo! Whatever you want."

She slapped his face, hard.

When he could get Joseph alone out on the front lawn, Emile gestured broadly, right over the covered Lamborghini toward Manhattan, where the greater glow hung in the sky. "I know there's more to life than work, and all this crap, Joey. *More!* But someone has to do the goddam work to get there. I don't mind, that's just the way the game is played. I never minded. Only remember: *all this was for you.* I want you to use the money so you and Emmy and Penny know all the best, and nothing but the best. Go to the opera. Buy art! Furs. Travel. See those expensive plays that are supposed to be so damn good. Maybe you'll go back to school and read the classics. Get Penny to read the classics. You should send her to the best schools, Yale, everything. It's all possible, Joey, do you get that yet? Tomorrow, maybe you'll get it. I want to see you and your family bloom. Bloom! That's what I've been working toward all these years," he repeated. "It's for you, son, you and your family now. To bloom!"

Again a long speech. He was an entirely different person. And the look in his eye was terrifying. But Joseph mustered all the maturity he could. "Dad, it's wonderful," he said slowly, "but we need to sit down and talk. Plan this out. I'm still pretty confused here. Let me see the paperwork, okay? I don't want to get Emmy involved until I understand all of this better, that's all. You say I don't need to work, but—"

"Your mother doesn't understand—how could she? She sees things small...her whole life she's been living in a little box. Tomorrow I'll buy her something. It was a mistake just to get the Lamborghini, without something for her. I think she misunderstood."

"She just needs time to re-adjust. We all will. I think she's maybe a little bit angry that you never told her about all this until today. I mean, I see how you—"

"I've had my eye on a bracelet," said Emile. And sure enough, the next day, after sleeping on the couch, leaving the Lamborghini under its cover, and heading to work as usual in his beat up old Ford, he brought home a little wrapped box.

Irene opened it. Inside was a simple, but glittering bracelet.

"They call it a tennis bracelet."

"I don't play tennis."

"It's diamonds and rubies, all the way around. A hundred percent real."

"And how much did this cost?"

"It's worth a lot...try it on. You can adjust the size with that little hook."

"How much?"

"Never mind that. It's beautiful, right? And they're all real. Every single one. When you get a present, you don't ask how much."

"Emile, you've lost your mind."

"Don't worry. I got it on sale—they said forty percent off."

Irene put the open box back down on the table, ever so carefully, and then looked at it as if it were an artifact from another planet—which perhaps it was.

On the third day, sitting behind his old metal desk at Testa Transit Storage, Emile died of a heart attack. He had only driven the Lamborghini once, on the way home from the dealer—though let it be recorded that he enjoyed that drive more than anything else in his whole life. Certainly more than telling his family they were rich. As it turned out, that drive was his actual greatest moment.

Joseph still hadn't told Emmy the big news—and as a result, forever after he remembered her shock and grief at his father's death as the last honest emotion she ever showed. Already at the funeral, he felt his mother drawing rapidly away from him, disappearing as on a train out of town. Everyone noticed how she seemed strangely unperturbed by Emile's passing. Indeed, she spoke hardly at all during the arrangements and the internment, and no one saw her shed a single tear.

"He was so young!" said everyone, apparently as a way to comfort her.

"Sixty-five," she would reply, as if informing them of a fact. When she didn't say more, they put it down to wordless suffering.

"You know, he didn't look so well at his party," threw in Cousin Louie. "He was sweating and breathing really hard. We all should have noticed. He worked himself too much. Emile was a great man, you know, in his own way—a rock."

After the funeral, back at the crowded house, Joseph saw that his mother wore the tennis bracelet. It sparkled against the black cuff of her mourning.

He and his mother were the only people invited to the reading of the will, which took place the next day in an extremely well-appointed office in Midtown Manhattan, on the thirty-ninth floor. The lawyer led them into a large conference room with a good deal of mahogany and a view of the East River. He was grave.

The will had been amended only the week before Emile's death, and it stated that the rest of their lives would go like this: Irene was to receive fourteen million outright, followed by thirty percent of the Testa shares in the Bay 500 Condominum Project then nearing completion. Joseph was to receive more. Much more. His name was already written into most of the contracts, accounts, debts, deeds, and outstanding lines of credit. The lawyer said it was difficult to assess the value of such complex assets, but the firm had done some rapid homework, and if Joseph sold out today, he could realize perhaps two-hundred-forty to two-hundred-eighty million. Selling out would not, however, be advisable. The firm's accounting and investments branch manager, the very reputable Mr. Arno Lucas, was waiting to meet with Joseph and his mother immediately following. Lunch would be brought in.

When the lawyer finished speaking, however, Irene simply reached into her purse, pulled out the keys to the Lamborghini, slipped them across the highly polished table, and said, "Drive carefully, son."

Then she rose and walked out of the conference room without a backward glance.

"Mother, don't be ridiculous," said Joseph, also rising. "We'll rethink this. It's just a will." Amazingly, his tone had changed to something stiff and sophisticated, as if from a movie about the upper classes—he heard the shift himself, as if the music of his voice had ceased from one movement of a symphony and had moved into another. For example, it might have been the first time he ever called Irene "mother" instead of "mom" or "momma," and he saw that it would not be the last. In a stark omen of the years to come, he did not run after her. Do not judge him harshly for this: he had never been on the thirty-ninth floor of a Manhattan highrise, had never heard a will read, met a grave lawyer, or been told he was worth perhaps two-hundred-eighty million. He had only been to state college, married a pleasant but competent accountant, had a daughter, and worked in snack foods, most recently as assistant manager of logistics.

That evening, he finally told Emmy. He waited until after dinner, when their daughter disappeared, as usual, into her room. He spoke for perhaps twenty minutes without interruption, putting the situation as soberly as possible, with all the serious ifs, ands, and buts—so as to keep her grounded. He cautioned that he would have to renegotiate the terms of the will with his mother, as it was so unfair to her. In any case, the joint property laws of New Jersey might void the will altogether.

But then, in one of the most startling experiences of his life, he watched his wife's personality grow larger—much larger, big enough to fill the room and dominate it. The spectacle both scared and comforted him.

"Slow down, Joseph," said Emmy, who was, after all, a certified public accountant. "Don't do anything rash regarding your mother. We need to talk through all the ramifications of this thing. Let's look at all the paperwork, and I mean *all* the paperwork, both with and without the lawyer. Let's take some time to figure this thing out before making any moves. What's the name of your father's law firm again?" And she rattled desk drawers until she could find a pad and pen.

"We have to fix this with my mother right away," insisted Joseph. "I don't know what got into my dad with that crazy will. It's nuts. Mother was devastated. It's all so overwhelming. Do you know, he bought this crazy sports car right before his birthday? It's worth, who knows, a quarter million and it's still parked out in front of their house, under a cover. If any of the local punks take a peek under that cover, it'll be gone in three minutes flat." He produced the keys and thought about recounting the speech his father gave to him about "more to life" and "sending Penny to Yale," but for some reason, he hesitated. This was not the moment.

"Do you trust this lawyer?" asked Emmy, pushing aside larger issues. "Don't tell anyone else. Absolutely no one else. What about your father's brother in California? Is he a player in all this? He didn't show up for the big birthday, or even the fucking funeral."

Joseph was pretty sure that Emmy had never before used the word "player" in such a context, ever. No doubt she was right to begin using words like "fucking." But yes, at that very moment, her soul began to separate from his.

The next day Emmy made a convincing argument, based on his father's own words, that the will should not be changed. "He wanted you to build on the beginnings of his fortune—a second career for both he and you. That was his plan: I mean he *told* you to quit your job. He knew your mother would not become involved in the development business, and he figured that what he left her was more than enough for her to live wonderfully, in fact *really extravagantly,* for the rest of her days. I think you two are going to have a *wonderful relationship* as this thing plays out. I can just see Irene dressed to the nines, escorted by her son to opening nights. It will be wonderful. What's she going to do with more than fourteen million dollars?"

Three years later, Joseph, Emmy, and Penny were living in an apartment on the Upper West Side of Manhattan, in the Seventies, with a big view back across the Hudson toward the lights of New Jersey. Penny was now seventeen, much thinner, and dressed in absurdly expensive jeans. She was no longer shy, but she had become rather gloomy, with a tendency to look at people with her eyes half-closed and eyebrows half-raised, as if enduring rather than listening. She was not yet hostile to the world at large, but she hated her new private school, "Where everyone is like, a fraud."

Emmy had also grown thinner and better looking, and come winter, she wore carefully wrought sweaters that hung in artistic folds. Indeed over the last three years, Emmy—or perhaps at this point we should use her more formal name of Emma—had become the leading partner in the marriage. It was Emma, not Joseph, who kept the family books, consulted the lawyers, and "arm-wrestled" the eight different developers working on Testa lands. It was Emma who found them new friends among charitable committees and private school governing boards. The lawyer Arno Lucas was a frequent lunch companion, and Emma felt a powerful bond with the departed Emile, speaking often and fondly of her father-in-law, and keeping a flattering photo of him on her desk. This desk, a modernist construction of pewter and glass, was situated in a corner formed by two huge windows which came together to point west. It was an impressive arrangement, particularly at sunset.

Irene continued to live in Jersey, though she had moved into a Bay 500 condo which looked right back toward Manhattan. Although she did not know it, she could have picked out the southern lights of the 20th floor apartment of Joseph and Emma across the bay from her own 20th floor unit in Jersey. She did not dress to the nines or go to opening nights. Friends had urged her to contest the will, but she had not, and she had rebuffed most of her son's further efforts to discuss the matter. She now seemed both older than her sixty-seven years, and largely uninterested in the affairs of others, including the doings of her granddaughter. Certainly, she never returned calls from her daughter-in-law. When Emma sold the Lamborghini and generously gave Irene all the proceeds—ten times more money than Irene had ever seen in one place before the Fateful Day—she did not even thank her. Everyone said that Irene should travel, but it hadn't happened yet.

Previous to the Fateful Day, and despite his knowledge of *more,* Joseph's own goals might be summarized as "steady career advancement, a safe retirement, a solid future for his daughter, the happiness of his wife, the purchase of a house in a decent neighborhood, and minor achievements in his chosen hobbies." But after these goals were destroyed, he found to his surprise that all his new goals were provided by the scattered and clumsy words of his father, spoken on the Fateful Day. Thanks to his wife, he no longer saw his father as a madman. Instead, Emile Testa had apparently "known what he was doing better than any of them," and had skillfully played out the forward lines of history to fulfill the highest mandate of his civilization.

Following his father's instructions, therefore, Joseph quit his job, but did not work to build on the family fortune: his father had already done that. Instead, he left the serious management of their affairs to Emma, and began to attend high-minded lectures and go to galleries. He bought tickets to the opera. Surely, he thought, it was now his job, over the remaining forty or fifty years of his life, to justify the long work of both his father and his forebears in bringing him this bounty. What else did all those previous men and women work for all those centuries? Lying in his bed at night, listening to the increasingly impersonal breathing of Emma, and looking out over her sleeping form to the Hudson, glowing like history itself beyond the picture window, he imagined his ancestors strung out in a long desperate timeline: grubbing in the forest, then farming in the dirt, losing countless children, struggling with terrible disease, fighting back barbarians, building and losing cities, preserving culture in dark times, building New York City—until they could finally found art museums and concert halls for his benefit.

Surely the purpose of all those centuries of struggle, as his father realized in his own inarticulate way, *was for Joseph to have and to know more: better clothing, better food, extensive beauty.* If he ignored this bounty, what was the point of those centuries of struggle?

Although he told none of these ideas to anyone, and especially not to Emma, Joseph felt a heavy responsibility to fully live out the human dream, with the weight of ten thousand generations on his shoulders. So even though he felt at first intimidated by great art, and somewhat bored by symphonies and operas, he forced himself to go to pre-concert lectures and after-hours gallery talks. He bought books. And yes, eventually he did begin to see the valuable rarity of great artistic moments, the shine they painted on life which he had not seen before. Emma was busy, but she made sure he had the right clothes, and sometimes joined him at cultural events, especially if she could bring their new friends.

It's hard to say when or why this life led to a near-cessation in marital relations, or how it was, when they did have sex, she treated him like a little boy.

Joseph tried talking Penny into applying to an Ivy League college, but she only stared at him like he was an idiot. The once-shy Penny became increasingly demanding, but dismissive of the very things her demands produced. After a ski trip with her "fraudulent" schoolmates, for example, she decided that she would devote her life to skiing. This sudden purpose greatly excited Emma, so she got the girl lessons, then a coach, then let her out of school for a winter in Chamonix. But skiing paled, Penny returned from France, and soon the state-of-the-art ski equipment hung forgotten in the front hall closet. For a time she focused on ping-pong, and they cleared a room for a table. Ping-pong faded when Penny fell in with a bad, if extremely wealthy crowd at her school, and on her eighteenth birthday, she demanded three months at a detox facility in the Florida Keys with her friend Bethany. She showed them the brochure.

It was about this time, around five years after the Fateful Day, that Joseph began to recall again the vision which had so startled his nine-year-old self. Late at night, not touching his wife and no longer looking out the magnificent picture window at the lights of the river and the works of humankind strung out into the sad reaches of time, he searched up into the dark ceiling and re-imagined the jagged hole in the sky created by the tall pines. The vision appeared perfectly above him, and he realized that through it he could see both our galaxy and galaxies beyond—but not a different universe. At some point after the age of nine, he had learned that despite the speculation of science fiction writers, our universe was large enough that we did not require additional universes. The Milky Way alone held two hundred billion stars, and nearby Andromeda galaxy, about a trillion. Beyond these flew billions more galaxies. Indeed, our universe was not just expanding outward, but actually *accelerating* outward. That meant his own personal expansion, no matter how startling, was simply part of a universal motion toward *more*. And even though the jagged hole offered no escape to a better universe, it did lead to the full expression of the present universe. One did not escape through this jagged opening, it seemed: one exploded through it like smoke.

So explode like smoke he did. In year five, Joseph became a leading, even a known consumer of high culture: He attended numerous well-reviewed plays, sat in the front row of dark poetry slams, wore a suede jacket in the lobbies of great hotels, rode taxis across steaming Manhattan grates at two a.m., participated in meditative retreats, blew cocaine with a woman from Bolivia, and cried out in ecstasy during sex in her tiny Harlem apartment. And though Emma began to chastise him for not building anything larger with his father's fortune, he demurred, for he felt he was on the track of something, and his understanding of the concept of *more* was deepening every day: He had begun, of course, by believing with his father that the highest purpose of the earth was to seek the perfect expression of beauty—the final joy of the most exquisite meal, the most delightful moment, the most finely wrought object. In short, to escape the warehouse and enter the opera house. His role as a wealthy man was to be the admirer, the appreciator, and the funder of noble human efforts lead by others: musicians, artists, and authors. This apparently robust philosophy of life, and his role in it, was encouraged by the owners of galleries, the development arms of great cultural institutions, and the better part of his new friends. Indeed, this philosophy worked admirably for some time, not just in the founders rooms of concert halls, but in Emma's decoration of the condo, which built on the theme of the pewter-and-glass-desk by sporting a good deal of modernist chic.

As his tastes developed, however, Joseph saw beyond this philosophy. After all, most artists and thinkers had come to realize that the purpose of culture was not to find any kind of ultimate beauty, but simply to create many new things—the more utterly new things that existed in the world, the better: art, architecture, graffiti on warehouse walls, dark statements in poetry and grotesque visions (often featuring things like blood or human hair). And if this sometimes led to ugliness and nihilism, to hard metal music and chaotic gestures of the soul, so be it. God the Creator wished simply to continue *creating*—and yes, way beyond opera and symphony, Jane Austen spinoffs, and French food. God clearly wished for all possible things to come into existence: the unlimited stars of the galaxies, the unlimited planets circling those stars, and the unlimited works of His creatures resident on those planets, including the lame, the absurd, and the irregular. Contemporary art proved this. It was not just Joseph's forebears who laid this responsibility for infinite creation upon him, but God Himself. *More* was simply required.

By year seven, however, a certain skepticism set in on this philosophy as well, as he began to notice that that all people and all their institutions, artistic, religious, charitable or otherwise, wanted more, pretty much *all the time, r*egardless of quality or direction. Artists wished to create more, of course. But Emma, too, was not content with two-hundred-eighty million, nor with four-hundred-twenty million when the fortune grew. Nonprofits were ever approaching him with their greater growth plans: new buildings, longer seasons, more children served, a bigger global reach. Mauricia, the beautiful woman from Bolivia with her lovely strain of native blood, the woman with whom he never ceased enjoying sex, wanted to be *more fair-skinned, more American,* and of course she wanted a larger apartment—in fact she was pretty angry when he did not provide a larger apartment. As he became known in the world of high culture, he could no longer go to any event without people hawking him: their causes, their ideas, and their expansive concepts of, well, everything.

Surely, he thought, it could not be his purpose on earth to further *all* such goals.

In year nine, Joseph began to see more clearly that the number and variety of remarkable new experiences did not necessarily improve the quality of his life. More travel, more galleries, more restaurants, more conversation with more clever and increasingly successful people did not necessarily provide, well, *more.* He noticed, for example, a real value to repeating the same experiences *over and over again*. It was worth seeing *Macbeth* more than once, he found, but even better was to haunt the same restaurant and see the same friends over and over again—difficult as that became. He tried revisiting certain paintings and listening to the same music again and again, and he found in this effort a certain comfort. Indeed, after the first novelty of redecorating the West Side condo with bucketloads of money, he began to dislike the way his wife was always *making changes*—new paint, new drapes, a sudden piece of art.

Just about every fucking week.

One day, he sat Emma down and said, in a rather disjointed fashion, "Emmy, I've been thinking. My father wanted us to have more than he had, but I'm not sure we really understand the concept."

"The concept?"

"The concept of *more*. I mean, it seems to me that the people who really understand *more,* realize it doesn't necessarily come from, you know, the kind of nonstop experiences and variety that come with serious money..."

"We don't have serious money. The Grahams have serious money. In this part of town, we're sort of upper middle-class."

"Right," he smiled. "But still, we have enough to pursue new experiences most of the time—what we forget is that new experiences have become the most common things on earth. On TV, there are a thousand channels to watch, a hundred new movies a day, planes and trains to all the exotic possibilities on earth. *Practically everyone can now have new experiences every day.* Every moment there's a new thing to see: Art. You name it. We might as well be sailors, ever out at sea with no home port. We might as well—"

"Joseph, I really don't think—"

"Emmy, who are the people who really understand the concept of *more?* The people who really understand how to be happy? Maybe a monk contemplating his 800-year-old stone garden, or a philosopher studying a raindrop like every other raindrop, maybe a deeply religious person saying the *same prayer* every day, dressing the same way every day, knowing the same people their whole lives, maybe the farmer tilling the same soil, raising his children to be farmers. I don't know, but when you think about it, don't the very wisest people advocate *repeating things?* Emmy, the other day I realized that I was happiest when we had spaghetti every single Thursday night with Penny, or when we watched the same old movie for the fifth time—or if wanted to see a new movie, how we enjoyed repeating the experience of sitting together with popcorn. Even my parents' horrible barbeques in the backyard were friendly in the way they were always the same. Wait.... don't make that face. I'm not saying that being practically poor all the time was a source of happiness, but the *repetition,* that was...well, I'm realizing that was a great joy: the same moment, repeated over and over like a warm blanket. So when you go and redecorate the condo all the time, with all those carpenters, or when you want us to go to the Galapagos—which does sound amazing, I admit—or you acquire more new friends for us, it is not, strangely, creating more." He paused, before stumbling on: "Okay, I can see I'm not making myself clear. It's more like... You see, it's just not what I'm now understanding as *more.* I'm seeing how our friends are always leaving behind their own happiness, again and again, just leaving it behind. All of which leads to something else, a 'much' perhaps, a 'much' across which we all find ourselves spread as thin as varnish." He laughed at himself then, and took her hand. "I just want us to be happy again."

She looked at him with a wifely smile. "I love you Joseph, and you should write all that down, for sure. Fredericka is a Buddhist—did you know that? She probably has some books to recommend. And if you don't like the red walls in the hallway, just tell me, and I'll have them repainted. Did you remember that we're meeting the Andersons tonight at Heather—that's the new restaurant on 80th? She's Nancy and he's Carl. Try to remember: Nancy and Carl. Nancy is president of Friends of the Met, and I want to talk seriously to her—so could I ask you to distract Carl at least part of the time? Your whole repetition theory of happiness is very interesting, he might like it."

As she continued to speak, however, Joseph saw his youthful vision of the tall pines and the jagged hole in the sky with a new terror. Yes, they formed a portal to the infinite unknowable, but the infinite unknowable was no longer the greater truth which kept a mundane life livable. It had become a palpable threat. He remembered now how terror was part of that night, a terror of being drawn up through the hole and disappearing into the sky. And he recalled now, this time without resentment, how his mother had drawn him away that night in haste. Maybe pulling him away had made sense, after all. Maybe one wanted to know that the infinite existed, but one did not necessarily want to *experience* it. In the same way, when God appeared with thunder and lightning on Mount Sinai, the Israelites knew that if they continued to hear His voice directly, it would kill them—so they made God stop talking to anyone but Moses. A regular person might glance up briefly into the infinite, but a regular person could not necessarily survive a journey into those distances—to places cold and airless and forever. Okay, maybe *someone* could, like Moses. Or people trained from birth to be astronauts. For the rest of us, it was no doubt more than enough to know that the infinite was waiting overhead, far above the pines, and out of reach.

When the divorce finally came, Joseph found that Emma was more than fair, especially since she'd found out about Mauricia. His wife had made an accurate accounting of every dime, and as Arno Lucas held her hand, she actually suggested a good lawyer for Joseph's own side. Emma wanted to keep the condo and the *pied-a-terre* in Paris, but he could have the place in the Berkshires. She even volunteered to fly down to break the news to Penny, again down in the Keys, during a week when they allowed visitors.

On the day Emma headed south, Joseph drove to Jersey to visit his mother in the Bay 500 condos. He stood sheepishly in her doorway, but she invited him in without hesitation. In fact, she offered him a motherly smile, settled him on her couch, and pulled up a folding char. Her tennis bracelet sparkled, and as he spilled out his tale, along with his slowly forming theories on the infinite, he realized it was one of the very same folding chairs the two of them had set up on the Fateful Day. When Irene finally got up to make tea, she only said:

"Well, I told you to drive carefully."

And just like that, Joseph knew that like most men, he would never be happy.

LOVES

FICTION
Part I

O cloud-pale eyelids, dream-dimmed eyes,
The poets labouring all their days
To build a perfect beauty in rhyme
Are overthrown by a woman's gaze
And by the unlabouring brood of the skies:
And therefore my heart will bow, when dew
Is dropping sleep, until God burn time,
Before the unlabouring stars and you.
　　　　　　　　　　　—W.B. Yeats, 1899

We begin our discussion of love with an erotic tale. Not for arousal, and not because the world is short of erotic intention, but because sex is rapidly becoming the only poetry able to stand up to the prose of the present day. In a world dominated by eight-lane freeways, five-acre Walmarts, thousand-foot container ships, million-square-foot data centers, two-million-follower blogs, employee-management software, old-age homes, Part A and B Medicare, transmission towers disguised as palm trees, 24/7 news, 24/7 fast food, and the 24/7 chatter of millions and millions, what else can really help us stay human?

We will have to depend on fragrant limbs and stroked thighs for our verse. Everything that used to serve, be it clouds or waterfalls, sailboats or hyacinths, loss or religion, just doesn't seem sufficient anymore. That's why the same people who used to say, "start with love and be patient in waiting for sex" now say, "start with sex and be patient in waiting for love."

Sex occurs in a realm sometimes greater, and sometimes lesser than truth. Imagination drives its true greatness. That's why, in this tale's realm of outright fiction, we can say whatever we wish.

Let's start with Jack, a Caucasian man of about thirty-three, with striking blue eyes, black hair, sharp chin, strong chest, flat belly, and muscular arms. He wears tight jeans and a white dress shirt with the sleeves rolled up. He has three tattoos: a bow and arrow entwined with a vine on his left arm, a cougar in full gallop on his right, and a pagan symbol of uncertain origin between his shoulder blades. And let's introduce him to Jessica, a black woman of thirty-two with exquisitely thin wrists, careless, ever-laughing eyes, and a full, but tight body beneath a purple shift.

Or so Jack notices when he encounters her in a large, brightly lit supermarket. Randomly, as it should be.

Okay, already we go on too long before the event. The erotic should offer only minimal preamble. Let's not, for example, get into the fact that Jack works the loading dock at a packaging concern here in Chicago but has ambitions for his future, pursues an on again/off again girlfriend named Naomi, suffers from a bad left knee (three operations), and lives with, but doesn't get along with his father, Gerald, who seems to care only about his dogs.

And never mind that Jessica is a former shoe salesperson, former manager of a Wendy's fast food place, and is currently interviewing as a floor manager at a store with the loud and prosaic name of Discount Everything!, exclamation point included. All such details would prove tedious.

In fact, sorry. Pretend I said nothing.

Let us forward:

Jack and Jessica encounter each other in the produce section of an incredibly large supermarket while picking out cantaloupe. The lights are glaring. Jessica is inhaling the fruity wonder of a perhaps too-soft melon when their eyes meet. Jack brings his own tawny fruit to his nose, and without breaking the lock of his gaze, he sniffs gently.

"I think it's ripe," he says.

"Maybe overripe," she replies. "Smell the back end."

"Got it," he says, and turns the melon around, places the slight pucker at the end of the cantaloupe against his nose, inhaling more deeply.

"Mmmm," she replies, and with the completion of those (if you count the "mmmm") four lines of dialogue, reality falls apart completely.

Jessica looks round the store to be sure that no one is watching, then pulls down a corner of her purple shift and lowers the right-hand cup of her bra to show Jack a large and suddenly released breast with a magnificent nipple, already stiff and erect. She holds the breast in her right hand a moment, then wets her left forefinger and rubs it on the hard nipple to arouse it further.

Soon it looks like a dark pink eraser tip on a pencil.

Jack, still balancing a cantaloupe in his left hand, takes her offered breast gently in his right, and closing his eyes, brings his face forward and tastes her nipple. It is a long taste, as if he had never tasted a nipple before. He has imagined that black would be different, and it is. For a time he sucks gently, and when he is done, he leans back with a certain indescribable propriety.

They're still in the produce aisle, remember.

"Wonderful," he says. "Salty. So soft around, and so rough in the middle. Ripe."

He releases her breast, just in time, for Jessica sees another, and fairly large black woman not five feet away, on the other side of a fig display, looking at her suspiciously.

"Dropped some cantaloupe," says Jessica.

"That can happen," says the woman, and turns quickly away.

Jack and Jessica share a smile of amusement.

"I've never made love to a black woman before," says Jack. "Never run my fingers down a black belly to the hidden places."

"It's different," says Jessica.

And she reaches out a hand to place it on the crotch of his rapidly tightening jeans, lifting his package twice, to test the weight, like testing the weight of a bag of fruit.

But there's no more time to lose on the preliminaries. It's already noon, Jack has to be back at the loading dock at four, and we have already seen that Jessica dislikes timid introductions. So Jack abandons his own, half-full cart, rolls up his sleeves to better display his tattoos, and follows her through the checkout with only her little basket of two bottles of wine, French bread, butter, salt, and cantaloupe. They hurry to load her car. Absurdly, she tells him to lie down in the back seat, as this is her neighborhood, and she doesn't want anyone to see him.

"Where are we going?" he asks, excited by this bit of drama, and readjusting the grocery bag away from his head. He wonders, obscurely, about the salt. The butter has already entered his dreams, but salt?

"Can you afford a really good hotel?" she asks.

"Yes," he replies.

"Sure, then. We'll head downtown."

And they do, moving right along the freeways as if freeways were suddenly transformed to something remarkable, beneath a sky suddenly turned to dark cobalt, electric, heavy with humid anticipation. In fact, the sky is cloudless but for a thunderstorm gathering to the west and heading steadily across the city toward a tall and elegant hotel of thirty floors.

As they take the exit ramp, Jack reaches both arms round between the bucket seat and rubs her thigh through her dress, hesitates at her crotch, then grasps her two breasts. He has to press his face to the back of her seat to reach properly. It's a little awkward, given the width of the seat.

"How'm I gonna drive?" she laughs.

"You're nervous?" asks Jack, trying to forget his schedule, the fact that he hates his job and most of what happens to him in a given day, a given week. Fuck it. Fuck everything. Fuck. Fuck. Yes, fuck. In this mood he would fuck the back of the bucket seat, the sky, the day, the universe. Now he's fully dreaming. He can already see it in his imagination. Fuck, fuck, fuck. It is an uncontrollable fiction now. The modern world is disappearing. The Walmarts and grocery stores. He is sweating. He even turns off his phone.

On the radio plays, of course, *The Productions of Time*. Which eternity, seeking production, loves.

The thunderstorm breaks out in unrestrained passion just as they enter the lobby of the tall and elegant and expensive hotel. Jack carries the grocery bag with Jessica's wine, French bread, butter, salt, and cantaloupe—all their luggage. He books a tenth floor suite, oh hell, a fifteenth floor penthouse with balcony. Out of discretion, he asks for only one key, and heads into the elevator alone as a precaution, and wonders if she will follow, after all. She could just disappear at this point. He doesn't even know her name...but then names would ruin the random irresponsible joy of everything, of afternoon, of sex, of life itself. Life! Life! Life! He enters the room, which is lavish. A suite he cannot actually afford. Where should he sit? What should he say? He chooses a fake antique chair. He opens the wine with a corkscrew magically available on a side table and lays out the bread and the butter and salt, but hesitates to mess with the cantaloupe. How would he cut it?

He rolls up his sleeves again, as they have fallen over his tattoos. Time ticks by, indecisively, but at last there's a timid knock on the door. He opens it, and sees that Jessica has gone a little shy, as propriety demands.

"Hi." she hesitates.

"Hi," he says. "Wine?"

The door closes. She removes her blouse, walks to the side table, rips the cantaloupe apart with her bare hands, and puts salt on it. "Here," she says, smearing cantaloupe into his face and over her chest.

And now we forget about dialogue, about clothing, cantaloupes, consequences, truth. There is no clothing. No dialogue. No consequences. No uncertainty. No Walmarts or freeways or employee management software. Not even any metaphors: no sailboats or hyacinths, no victory or defeat, no loss or religion. Only her body, redolent with wonder. Only his strong chest, slick with sweat. Only her long fingertips. Only her lips. Only his lips. Her flower. His member. Hair, poetry, wordless, and nothing else. Just humanity, again.

CERTAIN
INEVITABILITIES

"We are well aware of anti-evolutionists' fondness for presenting their audiences with numbers of dizzying magnitude that they use to represent incredibly low probabilities for such events as the chance formation of a protein molecule, the origin of life, and the like. Thus they argue that it is irrational to believe that the event in question could have happened naturally (they mean "by chance") without the aid of intelligent design. In some cases, such as the chance formation of habitable planets, one may avoid a technical discussion of the physical processes involved and respond simply by pointing out that the universe is a very big place, containing countless galaxies, stars, and planetary systems, thus providing so much opportunity for the natural occurrence of the event in question that the probability may be quite high that such an event would occur somewhere. Furthermore, if the universe is infinite, providing the event with infinitely many chances to occur, then the occurrence of the event is a virtual certainty."

—A scientist named Thomas Robson, in 2006

When he was sixteen, R.C. fell in love with his best friend Petey, but Petey did not know it. Petey, who lived a couple streets away in a dull suburb just outside Tacoma, Washington, was also sixteen, but sunny handsome, with a good deal of blonde hair that flew a bit wild. Petey himself was a bit wild, or would have been, but for R.C. From ages ten to sixteen, they were inseparable. Petey provided the excitement, but R.C. was the one who prevented Petey from shoplifting a camera at Walmart when they were twelve. From climbing out of Randy Johnson's second story window when they were fourteen. From skipping math class more than two times in a row during freshman year of high school. Petey would get that huge and mischievous grin on his face that both thrilled and scared R.C.: the grin that made him look like Peter Pan in the Disney cartoon in this, the halcyon time before digital technology.

At such moments, Petey became a demon of joy. An avatar of life. He would call for an "evil adventure," but then R.C. would be the one to "exercise some fucking sense."

They were "Petey and R.C.": an arrangement that worked for pretty long.

Midway through their sophomore year, however, Petey really got into bicycles, began reading bicycling magazines, saw the movie "Breaking Away" (just to nail down the precise timeframe for you) and come summer, started riding around the neighborhood shirtless, like every day. He started lifting weights, and he became ever more beautiful, his blonde hair more wild, his role in R.C.'s existence ever more symbolic.

Sadly, as Petey's beauty increased, R.C. began to suffer. He lost sleep. He had fearsome dreams. Several times he cried. Soon, he wrangled himself a decent bike, often removed his own shirt, and because sex is fiction, he began to imagine that he and Petey had a special understanding—something that went beyond friendship. Often, when they were together, R.C. imagined reaching out to touch the other boy. *Just a little touch.*

One late August afternoon found them working on their bikes in the shade of Petey's garage, with the garage door open wide onto the sun-drenched suburban street. Petey, thin and shirtless as usual, had his whole crankshaft apart to regrease the bearings. It was an Italian brand of crankshaft, which like the boy in the movie, made him extremely proud. He was using gasoline to clean the bearings, and the smell of it hung sharply in the air.

Then an odd thing happened.

"Hang on," said R.C., and instinctively reached out with a rag to wipe some grease off Petey's forehead. Petey looked up with something like a scowl. At that moment, an unnamed but unbridgeable awkwardness fell between them.

Over the next few days, without at all knowing why, Petey became annoyed with R.C.'s big words and constant worry. He became annoyed with his friend's inability to enjoy loud music. He grew irritated with the way R.C. let his hair fall over his eyes, in probable imitation of the way his own hair fell over his eyes. He suddenly realized that these things had bothered him for a long time. When school started up in September, they began drifting apart. Or rather, Petey began avoiding R.C., at first subtly, then obviously. He no longer sat with him on the bus. He turned down invitations to play Risk or to go for a ride. If you asked Petey why, he might have said, "It's high time I fucking grew up."

The moderating influence of R.C., of course, declined in parallel to this development. By winter, Petey was hanging with a faster, cooler crowd. He smoked a good deal more weed, and drove his parents' station wagon ever more dangerously. He got laid by the most popular girl in school—which made sense, because he was the most handsome guy. But he caught something from her which proved the very devil to shake. When it came time to pick a college, Petey looked for a party school. At the party school he joined a rowdy frat and barely kept a C- average before dropping out altogether. At twenty-six he was working part time in the back of a bike shop in downtown Portland, and was well on his way to becoming a negligent parent to a sweet little girl he'd fathered with a woman named Candy. At thirty-one, he took over the bike shop: but he was not sufficiently organized to make it a success, especially with his, as his sister put it, "fucked up tendency to head for Mexico for weeks at a time." He raced bikes some, but never really got that going either. Eventually, the shop failed. By thirty-five he had become something of an alcoholic, and Candy began to keep their little girl away from him. By forty-three, in his own words, he was "pretty goddam screwed up," and it became clear that middle age would not treat him well.

Not surprisingly, R.C.'s life followed a very different trajectory. During those last two years of high school, he did not easily forget Petey. After all, Petey was still displayed spectacularly before him every day: beautiful on the bus, beautiful on his street, beautiful at school events, and often grinning that huge, wild-haired grin for others. For a while, being separated from his Demon of Joy was a new, and much worse kind of torture than being in the Demon's untouchable presence. But as he slowly freed himself from all obsessive but impossible possibilities, he found new purpose in his studies. He worked hard and got super grades. His parents smiled. And eventually, of course, he did forget Petey. He won a scholarship to Cornell, where he was president of the debate club, labored feverishly in student government, and majored in economics. At grad school he worked slavishly for a professor who suggested that Robert Clarington (for he was no longer R.C.) pick up a law degree, so he did. In the course of time, this professor became governor of the state of Oregon, and Robert became an economics policy aide in the statehouse. Eventually he became known as a "key advisor," and was often quoted in the press. He wore good suits. He "met with lawmakers." Along the way, when he found time, he dated women. At thirty-four, he married Patricia Kent, a no-nonsense economist who hailed from Massachusetts. She was a bit younger, as well as tall, blond, and forthright. He liked that at first. They had two girls in quick succession. Patricia's parents, who had nearly given up on grandchildren, exulted. Robert's own parents were dead—with only a cheerful footnote in this history to mention that they had given Robert his focus, his honesty, and his ambition, which are all good things.

Robert at first tried hard to be a conscientious father, but he was gone a great deal for his job. As his responsibilities increased, he developed prematurely gray hair, a slight paunch, and an intimidating way of talking. This combination worked for pretty long, but his life sort of peaked at forty-two, when it became clear that middle age was not going to treat him well.

Robert's biggest single problem, at least according to Robert, was not really *his* problem at all: it was Patricia's once-beguiling forthrightness. She liked to "talk things out." She liked to "get things straight." This caused arguments over petty details, and because they had no "quote-unquote love," as Robert said out loud one awful morning, it was tough to ride out the petty details. Tough to enjoy life at all. He was a precise and highly organized man, and the chaos of the kids and the chaos caused by disagreement was more than he could stand: maybe, he thought, he was screwed up by being an only child, and maybe he had waited too long on the family thing. A coldness arose around him. Both his wife and his girls found him distant. At work he was, without his knowledge, becoming known as something of a scold and a naysayer: "tediously cautious," as one man said. It stalled his career. The governor lost interest in his opinions, which could always be predicted in advance and so became unnecessary.

At last, Robert Clarington was quietly moved out of the statehouse to a "liaison office" in Portland. A mild but palpable depression set in, and as he grew increasingly unhappy, Robert made a conscious priority of being away from home as much as possible. He worked later than necessary. As an escape and as an expression of unended youth, he bought an absurdly expensive bicycle with a carbon frame that weighed practically nothing. He purchased bicycle clothing in bright colors. Pedaling alone along damp Oregon roads, he could be at peace. No one wanted anything from him when he was on a ride. No one criticized him. If he heard any amusing echo of his teenage infatuation in the bicycle hobby, he did not care.

Robert was not a religious man. When pressed, he subscribed to a vague agnosticism: but late one April afternoon, something happened which proved to him that life is driven if not by a playful God, then at least by supernatural ironies.

He had taken to commuting by bike whenever possible. It was a long and somewhat dangerous ride along busy expressways, but he felt this ride did his soul good. That April evening of gray skies and mists he was caught by an unexpected rain three-quarters of the way home. And as he was pounding up a particularly treacherous climb with practically no shoulder, he got caught behind a ragged man pedaling slowly uphill on an old drop-handle bike from which hung a half-dozen black, rain-beaded trash bags. A sopping bedroll was strapped to the back. Cars were hissing by both of them.

At last, Robert shifted his smooth, $1500 derailleur into a higher gear. "Can I pass?" he yelled in irritation.

Startled, the man half turned to look, causing his bike to wobble toward traffic. A car clipped him, maybe without the driver even being aware. The bike went over violently, trash bags scattered and burst, and the man himself skidded across the wet pavement, long hair flying.

"Fuck!" said Robert, laying his own bike against the embankment, and dragging the man off the roadway. He saw that the victim was bleeding, and one arm was hanging at a strange angle. The man was conscious, but mumbling something indistinct. He smelt of alcohol and wet, unwashed clothing. And worse.

Robert called an ambulance, and propped the man up against the embankment, pulling a grimy army-green hood up against the rain.

"Just sit tight. The ambulance will be here pretty fast," said Robert.

"You know what?" said the man in a hoarse voice, admiring Robert's weightless bike: "You got a bitchin' machine."

A police car and an ambulance arrived together—the cop making a big show of stopping traffic while they loaded the man onto a gurney. The cop recorded Robert's statement on a clipboard, where his thumb held the ragged man's I.D. card. He'd written the man's name into the form, and when Robert saw this name, it was all he could do to keep from pulling the clipboard away to get a better look.

Strapped into the gurney, Petey had closed his eyes tightly, as if to make the whole scene go away. But sure enough, sure enough, there beneath the blood and the swelling and the tangle of wet wild blond hair and the twenty-five intervening years of progress and misery, Robert could see the clear resemblance.

The world became strangely quiet, experienced as from a distance.

"I'll just be going then," Robert heard himself say to the cop, who was roughly heaving Petey's bike into his trunk. The cop offered Robert a ride, but the rain was lessening, and he said he still had enough daylight to make it on his own.

Robert Clarington had ridden those last three miles home a hundred times, but this time the sky was preternaturally large with sunset. Time seemed to flatten. His life seemed to collapse like an old telescope. Had it all been some kind of dream? The career? The marriage? All some tedious movie and he was just emerging from the show?

Now he was eager to get home. Eager to see his kids. Eager to see Patricia, even to hold her. But when he came in the door, the girls were playing with large bright plastic toys and waved him off. Patricia was cooking dinner, and when he entered the kitchen, the usual chill arose, as he often said, "like death." He kissed her on the cheek, and she gave him a slight smile.

He had meant to tell her about the accident, but now, somehow, he could not.

That night, unable to sleep, Robert dwelt again in Petey's garage. He was again sixteen. He saw the crinkled smile on the beautiful face. Felt the summer heat. Smelled the gasoline. Heard the boyish laugh of his personal Demon of Joy. And yes, he recalled the fearsome dreams. Remembered even the actual terrible moment he wiped Petey's forehead with the rag. The actual odd look on Petey's face when he did that. The awkwardness.

In the morning, he called the ambulance company and found out where they'd taken Petey: a grade B hospital in a bad part of town. All day, however, he couldn't work up the courage to call. "Fuck, fuck, fuck," he said ever more rapidly, and aloud.

At last, on the second day, just before lunch, he called the hospital.

"Are you his brother?" asked the nurse.

"Brother? No, I'm just concerned because I was there at the accident," said Robert Clarington.

"Okay. That's real nice of you. He keeps saying his brother is coming to pick him up, but we can't get ahold of nobody at the number he gave us. His sister and his ex-wife also weren't interested. Anyway we can't wait any more. We're going to have to discharge. Legally *required* to discharge, you understand. So if you want to talk to him, you'd better do it now. I don't think he has his own phone or anything."

"Is he okay?"

"Just scrapes, as in lacerations—and of course, the fracture."

"The left arm."

"You want to talk to him or not?"

Robert got in his nice car. He started the engine. On the road, he observed stretches of long white cloud like a foamy wake across the purposeless blue ocean of Heaven. It was all very odd at this point: his whole fucking life, that is.

At the hospital, the nurse nodded him down the hall. He opened the door. Middle-aged Petey was asleep. The left arm lay in a full cast. The face had been cleaned up, even shaved, and he could see that its essential pixie-like characteristics persisted, if much ruined—no doubt by too much alcohol and too much outdoors. The blond hair, still as always uncombed, fell across the pillow.

Robert chickened out and turned to go.

U nfortunately for the once-key advisor, however, God takes such an inexplicable interest in human beings that He likes to create certain inevitabilities. Not "fates," perhaps—that seems too strong a word. Just certain inevitabilities. Things that just have to play out, you know, eventually. In the Biblical story, for example, God decrees that Jonah must go to Nineveh. What happens at Nineveh is partly up to Jonah, partly up to Nineveh, and partly up to chance, but God sends both an ocean squall and a whale to *ensure* that Jonah at least completes the fucking journey: that much, it seems, *has* to happen. The rest, who knows.

Some inevitabilities seem entirely trivial. It's a safe bet that God sometimes creates a river just so that someday someone might go skinny dipping in it. This might happen in 1650 or 1750 or 1850 or 1950 or 2050, but it apparently damn well *has to happen* before the river fulfills its purpose, dries up, and the universe moves on.

You think I'm making this up, but if you read any novels or especially if you see any movies, you know I'm right. Some things just have to happen. Such is the basis of almost every story we desperate humans tell. We sense a great truth, so we create books and movies to prove it true. Those two great generals just have to meet. The villain just has to make a mistake. If nature itself must bend to this purpose, nature will be bent. Just when or how, well...randomness is preserved, but certain inevitabilities get their due.

In the present situation, God stepped in to blow a cloud away from the sun, so that at that moment, the actual purpose of this great and astounding celestial body, weighing in at 2,000,000,000,000,000,000,000,000,000,000 kg and floating 93,000,000 miles away – the total purpose of the sun at that brief moment was to shine directly through the hospital window and strike Petey in the eye, just as Robert was turning to go.

Petey put up a hand for shade.

"Do I know you?"

Robert smiled awkwardly, and looked into the familiar blue eyes.

"I'm the guy who picked you up off the road a couple days ago. I came by to see how you were doing."

"Right. Very nice. Guy with the awesome all-carbon Scattante. Thanks." And then he squinted. "But we've met before, no?"

"Yes."

"And...?"

Robert's nose twitched just enough for Petey to notice. "I think we knew each other ages ago," continued Robert in a businesslike manner. "Up in Tacoma. When we were kids."

"No mind trips, man."

"I'm Robert Clarington. Remember? We were friends when we were kids?" He paused. No light dawned. "And then for a while in high school. You called me R.C."

An amused light dawned in Petey's eye. "No shit? You're R.C.? Of course I remember. Not sure I ever knew your last name." And thanks to the way not God, but humans organize the universe, their relationship immediately fell into the same old pattern, even though interrupted by twenty-five years. In other words, Petey took charge.

"R.C., no shit? That was you, by the side of the road yesterday? You pulled me off and called the ambulance?"

"Yeah, that was me."

"Pretty wild, isn't it? How weird is that."

"Yup. Pretty wild."

"No shit," repeated Petey, and shook his head. Then, being still Petey, began to laugh. "You gotta laugh, right? You gotta laugh about that one. Of course I remember you. Remember Walmart?"

Robert forced a second smile as Petey laughed, loud and demon-like. "Those were the fucking days. Sit down, R.C., sit down and tell me about yourself."

"They're going to throw you out of here in half an hour."

"So tell me fast. Give it to me fast. I can see you done well. The suit. Shit, a wicked Scattante with a Dura Ace train."

"I'm a kind of lawyer, but I work for the governor's office here in Portland. I'm married with two girls. They're seven and five."

"Of course! A lawyer, of course! Me, I'm a fucking bum. I fucked up good, R.C." He smiled big. "I've got a kid, too, or I did – but my ex won't let me see her. I stuck with bikes, no kidding, even owned a shop once. I still got a bike, though, and even though it's shitty, it gets me around. I lost touch with everyone, even Tommy and Evan. Or maybe you didn't hang with Tommy and Evan."

"No. I don't think I remember a Tommy and Evan."

They stared at each other. There didn't seem to be a lot more to say, life-story-wise.

Petey smiled again, with something of the old charm: "Can you do me one more favor, R.C.? You got a car? Can you give me a ride to the police station? I have to pick up my bike and shit."

Robert looked at his watch. "Sure, Petey. Why not? I can give you a ride over there."

Petey admired Robert's car. He played the HD radio. But of course, when they picked up the bike, they both knew Petey couldn't ride it with a broken arm. Plus, this being Portland, a cold rain had started. They stood outside the grim and darkling police station, just under the overhang, watching the rain chatter across the parking lot.

What could Robert do?

"So, let me offer you a place to sleep tonight. Just for tonight, you see, my wife—"

"That would be really cool, R.C. Just for tonight, I swear." And this time Petey really showed the old Peter Pan grin. "You say you have two girls? I'll show them my card tricks. I have killer card tricks."

They had still not shaken hands, nor had they hugged, nor had they touched in any way.

Patricia, whose influence and meaning in the story of Petey and R.C. will prove to be surprisingly unimportant, was, of course, uncomfortable. Her normally tight, New England features quickly became tighter and more New England-like. Okay, so this Petey was an old friend of Robert's, but not from out of town—so why did he need a place to sleep? Trash bags filled with clothes? You're kidding, right? And surely, his clothes smelt awful. The girls, at least, were charmed for twenty minutes before bedtime. Petey's card tricks were not particularly killer, especially one-handed, but they had not seen them before.

In the bedroom together at 11:23 p.m., Patricia put on her most sexless nightgown, which was thick and navy blue, and said, "Well?"

"Well, he'll be gone tomorrow."

But Petey was not gone tomorrow. Nor the day after. He got the old TV in the guest room working. He took apart his bike in the garage, one-handed. He laid out his clothes to dry on folding chairs with a space heater blowing. He walked down the hall in Robert's sweat pants with pink earbuds plugged into his ears. He taught the girls to play a card game called "Pass the Trash." He told stories about laughable customers who visited his old bike shop. He pulled a ragged sketchbook from one of his horrid plastic trash bags, and did a passable sketch of the tall pine trees that waved wet and dark just beyond their backyard deck. On the third night, Petey's own daughter visited, thanks to a weak moment on the part of his ex-wife. The daughter was no longer sweet, but now sixteen and morose, with a grim tattoo on her neck. She said not a word through dinner, and then sat in the family room texting until her mother picked her up.

Here we might pause to note that just as this is not Patricia's story, nor the story of their two girls, it is not Petey's daughter's story either.

God Himself may be handling all these other multiple storylines, each with their inevitabilities, and He may be directing the great and noble sun to shine more or less brightly on each—but we are here to focus on the story of Petey and R.C. That's just the way it works when we are forced to explain the actions of God.

By 10:23 p.m. on the fourth night, Patricia was openly angry. "I'm not hearing a plan here," she said to Robert. At 10:28, they had a titanic marital argument. As with most titanic marital arguments, it was only peripherally related to the problem of Petey, it was more about "respect." Petey's visit was part of a "pattern of disrespect," which included Robert's disrespect for her ideas, his unhelpfulness to her job-hunting brother, and his failure to aid the girls with their homework, their soccer practice, or acknowledge their incipient sibling rivalry. In general, ran her quite lucid and well-evidenced argument, Robert didn't seem to give a shit about his family. Or care about his job anymore, either. Robert objected, but being a lawyer, he knew better than to defend himself directly; he knew he had to shift the agenda. He attacked her "nonstop criticism," and then really pissed her off by discussing the future.

He said, "If you convince me I'm a creep, what then? Will we be happier people? What will be the probable result of that convincing? Will I become a different person?"

It had been raining all week, but that evening in a second or perhaps third demonstration of God's strange interest in the story of Petey and R.C., the wind really kicked in. Heavy drops beat against the windows as Robert and Patricia yelled. The dark pines creaked. Separately, in their two bedrooms, the girls covered their ears against both the argument and the storm. Petey, accustomed to noisy public shelters, slept like a log. Just after midnight, the wind tore the plastic sheeting off a little greenhouse where Patricia had been forcing tulips. She immediately recognized the sound. "Shit," she said, and broke off the titanic argument to run out the sliding glass doors of their bedroom, across the slippery redwood of their new, custom-built deck, and then down into the invisible back lawn.

There a branch fell from a dark pine and killed her.

The governor himself called. It had been some time since that had happened, but he spoke as if he and Robert were still close: "Who can figure anything, Robbie? Patricia was such a wonderful lady, so full of life, such a terrific mother. It's so unfair. It's so unfair to you and the girls. Reverend Paul will be saying a few words, and dedicating the legislative session to her tomorrow."

The governor's words seemed to come from down a long tunnel. They seemed to be words spoken by a stranger. Once again, Robert had the weird sense of the universe collapsing in on itself like a telescope. You looked through this telescope without hope because you could not distinguish the distance between things, because within this particular telescope everything was more or less the same size and weight, and packed horribly together as within the too-tight metal casing of the known realms of man. Was this strange feeling just grief over the death of Patricia? Two days had passed. The girls were at the Sheraton with Patricia's parents, who had flown in and set up shop in the Honeymoon Suite.

"Robbie, you still there?" came the concerned voice of the governor.

"Thank you, Governor," he heard himself saying. They were the last words he would speak to his one-time mentor, friend, and sponsor. No more governor for Robert Clarington.

When he hung up the phone it was about eleven a.m., and Petey was, as usual, asleep in the back room. On impulse, Robert walked back to see again the ruined face, the puffy eyes, the tangled hair— and evaluate them, as he had taken to evaluating them each day. Was there any meaning in all this? It was more like a story in a book than like real life. Surely, some wonderful Spark of Life still burnt somewhere within the knowable realms of man, but only in the hearts of other, probably younger men. He and Petey were surely too old to host the Spark of Life, fucking either of them. They were both failures. He said it aloud to the sleeping form. "We are both failures, Petey—it just took me a little longer. But how is it that we are now in the same house? How is that possible? Is it a joke? Surely, it is a joke."

Petey did not awake, so Robert went back into the living room and switched on the TV.

Two months passed, and a curious thing happened. Robert Clarington declined, but Petey thrived. Robert now could not get himself to go to work at all. He tried to see his lovely, sweet girls, but he would break out crying each time—not because he missed Patricia, but because his girls seemed like strangers to him. He seemed to have nothing to say to them. Patricia's parents thought that maybe it would be for the best if the girls lived with them for a bit, back in Massachusetts. No doubt, the grandparents were right.

Petey, on the other hand, began to work out on the cross-training machine in the rec room. He rode Robert Clarington's weightless bicycle out on the damp green Portland roads. He stopped drinking. He ate salads. He listened to loud music in the pink earbuds. And even if he did not get a job, or even *try* to get a job, he nevertheless, little by little, became beautiful again.

Okay, he became more ruggedly, even craggily handsome than *beautiful,* but at all events, possessed again of good cheer and an attractive wildness. In fact this good cheer and handsomeness and wildness returned with such force that we have to ask: maybe he never really needed a "job" job to be a proper Avatar of Life. Maybe being Avatar *was* his job.

For a long time, Robert did not notice this change coming upon Petey. He was too depressed. He was trying too hard to figure out what to say to the people at the office about his absences. He told them he needed to take a couple of months off, and they gladly let him. He was trying too hard to keep Patricia's parents convinced of his sanity so they would not file some legal motion regarding the girls. He kept trying to script out his conversations with the girls, even writing them down. But nothing seemed to make his brain work properly. He was thinking too much about telescopes. Staring too long at walls.

You may not believe my earlier assertion that some things just *have* to happen. That not just human authors, but God Himself believes in certain inevitabilities. Believe what you may, in this case a thing happened on a Tuesday morning in April at 8:17 a.m.

R.C. had awoken early from a dream about sex and wheat fields, though he did not remember either. He made coffee and sat in the t-shirt and gym shorts in which he usually slept. Then Petey entered in glory. Like the spring itself he entered: shirtless and hooting and headed through the kitchen for the Scattante stored in the garage.

"What's so funny?" asked R.C.

"Nothing's funny, R.C. That was a cry of happiness. It's just a gorgeous day, that's all, after a week of crap rain. My arm's all better, and after I tinker with your wicked machine a bit, I'm going for a ride."

He paused and shot R.C. a look. "Maybe *you* should get *your* shit together and go to work."

It was a statement about everyone's proper place in the cosmos, and it seemed to put things into perspective. Everyone had a job, perhaps even a purpose in the proper universe: R.C. working. Petey bicycling. Morning arriving. The girls playing somewhere. Patricia finally at rest. God in His heavens. Soft wind along the avenues. Sunlight following the kitchen conversation like an angel perched outside the window, doing its job, too.

"Oh," said R.C. He sat for a time drinking his coffee. And then his depression seemed to pass. To pass! This too! He rose. He went to the bathroom. He shaved and showered as in music. He put on fresh clothing. And then he went out to the garage, where he saw Petey in full tight biking garb, standing in the richly attendant light—the sunlight from God's chosen heavenly body pouring in from morning. God existed, after all. "Let there be light," he thought—that being the only command of God R.C. really knew. Petey's blond hair was long but tied with a bandana. He had a slight belly and a battered profile and a hoarse voice, but he was again the Demon of Joy.

"Petey, I have a confession to make," said R.C. "I— "

"Oh what the hell," said Petey, and kissed R.C. full on the lips. It just seemed like the thing to do. Then he shrugged and went for his ride.

The BRIGHT FOREST

My beloved spoke, and said unto me:
'Rise up, my love, my fair one, and come away.
For lo, the winter is past, the rain is over and gone;
The flowers appear on the earth;
The time of singing is come, and the voice
  of the turtledove is heard in our land;
The fig-tree putteth forth her green figs,
  and the vines in blossom give forth their fragrance.
Arise, my love, my fair one, and come away.

—from 'The Song of Songs,'
attributed to King Solomon, circa 950 BCE

This planet may host a thousand worlds, or maybe millions: worlds within worlds, each nation a deck of cards, each citizen a new deal. But as certain as Gregory might be that many worlds must exist, he knew that he had claims in only two. He could live in the world which contained Sylvie, or he could live in the world which did not. He had a secret name for the world with Sylvie. He called it the Bright Forest.

Sometimes she could draw him into that world merely by speaking his name on the telephone. "Gregory?" she would begin uncertainly, and then pause. The uncertainty itself seemed to undo the normal world. It was like a fairy-call, and in that brief silence, Gregory would be drawn, sometimes against his will, into the forest ruled by the misrule of Sylvie: a fairy queen and dark, with the serious expression of a girl, not of a woman. In the forest, she was at times openly a child, but no less the author of the tale. Much later, when he lived in the other world full time, the world without Sylvie, the Big World as he called it, he liked to say that he once knew someone who had thought about growing up but had thought better of it. People would smile when they heard this kind of thing, would joke about Peter Pan, but later, privately, he felt bad. Privately, he said, "What if innocence matters?" And he admitted to himself that when young with Sylvie he had looked up into windy sunlit birch trees and they had both seen the leaves flash in great numbers. And only when together! This was tantamount to a confession of faith by a fallen child, and it tore at him so much that sometimes long later he would pick up his phone and call her, and begin, uncertainly: "Sylvie..." then pause for the fairy-call in return...and say, again like a child himself: "Oh Sylvie, today I turned forty-one."

As a boy, Gregory was pale, with pale eyes that you could look straight through without interest. Drive into the suburbs and you might see dozens like him—boys with bikes and the pettiest temptations. He had gone to college as a studious lad without a clue on how to make friends or find a lover. He wrote to his parents: "Dear Mom and Dad: All is well. It looks like I have made peace with my Econ 12 T.A., and have been to the beach three times. I should be able to make your check last until February." When it rained outside his dormitory, however, he opened his window for the wet smell. And sometimes, like a premonition, he would walk out into a night of crickets and feel a largeness in the sky—but nothing much more than that until he met Sylvie.

They met as freshmen in English Lit 221: The Romantics, where they were in the same section, and Sylvie was the only one who really cared about Byron, who she called an elitist pig. He just thought Byron a bore, though there was something to some of that stuff by Keats. She loved Keats, and Shelley too, but hardly bothered to turn in assignments. Sylvie was no "college girl," but merely "in college" the way an animal wanders into a serious place, an office or a classroom, sniffs and wanders out again. She told him seriously that professors murdered all poetry. That poets were in fact real people who really cared about what they were writing, and not in the least what stupid college students or professors said about it. That poets had actually seen the magic in the world and tried to communicate it, and that he should try reading their stuff under a tree without looking for the fucking underlying themes. "Seriously, Gregory. Tonight." And she took him out at ten p.m. with his book and a flashlight and a jar of peanut butter in case they got hungry.

Of course they kissed, and her hands roamed, and they fell in love.

In love! There came a day when he walked into a city park in the full knowledge of being in love—looking at the other people in wonder, as if they must know. Of sharing secret amazements in the eyes of other young people, who must be, like himself, *in love*. If only he had known that it was all true, all along, all of it. Neither Gregory nor Sylvie were handsome people, but love does not require physical beauty, it only requires an alliance with beauty. So the two of them forgot about literature and sought beauty together everywhere—parks, houses, restaurants, bed.

In the face of this alliance with beauty, other things fell away. And so there came another amazing day when Gregory walked down the main street of the college town in full knowledge of Sylvie failing in all her classes. Not just one, but all. This information overwhelmed his previous knowledge of how the world operated. He saw how *provisional* and *fraudulent* the Big World was, and he ran into a store to buy champagne and potato chips to bring them back to her for a celebration of freedom. In the right light, this was a magnificent act, the act of a prince to his princess—and of course, after that, there was nothing for it but to fail along with her. He wrote to his parents, announcing his decision to drop out of college: "Dear Mom and Dad, I am finally taking responsibility for my own life. I think I'm about to discover a great truth, but I'm not sure what it is."

He was, of course, about to discover the deepest extents of the Bright Forest, a world where anything might become beautiful. In the Bright Forest were green bottles and mossy curbsides, wet iron railings, bits of colored paper caught in the trees. A world like a fine photograph. He could see roads leading to dilapidated gas stations, sudden rocky overhangs, rows of maple, the gathering places of strangers. In the Bright Forest no one read newspapers on trains; they ran their fingers across the cold windowpanes, drawing circles. Later, at the station, people did not speak of schedules, they huddled against each other on benches and whispered. Or played guitars. Sometimes these same men and women would walk into the alleyways behind restaurants, or lie naked together behind the hedges in a public park. In the Bright Forest, goals did not matter, *only each step mattered,* each momentary act—each meal of crackers and cheese, each raindrop in wintertime, each glance, each motion of the hand before the eyes. Sylvie and Gregory rented a shabby room together, got low-paying jobs, and before long the Bright Forest was everywhere: painted on the vinyl cushions of diner booths and tall against the blank stares of cars in parking lots. Each object in the natural world was but a marker for a potent force in the Bright Forest, each work along its paths a work of gods. In the distance, somewhere, was a lazy conductor beating a slow baton: Now you will sleep, will sleep, now you will make love. They would listen and lie together on long afternoons, would lose jobs for lying together on long afternoons.

Months passed effortlessly and grandly. Gregory let his head grow foggy and warm for whole weeks at a time. Sunlight would cross dusty rooms, grow weak with winter, strong with summer. He was for a long time a kind of prince, and in these, which he considered his finest hours, he was capable of the most royal actions: a quarter to a bum, a long night holding Sylvie when her father died. Prince Gregory could open his eyes to the near and the far and see them both as his dominion. Up close was Sylvie, her face, her hands, her frequent illnesses, her fears. In the distance were palaces: deeper glens, sea cliffs. Each palace they must find, or each palace would never be found by humankind, for there seemed to be no sight but their own. One afternoon in the year he was twenty would remain with Gregory for the rest of his life, a moment of greatness few people in this world can claim: the two of them standing on a small grassy hill in a public park. A breeze was blowing, and hand in hand, the whole earth was telescoped into the power of Sylvie and Gregory, young and in love and *owning it*, just owning it all. Looking out, Gregory felt *benevolence* toward the scene, felt *benevolence and generosity of spirit*, as would any great man.

Over the course of four years, however, Sylvie and Gregory changed from eighteen to twenty, and then to twenty-two. Despite the best efforts of the forest, Sylvie discovered that Gregory retained ambitions. He found that she could sometimes look strong and serious. One night he brought a lamp up close to her face and declared that she had become a woman.

"Really?" she asked.

"Really," he said.

She had no secrets from him, of course, and they began to talk about children. Carelessly, but they talked. "Imagine me having a baby," Sylvie would say, squatting and pretending to pull a baby from her womb. "It would just come out, like this." She did not know his secret term for their relationship, the "Bright Forest," but she knew that theirs would be the first baby of some amazing world. This baby would walk with them hand in hand among its trees. They would found a dynasty born in the poverty of the Bright Forest. A dynasty!

Nevertheless, talk of a child triggered an ancient male fear which lay dormant but deep inside Gregory. Time, he saw, was hotting up. Conversations such as the following began to occur:

Gregory (condescendingly): "I don't understand how you could have lost your fucking keys again. Look, I keep mine on this nail by the door. They're always there and I can always find them."

Sylvie (in tears): "What does it matter, Gregory? What does it fucking matter?"

Though such scenes became common, a greater threat arose. For the Bright Forest had a determined enemy, and his name was "Morning." All was well when they slept in and kept the shades drawn, but sometimes Gregory would awake early with a curious restlessness, and leaving Sylvie in the humid bedroom, he would walk out into the Morning. At Morning he heard the brass of trucks and streetcars, the cries of work and doing, could smell the clean hard smell of dew evaporating from the Big World, see mailmen. Eventually, Morning became a kind of religion with him. "Sylvie just doesn't understand this," he told himself, observing the early people and secretly smiling at their purpose. "These people understand something she just does not understand at all." And when he returned to find Sylvie still asleep, the bedclothes warm to the touch and the shades peeking pinpricks of sunlight; when he touched the damp shine of sleep on her forehead and smelled the smell of long untidy human habitation; he began to be repelled.

Frightened, he'd close the door and go into the kitchen to make coffee. Once, he even called his parents for advice.

Sylvie began to sense a change in Gregory, and it became an uncomfortable joke between them that he was never home when she awoke. "I want to wake up together," she would say. "We can open our eyes at the very same instant and then just lie there for a while before going to work or whatever." And often, after his new routine of newspaper and coffee, Gregory would return to the bedroom, and, consciously steeling himself against—what, he didn't know—he would crawl back into bed, and awaken her with much charm and grace. But this effort became deception and acting.

Gregory began to ask: was the Bright Forest merely a stepping stone to another, even finer world? And once that question had been asked, Morning was no longer enough. The idea of a baby born in the Bright Forest became more and more a threat. The Big World seemed more and more a release.

One day, Gregory got a real job downtown, to which he went at the appointed hours and worked not just for cash, but advancement. Such joy he took in arriving at a cold office in a gray a.m. would be hard to describe, but there he'd be, beaming inwardly to himself as he wrote things in files and passed messages to people in well-chosen clothing. At lunchtime, he would walk into the hustle of the city with a serious smile, and he would rejoice in the wind that tunneled through the office buildings and set the pant legs of busy men to flapping. The wind! Puzzling movements! Men themselves! The Big World held less beauty than the Bright Forest, but he found it strangely satisfying. He began to look collegiate again, tall and thin, with round glasses and a preppie vest. In the office he became liked, for he had a way of fixing his eyes on a person with an innocent concentration which brought him much good will.

His parents rejoiced that he had finally made a job last more than a few months. Hey, maybe he'd go back to school.

When Gregory told Sylvie that he enjoyed "this cycle of coming and going each day, being away from you and then with you again," she at first believed him. She was too naive, perhaps, to realize what was going on. After all, what could really threaten the beauty of the Bright Forest? When he came home each day she would throw herself around his neck and try to drag him into bed, but he would demur, would say he was tired, and again she would believe him. She didn't realize that he had brought the Big World in with him, and that she, in her old sweater and sneakers, and with all that undisguised love in her eyes, looked merely out of place. Little by little, Gregory grew impatient with "her" cheap restaurants, and "her" back roads, and he began to be repelled by sex. Seriously: a certain American Puritanism rose up in him against a life of pleasure. Worse, he now saw not a determined "poetry-in-real-life," but a kind of desperate quality to all his days with Sylvie, an excess of beauty which might well appear ugly to the outsider. To people, for example, from his office.

At night, lying awake by Sylvie's side, keeping a precious inch between himself and her flesh, Gregory would actually wonder how he could have given himself to this woman who was like none of the women he knew in his other, Big World of men and ideas. She, for example, could not keep facts straight and ask the right questions when taking a message over the phone. Just now, she was, for heaven's sake, working in an organic food collective. She had no shine of rapid plans in her eyes, she wore no masculine jackets, and touched no colored shadows to her eyes.

"You should throw out that shirt," he'd say. "It's falling apart."

"You look like a college boy in that jacket," she would reply, as a joke. "Do they laugh at you at work?"

But he did not smile.

Late at night, he could hear the wind curl around the edges of the apartment building like a kind of warning, and sometimes, rising noiselessly, he would walk out onto the balcony and feel a kind of tremendous and lonely power in the darkness. At such times, even though it was not Morning, he would let a strength come into his limbs which thrilled him, which reminded him that he was young and might do anything. For a short time, at least, young.

In such a manner, little by little, Gregory became utterly alone from Sylvie, and entirely left the Bright Forest for the Big World. This should be no surprise: a new world is all we ever ask, and for the second time in his life, counting the moment he quit college, he felt mighty and free.

The final separation came in the worst way, when Sylvie was out of town, visiting her mother. Indeed, a whole month passed without a visit to the Bright Forest. Under the circumstances, far too long for it to survive.

During that month, Gregory relaxed visibly, and worked late hours. So little did he think about Sylvie that he imagined that she did not think of him either. When he finally wrote his letter, on actual paper with a pen, he was sure it would come as no real surprise: "Dearest Sylvie, I'm sorry to write you a letter, but it must be done in a letter, if it is to be done at all. If you would find your own true strength, I know that you must leave me for a time. I am holding you back every moment we are together. We once said that the present should never destroy the beauty of the past, and in that spirit, I say that it has all been so beautiful that I am brought only to joy in looking back. You know what you have taught me, and I only hope the world can teach you what I cannot as time goes by. Write to me. Gregory."

Lying face down on her childhood bed, Sylvie could only think of that word "strength." Strength? What did strength have to fucking do with it? Either you stick with someone or you don't. The letter had come at a dark moment with her mother, when she was hoping for a word from Gregory to cheer her, and now she thought the world had come to an end. Who was this jerk masquerading as Gregory, who had signed such a letter? A letter so full of ugliness and distrust? She reviewed the few weeks before their parting and could not remember having met this other Gregory, though looking back, she could see the signs that he had been growing inside her true Gregory.

"Now I am alone," she thought, correctly.

This other Gregory grew a moustache, moved halfway across the country, enrolled at a new university—and after a few months he was no longer a child in the Bright Forest, but an adult in the Big World. City streets began to lose their shine and glimmer. He completed a tax return. He graduated. He obtained a job in a sales statistics firm. He fixed his own lunch to bring to work, and he began looking at advertisements for cameras and stereo systems and folding couches. In time he forgot the smell of women, or rather the women around him were so clean that he could not smell them through their blouses and sinless colognes.

About a third of the way into the fourth movement of Beethoven's Ninth Symphony, there's a curious moment when the chorus pauses for the orchestra to play a theme like a little brass band—a brief, bouncy military march, revving up for another grand entrance. Gregory whistled that little tune to himself almost every Morning. If he thought back to his time with Sylvie, he would say things like this to himself: "Is it only the first moments of any new enterprise that set the whole image and beauty for what is to come? Surely everything that happened in that first moment beneath the oak when Sylvie's hands roamed created everything that occurred in the next four years."

Again and again he recalled specific moments of joy in the Bright Forest, but always he heard himself describing his former love to his new friends in disparaging terms: "Those were awful days after I left school, just floundering around. There was this girl who flunked out and took me with her. She, like, never grew up."

But Gregory found no new woman in the Big World. And sure enough, six years further on, when he was nearing thirty, he began to dream again of making love to Sylvie. The dream of her would arise against his will around him in the night like a close and familiar room. He began to telephone her in Phoenix or Boulder or wherever she had moved that month and found himself talking to her in the small, childlike voice of his previous love.

"Sylvie?"

Sylvie was at first hesitant, and kept her distance over the phone. Gregory took this as a sign of strength, and in his mind, judging by the new tone of her voice, his heart began to dress her in sleek, adult working jackets and straight slacks; he pictured her wearing makeup and staring him directly in the eye. Then she began to call, too. "Gregory," would come the call. Each time, after they spoke, he would walk out into the city with new eyes and look briefly down graffiti-laden alleyways and into the beautiful shadows of the trees, revisiting the Bright Forest. But safely.

At last, one long holiday weekend, Gregory boarded a plane and met Sylvie in her latest town. Over the course of those six years, she had known many men and many jobs. Gregory had become the poet who was her first love, and her best, but who had abandoned her in some vague, artistic confusion. She lost her anger, and told herself they had had to part in order to grow up. She could now speak in a more direct manner, dress in well-kept skirts (though not sleek adult jackets), own a car, make plans in advance, offend people less often, and generally pass as a citizen of the Big World.

When Gregory arrived, therefore, he was at first perfectly enchanted. He felt his fondest wish had come true. Sylvie had gained all the strength he had spoken of in his heartless letter! They went out to dinner without even holding hands, and Gregory was magnificent with charming talk and generous public behavior. He had learned how to smoke cigarettes, and he displayed this new talent with bravado, blowing smoke into a warm summer night. Sylvie, in her turn, acted witty, and she looked at him with the indulgence of a former lover, now grown mature, gently hinting at the secrets they had in the past, and laughing indulgently at the right moments.

Like in a movie made by the Big World.

No one in the restaurant looked at them oddly, or suspected them to be refugees from another world altogether. And back at her apartment, they went about the business of getting ready for bed with coy efficiency. When the lights went out, Gregory crawled into Sylvie's bed with confidence, eager to make love like men do to women in the Big World.

On the second day, however, Sylvie didn't bother to comb her hair as carefully. Gregory overslept.

On the third day, spent idly at a beach, they didn't walk as they'd both intended, with pants rolled and shoes held discreetly, but instead sprawled in the sand, making a mess with sandwich wrappers. Sylvie forgot to mention the plans she had for Gregory to meet her new friends—annoying and confusing him.

And by the end of the fourth day, when he awoke dreamy and lost, and looked deeply into the waxy magnolia leaves that rattled outside Sylvie's window, he lost sight of Morning. He saw only that the Bright Forest had sprung up lush and fantastic from the ground all around them, once again. All day they slept and woke, slept and woke, missing the appointment to meet her friends. It wasn't their fault, Gregory thought. When they got together, everything just went to hell.

As anyone will tell you, much is changed in one's life merely by having a regular job. And so, even though he delayed his return flight until late into the night, Gregory did eventually drag himself to the airport.

For a time, as they sat together waiting for his flight to depart, it's true that everyone else looked like a stranger.

Only after their final kiss, and when he found himself alone on the airplane, did Gregory begin to think about how to organize the next day. He checked his messages. His calendar. A few minutes later, he felt the vast cool relief of flying into the Big World forever.

The DIGNITY of MAN

"We scatter the seeds of the future randomly and unknowingly. They drop unnoticed from our pockets into the fecund earth where they begin to sprout aggressively and immediately into fields and forests, unseen as we stroll on without a backward glance."

—Your Author, 2019

In the first three decades of his life, Mohammed Mafaz Karim experienced three great loves, one after the other. They came in this order:

As a child, Mafaz loved God—a love built in his heart by affection for his father. He had loved praying next to his father on his own janamaz; loved trudging beside his father through dusty streets, listening to the call of the muezzen at dawn; loved hearing his father read high-sounding words from ornamental books. He had especially loved the ritual of the washing before prayer, and even the times of fasting, both of which had made him feel virtuous, clean, and right with all things.

But when he grew old enough to see that his father was not a happy man, the love of God passed away.

In his twenties, Mafaz loved the Nation. He felt part of a great experiment in history called Pakistan, and saw that experiment coming to fruition despite the most terrible of odds. He had read history in his spare time, worked hard to pass the civil service exams, and was lucky enough to be assigned to the staff of General Nasir Ul-Farooq, a man he considered to be steady, honest, and of admirably stern character. The famous Ul-Farooq had left the military to confront waste and corruption in the civilian sector, and for several years, like the General, Mafaz had walked proudly in suit and tie, special among the crowds. Unfortunately, however, General Ul-Farooq was closely allied to a Prime Minister who was ousted and even hung. Naturally, the General was also forced from government, along with his entire staff. Mafaz lost a fine house in Peshawar, and his wife moved back in with her parents in Pabbi, taking his two children with her.

As a result, Mafaz's love of Nation also passed away.

The third great love of Mafaz was the West, though he had never traveled there. Once again his love was tied to another man: in this case his good friend Ahmed "Alvi" Al-Shiraz, who had traveled to the West often—and had actually been educated in an American university. France, Germany, Britain, and of course America, Alvi told Mafaz, were not lost in religious fetishism. Did not allow unpaved streets to persist in major cities. Did not experience rampant corruption in high places. Did not hang their prime ministers. In the West people built magnificent skyscrapers. Made magnificent movies. Allowed women to walk beautifully unclothed in the streets.

As the monsoon season neared its end in the summer of 1982, Mafaz Karim was unemployed and living alone in the unfortunate Kashmir Victory Hotel, but he watched every Hollywood movie he could on scratchy VCR tapes, read famous English novels, and listened to the dangerous Western music that made its way to the bazaar on pirated cassettes. In the absence of other affections, this love became his joy.

Someday he would be allowed to rejoin the government. Someday the government would send him on a mission to the West, perhaps even to America. Meanwhile, all he had was the Kashmir Victory Hotel.

Like the other residents, Mafaz rose early and went to bed late, taking the balance of his sleep in the heat of the afternoon. Unlike the others, he wore a suit with pockets, had a sign on his door, and made calls from his own telephone. His business card, though printed poorly on cheap stock, read: *Government Consultants International, Kashmir Victory Center, Quissa Khawani Bazaar, Peshawar, Pakistan.* In a city that lived on rumors of the outside world, he hoped this card made him an indisputable fact.

The Kashmir Victory, however, was also indisputable. It was in fact a dark and immeasurably dirty establishment of many windowless rooms and spider nests, wreathed in the faint stink of faulty plumbing. The walls were decorated with water stains, and light emerged from dusty bare bulbs switched on just before dark and switched off promptly at eleven. Most nights, the patrons dragged rope beds out onto the roof: the regulars in regular spots backed by a corner or a wall, and transient Pathans, many of them Mujahadeen, face up in rows along the center, sleeping with their rifles—"Keeping watch for their God," joked Mafaz, who did not sleep with the others, preferring his own quarters. But though he slept ill and woke up panting—as if he had been running great distances in his sleep—yet he woke before dawn, and had tea served no later than six a.m., regardless of the season. Tea arrived on an antique English service carried by Ashfaq, the taller, thinner, and quieter of the two brothers who owned the hotel. Mafaz enjoyed the routine of this awakening, as he enjoyed all the small conceits of daily life. Ashfaq would smile deferentially with his bad teeth while setting out the tea things, and sometimes they'd play a little game in which Ashfaq would count out biscuits from an imported box.

"Oh, just one more, dear Ashfaq," sang Mafaz.

"No, Mr. Karim, you pay for five English biscuits with breakfast, five is what you get."

"Oh, don't be so scared of your brother. How long have I been living here? This week, you can give me seven."

"No, Mr. Karim. I am an honorable man. I would not lie, even to my own brother." And they would laugh.

"Very well then, six." Ashfaq, Mafaz knew, was always impressed by this kind of talk, and he would later impress the men gathered in the tea shop downstairs with tales of Mafaz Karim. Mafaz, once an aide to General Ul-Farooq himself; Mafaz who had the best room in the hotel, with a view of the Afghan mountains and an actual private toilet; Mafaz who insisted on eating foreign-made sweets; Mafaz the grand, Mafaz the eloquent, Mafaz the frivolous.

"Dear God I love this life. Dear God I despise this life," prayed Mafaz, completely ignoring the obligatory verses. "But you, God, I thank for this life always. Of course." And then, God having received His due, Mafaz would add various entreaties on behalf of his letters—for after breakfast, Mafaz would dress and shave carefully and then get right to work on his battered black typewriter, often getting out a half-dozen letters before the heat of the day drove him from his room. "Dear President Ronald Reagan: This is your friend Mohammed Mafaz Karim. How is your family? Perhaps you are familiar with my current project, Government Consultants International, which is helping to create an unimpeachable economic base for South Asia." Or, "Dear Mr. John F. Bookout, President, Shell Oil Company: Perhaps you are familiar with Government Consultants International. As we develop our nation's untapped resources, we find ourselves reaching out to companies like yours with our proposals for unlimited opportunities." And, "Dear General and President, Mr. Zia ul-Haq: Congratulations on your efforts to Islamicize the nation's economic systems. I have always been a great admirer of yours. I'd like to contribute a number of points regarding leveraging foreign company interests, if you could make the time." The envelopes were made of fine, imported linen, and he had a habit of signing them across the rear flap, like a seal. He had beautiful, clerk-like handwriting. To his inner eye, these envelopes flew as white birds, messenger pigeons winging their way to the weighty offices of Islamabad and the sparkling great towers of the West. Mafaz was given to poetry, and he once wrote:

> We who seek the sky with kites,
> With banks and bridges and wings,
> We know that beauty is infinite,
> And everywhere a pale blue.

Come evening, after his afternoon sleep, Mafaz generally descended to the tea shop on the ground floor, where he joined his political friends in a scatter of outdoor chairs which sprawled right into the dusty street. Here they talked and argued as they watched the heat of the day lift into night. Come eight or nine, each man would drift off to see what the wife had cooked for dinner. Like Mafaz, they were all slightly overweight, balding men in their late thirties—either in government or, like Mafaz, temporarily out of government.

Tonight, Mafaz is the especially round fellow with the short, wetted-down hair, a bead of sweat on his forehead, dark circles around his eyes, a thin moustache, and a wide smile on his face.

The smile is beautiful. His Western clothes are ill-fitting but well-kept, and they are something of an amusement to his friends, as Western clothes are rapidly going out of fashion in the government. All the others sprawled in the chairs have returned to a traditional *salwar kameez*.

Mafaz has been praising America, which, in his words, "might be clumsy and naive, but does try to do good."

"Mafaz, I confess that I too love the Americans," puts in one of his friends. "For they are presently sending us their most excellent F-16 fighter jets, along with bagfuls of money. And I also fully appreciate the Russians who are diligently prompting the Americans to send us all this fine stuff."

"Americans are fickle heathens," cheerfully replies another as he joins in the resulting laughter.

"America is not the West, my friends," says Mafaz, raising a finger. "America is merely a *manifestation* of the West. The West is not a place, but an idea. It is the idea of a society built not on God, but on the pursuit of happiness, as Mr. Thomas Jefferson proclaimed in the year 1776. This leads, surprisingly, to a highly rational, efficient, and well-ordered approach to business and to government—for without rational efficiency, how can one have happiness? It also leads to all kinds of lovely, well-made things: architecture, fine art, excellent pastries. The lack of religion leads, unexpectedly to great respect for the rule of law—often more respect than here in the Land of the Pure. No, no, hear me out. You will see the contradiction: without the *Quran,* the Westerners have more law than we have with the *Qu-ran.* This is a shame on us! And very odd, for in the godless society, they believe in constitutions, laws, no man above the law, and expe-rience a very low level of corruption. Why is that? We should stop worrying about why, and certainly we should stop feeling inferior, but we should learn from the West! We should learn to emulate their beautiful efficiency, their handiwork, their honest government. Our wise president, General Zia, understands that we should learn from the West, and take what we can from their civilization, while leaving behind what we, as Muslims, should properly leave behind. The Na-tion should take only the best of the 'Western' and use it to build our economy, while maintaining and strengthening our Islamic charac-ter and values."

A momentary pause ensues while the others ask themselves if Ma-faz has been mocking them along with Zia (who did, after all, hang the prime minister and cause the loss of Mafaz's job), or if the man speaks in earnest. They decide he must certainly speak in earnest. Still, just to be on the safe side, one of the men says: "Americans are given over to pornography and worse."

"Another manifestation of the West, I admit," laughs Mafaz. "In France, they make the best cheese. In Britain, they make the best bis-cuits and brew the best tea. In America, they brew the best women— and here is our friend Alvi to attest to this great truth. He will tell us if California girls, as the song demands, cannot be beat."

Mafaz's great friend going back to childhood has been standing a few feet off, listening with folded arms and a smile. Now he joins the group, which does him the honor of rearranging their chairs. Ahmed Al-Shiraz is certainly the most important of the men who drops by the Kashmir Victory for tea: tall, lean, handsome, and wise beyond his thirty-six years, he's presently well-placed in the Governor's office. The man has recently seen a paper on Islamic economic systems re-ceived at the highest levels, and everyone knows that the local *Bettani* leaders, at least, consult him almost exclusively on national politics. More importantly, Ahmed Al-Shiraz has been educated in America, at U.C. Santa Barbara, in California. There he had obtained his nick-name, "Alvi," from those who could not pronounce his real name.

Both Mafaz and Alvi know that Mafaz's best and perhaps only chance of re-entering government lies with Alvi. But they do not let this fact interfere with their friendship.

"For the public record, I know nothing of American women," says Alvi with a smile. "And certainly not in the plural."

"I have seen the pictures, my friend, of your extreme handsomeness in your college years. Indeed, I have seen a picture of you, shirtless, holding a surfboard with scantily clothed women not far away." Switching momentarily to English, Mafaz adds: "Your silence on the subject of American women speaks volumes."

"But alas, my silence must continue to speak: Not as eloquently as you, Karim, but it will have to do. I could not help but overhear you lecturing about the fine qualities of the West, which you have never visited."

Mafaz, again in English: "Alas, I have never left the Land of the Pure."

And Alvi, back in Urdu: "I must tell you that those Western qualities are a mixed blessing."

"Let me see that!" cries Mafaz. "I think you should hire me as your liaison to Paris—or no, San Francisco, which I hear is much more exciting these days."

The shop boy comes running with tea for Ahmed Al-Shiraz, and as another mark of respect, the conversation halts while he takes a sip. He pushes up the fine wire-rim glasses he acquired on one of his trips to Europe. He adjusts his fashionable pink *salwar kameez*. "In America, they may be more educated, they may have better clothing, better music, better buildings, better cars, and better pastries—how can one argue? But they know little of loyalty, of true friendship, and are not better men than we Muslims at being *men*—that much is clear. Indeed, Americans sacrifice their manhood every day. I have seen it. Remember that. Ashraf is right, the current friendship of the Americans to Pakistan will prove fickle in the long run. It always does."

"And you, Alvi, are you not fickle? If only I were ten years younger, you might look at me with more loving eyes; but alas, you are now much too beautiful for me."

Alvi leans over and kisses Mafaz on the forehead, and Mafaz stands up as if smitten with love. "Allah, take me, take me, now I may die happy!" It's an old schoolboy joke and all the men laugh. They drag Mafaz back down to his chair.

"Enough, sit down and drink your tea," puts in one of the men. "Haven't you seen the headlines today?"

"I've seen the headlines and I don't give a royal damn. Alvi here has to give a damn, he gets paid for it."

Alvi gives a little smile and sips his tea. "I read that the Nation makes great strides, the war goes well, and elections have again been postponed. I find it certainly possible that these are related developments."

"Quiet, Alvi," jokes another, "spies are everywhere."

"No one needs spies in Peshawar," says Alvi, his eyes shining with his humor. "Information travels in the very dust, and we have sufficient dust to carry all possible gossip." Although he's thirty-six, Alvi might be yet a young man, thinks Mafaz. He once wrote a poem about Alvi, which he sang only once, at a drunken evening. It was in Pushto:

> *I am not a believer in dark eyes,*
> *As I am not a believer in secrets.*
> *When I was young I believed in many things,*
> *Djinns and saints and sinners.*
> *I am not a night traveler,*
> *Just as you are not the night.*
> *When I grow old, I will light candles*
> *And place them in all the windows of my house.*

The song went on, but got confused by the third verse. The words did, however, express the nuances of a great friendship. Strangely, Alvi told Mafaz that in America, people are not so much interested in poetry.

Alvi lowers his glasses mischievously. "Mafaz, do you remember when Farooq drove halfway across the damn country just to chew you out for signing his name to some letter to the President?"

Mafaz starts to giggle.

"And then it was all a mistake and he looked like such a fool?" Alvi presses on, gesturing with his hands. "He had that little aide with him, the skinny guy with the dirty *kameez* who got all the fallout? I saw that very same man today, sitting in an office at the Ministry of Housing and Works. Apparently he has found his way back into government—so I am certain there is hope for you."

The joke is not unkind. Mafaz slaps Alvi on the back and finishes the tale to general laughter. "Excellent! Farooq realized the mistake of his aide, and began shouting at him instead of me. They climbed back into the jeep and were gone instantly, Farooq yelling into the sunset. It was an excellent moment." It pains Mafaz to make a fool of General Ul-Farooq, but it is, of course, necessary.

"Still, Farooq was a good egg," intones one of the others, after another little pause, again as if speaking of the dead.

"Yes, he was a good egg," offers a third, his smile softening. "Worked hard his whole life. Has three sons in the army, you know. One's a fighter pilot."

"And his brother found me a position with the press."

A moment of silence falls. Better not to say more.

Mafaz knots his fingers and stretches them out in front of himself. "We're not such young men ourselves anymore gentlemen. One day we'll be the old men in the cushy offices that the bright young fellows make fun of. 'Old Mafaz Karim, there,' they'll say, 'I wonder what dancing girls he keeps on the side. And Ahmed Al-Shiraz, that old stick in the mud, posing for pictures in Shalimar with heads of state, goosing the wife of the Ambassador from Italy.' They'll be figuring out how to ease us gracefully into our graves."

Alvi laughs, then grows a bit serious. "Only too true, Mafaz old friend. We are merely part of this particular moment in time, this tiny bit of national history. This moment will not last. We ride it like a leaf in a river, and we cannot escape our fate. So...we might as well enjoy it. *In Sh'Allah.*"

His worthy comment has resolved the embarrassment of all, and one of the others follows with a lengthy quotation from God. They all listen with enjoyment—even the shop boy, who pauses with the teapot as the moment continues to develop.

Alvi does not tell them that General Ul-Farooq died that very day. This will not become public knowledge until certain safety measures have been taken: perhaps three days hence, the papers will be full of the news. When the others hear, he knows, they will relive this conversation and realize that Alvi knew all along—increasing his stature. Like all deaths of important persons, this death opened up avenues. With Farooq dead, it will likely be safe to bring men like Mafaz back on board. Indeed, Alvi himself will make that recommendation. He thinks: "Brace yourself, old friend, the wind is about to blow." Then he leans over and whispers in his friend's ear, inviting him to join his family for dinner. Mafaz raises his eyebrows in surprise and delight.

The wind, of course, is already blowing quite hard. Just over the mountains in Afghanistan, the Mujahideen are fighting the Russians and radicalizing the countryside. American weaponry flows freely across the landscape. The Nation teeters on the verge of obtaining the nuclear bomb.

At Alvi's house, the men sit on the floor, around a cloth, while the women flutter in to serve and remove the food. Tonight the men include just Alvi, Mafaz, and Alvi's younger brother, seventeen-year-old Khalid, visiting on his school break. After dinner, Alvi and Mafaz share a small sofa in a rather barren sitting room. A single light burns. Outside the rain comes again, hard. As the old friends speak, they look down at the sleeping but beautiful form of Khalid, sprawled with rumpled abandon across the small carpet. Whenever they pause, they can hear him breathing.

"In America, there was a girl," says Alvi after a pregnant silence. "Her name was Elizabeth, and she said she understood all about men. She was eighteen and I was twenty."

"The girl, Alvi? Am I finally to hear about the girl?" asks Mafaz with whispered glee.

"Only if you are very quiet."

Mafaz makes the motion of a zipper over his mouth.

"Truly, she said she knew all about men," continues Alvi.

He pauses for a response, but Mafaz again mimes the zipper.

"We would go walking in the hills above the university where we had a view of the sea. We walked hand in hand, in plain sight of everyone. I suppose she thought me very stiff and formal. I believe she found that ...." And here he waits rather long before adding the word "...charming." And again a long pause. "Every day she wore shorts so that her legs were entirely bare."

Mafaz catches his breath.

"Entirely bare."

Wore shorts so that her legs were entirely bare, repeats Mafaz to himself, and the words make him actually suffer. *She was eighteen and I was twenty.* In the next and again lengthy pause, Mafaz begins to compose a poem, aloud:

> "*She was eighteen and I was twenty.*
> *The hills were green,*
> *With views of the sea.*
>
> "*Or no, better:*
> "*If I were twenty and you eighteen,*
> *Would you take me to the hills*
> *With green views of the sea?*"

Alvi smiles in deference to poetry. "She would say things such as, 'Men like to think they're boyish and awkward; they think it a kind of excuse.' Outrageous things like that—but you read those magazines from America, you see those movies. They all talk like that in America; believe me, especially in California they like to hear themselves say outrageous things. At the time, I found it invigorating."

In *California,* in *America.* Mafaz has never been to America, but he can imagine the freedom of that moment, both of them so young, and walking in the green hills—Alvi *an American college boy* and she *an American college girl.* The image could be in a movie, and it brings tears to his eyes. "It's like a movie," he says. "Like a song in a Hindi movie." Meanwhile, to himself, *My God,* he cries. *My God, if I am no longer young!* And he tells himself this version of the poem, privately:

If I were twenty,
You would take me to the hills.
But I am not twenty, and I live
Far from green views of the sea.

Then he watches closely as his friend removes his fashionable wire-frame glasses and wipes them on his sleeve. Should he speak, after all? Mafaz moves forward, raising his eyebrows and licking his moustache:

"This girl, was she beautiful?"

"Blue-eyed and blond-haired, Mafaz old friend."

"And were you in love?"

"As I said, Americans are a disloyal race. They don't recognize any code—or perhaps in recognizing the value of *every* code, they recognize nothing at all." This is, perhaps, something Alvi read. Something which serves to convince him of his good decision to move back home, marry a Pakistani woman, work in his tedious office. "Consider how they call themselves America when their country is just a fifth or less of the continent. This attitude is naive, but not benign." Alvi here pauses in frustration. "And yet everyone is their friend, everything is 'o.k.' I found it very frustrating, if you must know."

A passionate animal, thinks Mafaz to himself, *a passionate animal educated by the touch of many men, rich in her conversation and in her sex. Alvi, you don't even understand what you know.* "But did this Elizabeth say she was in love with you?"

"She did."

"And you felt nothing?"

Silence from Alvi.

"So...you were young and in love. In time she would have introduced you to her family—one thing would have led to another, and no doubt they would have understood when she converted to Islam." Mafaz lifts his hands to express opportunities lost, and he takes a large sip of the mildly sour illegal whiskey he has brought back from a little back alley he knows in Pabbi. In his mind yet play the movies. In the movies the young always triumph. Fathers are overthrown, young lovers come together against impossible odds, defy their families and are made whole in the fire of their love. In the movies, lovers are forgiven not only by their God, but by their parents.

Alvi has to laugh. "Ah, old friend, the things you can't even imagine," he says, "Her parents didn't figure at all in that equation. Imagine this: Elizabeth didn't give a damn about her parents. And they didn't give a damn who she was seen with. And that's—"

"Yes?"

"Well, that's the size of it," says Alvi, sipping his own whiskey and making a face at the taste of it. "If I could explain America to you, we would no doubt both be lost entirely. The trick is to understand, but not to be conquered by knowledge. Alas, the *Quran* has warned that such a balancing act usually proves impossible for we weak humans. Impossible. That is why we must *not* know."

In a single gulp Alvi finishes his whiskey, then falls into a long silence which Mafaz takes to be philosophical—until he realizes that Alvi has begun to snore. From upstairs comes a stirring. A woman appears briefly at the head of the stairs and then shyly turns away. Mafaz catches just enough of a look to recognize Alvi's wife.

Now the monsoon leans in over Peshawar with its full weight, shaking the windows and blinding the street outside. Young Khalid shifts position, rolling right off the carpet onto the hard floor, face up. Mafaz can now inspect the boy's fine chin and slight beard. Khalid often strokes this beard proudly, denoting a growing religious fervor—though Mafaz feels, as he often feels about these religious young men, that the beard takes away from the handsomeness of youth. Mafaz lets himself yawn. He does not feel quite content with the remarkable conversation he has just had with his old friend. Something is wrong on which he cannot place his finger, and which continues to bother him as he too falls asleep on the couch, unconsciously leaning against Alvi in a comical fashion.

As the breathing of Mafaz becomes regular, however, that of young Khalid quickens. The seventeen-year-old has only been pretending to sleep all this time and has heard their entire conversation. Now, with both his elders lost in dreamland, he rises soundlessly and goes to stand at the window, where he can watch the rain. Instantly, he feels part of the monsoon, and again senses within himself a growing storm. He looks at his older brother, whom he once admired. He looks at the pathetic Mohammed Mafaz Karim. To be laughed at by a woman! To maneuver for position in a puppet government, manipulated by the Americans! To slavishly admire the West! These are not the marks of true men. These are not the ways of greatness. *Only Allah knows the ways of greatness.*

Next afternoon, Mafaz does not take tea with his political friends. Instead, when evening falls thick and rank and the heat grows almost unbearable, he gets into his still-shiny car, and drives to the small town of Pabbi. It's a weekly ritual. Mafaz has a wife and two children in Pabbi, but he does not live with them. Within a few days of the fall from power of Ul-Farooq, there began a time of disagreement with his wife and his wife's family—well, more specifically, his father-in-law. As a result, his wife had moved back in with her parents and uncles and brothers. Everyone understood this as a temporary arrangement. The children were too much for Nusrat alone, and now that they could no longer afford a nurse—or for that matter, the house in Peshawar—she just had to live with her mother. Mafaz, of course, had to stay in Peshawar and build up Government Consultants International. *No kiss when we parted, no kiss when I return,* thinks Mafaz, remembering a phrase he had once worked into a poem.

Tonight, by accident, he is left alone with his wife. The children are in another room playing with their grandmother. The other men have gone to prayers. Mafaz, by long and obstinate custom, has declined to go to prayers, but he forgot that tonight that might lead to sitting alone with Nusrat. She reads a tabloid magazine. It is in English with glaring headlines and ugly colors. She wears a kaftan of the latest fashion—purchased how? No doubt her mother has given her money. He knows she's wearing the kaftan and her best jewelry to intimidate him, and that she's reading to make a point of ignoring him, but she does it all so awkwardly and childishly, that he cannot get angry. In any case, he finds himself too weary of their battles to care anymore. "Woman, you have my time," he once said aloud. "Do you want my heart as well?"

Tonight, for some reason, he regrets such words, and does not have a similar angry resolve. His regret has something to do with the story Alvi told him, but again, he cannot quite connect the dots. As he looks on her face all he can only say to himself: "Are we still children together? Can we at last be adults?" She glances up as if he had spoken, and then looks back down at her tabloid and turns a page. It is all too ridiculous. Mafaz feels an anger at the world rise up: Their dignity has been offended, the dignity of both of them, by *someone*—but exactly how or by exactly whom, he cannot say. One moment he is sitting on the couch in dignity, and the next that dignity is removed by some ungodly outside force: Her family? Perhaps. The person who designed the ugly furniture in the room? Perhaps. He cannot say. *Perhaps a man must be poor before he really sees how the world is organized,* thinks Mafaz to himself. *Only when he is poor does he have no protection against the truth.* At last, thank Allah, the children appear. They are small children and want to play with their father.

"Would you like some water, Karim?" asks Nusrat, rising. She apparently cannot bear to sit and watch him play with the children.

"Yes, yes, thank you," he replies, too exercised to be embarrassed. *It is not her fault and not mine,* he tells himself. If everyone just worked harder, no doubt they could overcome this indignity, whatever its cause. But what work?

When his father-in-law returns, solemn after prayers, and stroking his lengthy beard, he sits the other men in the room around Mafaz, and they enter into a discussion of politics which lasts two hours. Mafaz nods a great deal, even when the President of the Nation is insulted as being insufficiently religious—"Though he is much better than that idiot Bhutto"—a purposeful sting to Mafaz, who was, after all, a Bhutto man. Again the name of God arises naturally, as if He were in the next room. "Allah does not admit of mysteries, Mafaz," says his father-in-law, pointedly. "He has made everything very clear." And later, during a lull, "It is not too late for you, Mohammed Karim. You are wasting your time in Peshawar, which is anyway a den of thieves. Go into the countryside, pray with the simple people, the faithful, cleanse yourself, and then come back and get to work supporting my daughter."

"I'm sure you offer good advice," nods Mafaz, with a submissive smile. "Indeed, excellent advice, *jenab*. I shall consider it carefully." Sweets come and go, carried by Nusrat and her mother. In the back room, other women are talking, talking. "Dear God," prays Mafaz, "I was no child of fortune, but you have made me poor before my time. Are You, as they say, the God of charity, and close to the pauper? Do You go with me as a man, as Mafaz Karim, or do You travel only with the Nation as a whole? I confess to you, Allah the great and merciful: as a *man* I would take a lover even now, would lay myself on the grass with her and look at the sea. Let me be a man!"

After a while Mafaz altogether stops listening to the conversation. Naturally, he is restless to leave, and despite his best efforts, this restlessness suddenly rises up and takes him by the scruff of the neck, pulling him out the door. It is unlike him to be sudden and impolite, but his brain is on fire. "What is wrong? What is wrong?" he wonders. "Something beyond the obvious!"

Nusrat comes running out after him. "Do not be angry, Karim," she says, though in the dark he cannot see the expression on her face. "You do not look well. Are they feeding you properly in that hotel? Remember to eat plenty of fruits and vegetables, but insist in the kitchen that they wash them thoroughly and dip them in bleach. You can't trust them." He identifies a searching look in her eyes which is in contradiction to her earlier hostility. He cannot understand it, but he appreciates that she has said something nice.

"Thank you, Nusrat. I am doing extremely well, actually. The business looks promising. Don't worry about me. Please greet your mother on my behalf." They do not, however, kiss.

Along the road, the moon has risen full and smoky, and a vast ring hangs around it, indicating that although September has arrived, the monsoons will continue. Mafaz drives with great concentration; not only because the road is dangerous, but he is too impatient a man to be a good driver, and he knows it. Through the windshield, the light shines white on his knuckles, and white on the dashboard of his old Volvo. On the road at this hour are only trucks and buses, large and terrifying in the moonlight, hurtling past at breakneck speeds. No streetlights. Here and there the open fire of a tea stand becomes visible, but most have closed, their owners and patrons stretched out on rope beds beside the shuttered shacks, ready to move inside when the rains begin again. Mafaz forces himself to think of California, picturing it like the hills around Murree, where he spent a vacation in more prosperous years.

Well, if Murree had views of the sea.

In the West, he thinks, men have no illusions. They don't claim that God has no mysteries, they accept that such mysteries are inevitable or they do without God altogether. They make their houses beautiful. And the women! The women are free and available, lovely blond hair in one's hand, perhaps silver-white in the moonlight. In the West, one need not cheat and sneak around to enjoy life. A few lines of a poem spring into his mind, and he says them aloud to the bus drivers and truck men passing him in the bright dust of the road. He plays with the verse and tries to work out another.

> *Are women the keepers of the home,*
> *Guarding the inner sanctum*
> *Like a sweet body hidden in a cloth?*
> *Or are women our road companions,*
> *Their colors billowing out*
> *Like wings to lift a man to flight?*

The image pleases him, and he drums his fingers on the steering wheel, putting the words to an old melody. Why has he never before enjoyed driving? The beauty of the white dusty road? To drive forever, that would be the ticket! To continue across borders to other lands, to leave this Pakistan, this after all dirt-hole of a country. He thinks of Alvi and looks at his watch. Nearly too late to visit his old friend, but with old friends nearly means nothing at all. In his heart he feels the freedom of another full week without visiting his wife's family, along with other freedoms, blossoming along the roadway with wide petals, as in those Hindu paintings. As he reaches Peshawar, Mafaz turns the car off in the direction of the old cantonment area, now the ground of fashionable western-style houses, laid out on neat square streets. Here again he finds Alvi's house, this time with more lights burning.

Mafaz guts the engine. *A man need never be alone, if he doesn't want to be alone,* he thinks to himself, and gives the steering wheel a bang. Already he has recovered his good will—and as he opens the door, the moonlit drive is still with him, ringing with the next verse of his poem:

Do not go alone, my friend!
To go alone upon the road
Is to travel only with one's God—
Do not go alone, my friend!
God is too great to be your companion.

Inside it's late Friday night, but every light blazes. Alvi greets Mafaz warmly: "Ah, old friend, you must be psychic! I tried calling you earlier tonight, in fact! Come, come, sit. I have Turkish Delight, and some news that should interest you greatly. We must speak a bit quickly, however, for other guests are coming soon."

"Oh, perhaps I should not have intruded."

"Not at all, not at all. In fact I would like you to meet these guests. It is a matter of business."

"Business, well!" says Mafaz.

Mafaz and Alvi sit on the sofa. This time alone.

"I was on my way back from Pabbi," begins Mafaz by way of further excuse. "I thought I'd drop by to see if you could cheer me up." He is for some reason feeling a tad awkward. Something in the manner of Alvi has changed. He seems, perhaps, more formal.

"Your father-in-law has been at it again?"

"Alas, he's right, as usual, about everything. Of course, he's only concerned about his daughter and his grandchildren, which is only to be expected. Still, his lecture proves tiresome week after week. But I do not want to talk about him," ventures Mafaz, plowing forward, "I want to hear more tales of California."

"Mafaz, old friend, read this."

Alvi hands Mafaz a poor photocopy of a typewritten page. At the top is a newspaper-style headline:

UL-FAROOQ DEAD OF HEART FAILURE

General Nasir Ul-Farooq, the much-decorated lead-
er of the Air Force for over fifteen years, and later a
key figure in affairs of state, has passed away from a
natural heart attack early Tuesday last.
News of his passing was delayed by an autopsy and
the compassionate need to inform his family.
The President has expressed his deep sadness at the
passing of the General, calling him, "A great servant
of the Nation and a superb Muslim. His talent has
been missed by the government, and will now be
missed deeply by family and friends."
General Ul-Farooq retired from governmental service three years ago, citing health concerns which
have now shown themselves in this tragic manner.
The general is remembered honorably by the Air
Force, and was cleared of all possible wrongdoing associated with the actions of the late prime minister
by....

"This will appear in *Dawn* tomorrow morning," smiles Alvi. "I
thought I would let you know first." He pauses as Mafaz continues to
read. "You realize, of course, that Farooq's death changes everything."

The rugged, earnest, and ever-troubled face of Nasir Ul-Farooq
arises before Mafaz. A face that had seen and suffered much. He was
a man, after all. A soldier. *A good egg.* Mafaz looks up at Alvi and
manages his own smile.

"Does it?"

"Of course," says Alvi, grinning quite broadly now. *"Al-Barzakh*
will be coming to an end for you. You may come out of the shadows
of the Kashmir Victory Hotel. You will be a new Karim!" And he
slaps him on the back.

"You say that with certainty, dear Alvi."

Alvi glances at his fine watch. "I do. In fact, I have an idea of a
position for you already—not precisely in my department, but I have

a finger in many pots these days. We have to have civilian oversight of these weapons systems, Mafaz. And here in the territories, as the goods and monies come in from the American 'Cyclone.' Not all of that money is well spent by the military, I am afraid. Not always well spent at all! Your own experience will tell you that. We see too many middlemen, and we have to sort them out...and sometimes, of course, we must redirect the money to a more worthy cause than the military. I do my best to keep tabs, but I need a right hand man involved." And he holds up his right hand. "Someone I trust. Someone I know extremely well. So why not my oldest friend? We'll start by getting you invited to the Governor's Luncheon next week."

Four seconds pass during which Mafaz smiles more seriously and nods thoughtfully. He of course immediately understands the parameters of the offer. His job will be the redirection of American aid, the collection of subtle bribes, the arrangement of quiet skims. Of course his old friend wants him for this job, for his old friend can trust him without question. Especially now that Mafaz has become a man with no other recourse or influence. He sees the future in its entirety: He will serve his old friend, and his old friend will make him whole again, perhaps even wealthy. Hence the slight formality as their roles shift. Mafaz will, of course, accept—what other choice does he have? His father-in-law will respect him again. His wife will kiss him. Rapid thoughts follow: The letters to Shell Oil were always foolish, but are, as of today, dangerous.

Knowing he must make some kind of response, Mafaz pats his old friend on the knee as if in complete and joyful astonishment. But he finds himself unable to speak his acceptance: some kind of strange coldness has come into his chest and throat, making it difficult to breathe. Soon he will remember this as the feeling which always accompanies the departure of love. But just now he has no time for reflection, as a knock has come at the front door.

Alvi rises. "It's settled then," he says. Mafaz rises too, smiling, moving to leave. But, "No, no, stay, stay," says Alvi with a raise of his eyebrows. "You will enjoy this."

Mafaz hears English greetings in American accents, and the West enters Alvi's sitting room. It comes in the form of an American man in casual Western clothing and an American woman who wears pants. The man is middle-aged, fit, clean-shaven. The woman is young and magnificent, with blond hair and blue eyes. This is not, of course, the first time Mafaz has seen Westerners, but he has never been entirely in the same room with them, at least certainly not a room this small. Peshawar, is not, after all, Karachi or Islamabad.

"Alec Black, Karen Armstrong, I want you to meet my associate Mr. Karim. He will be working with me closely on these projects – out of Regional Affairs. Alec and Karen are with Beachhead Consulting, a private contracting firm."

The two of them become momentarily interested in Mafaz. They look him up and down, like a new servant. Trustworthy? Reliable?

"Oh, of course," Mafaz manages. "Excellent."

"Ah, okay, great," says Alec, and gives Mafaz a quick shake. "Welcome to the party." And then...Karen takes his hand too! A Western woman's cool hand in his own! He holds it oddly, by the fingers only, and he shakes it up and down in a foolish manner, conscious of appearing idiotic. Karen looks exactly as he pictured the fabled Elizabeth of U.C. Santa Barbara. He wonders if she is wearing a bra.

"Mr. Karim," says the vision. It's the last time she looks at him for the entire evening, but he's shocked to find that she looks at him with a slight repugnance. Is he repugnant? Her hand feels lifeless.

"Well, sorry to bug you at this hour on your holy day and all," says Alec. "But like I said, the reqs have to be in Monday, and I figured you needed time to look the whole deal over."

"You were absolutely right to come by," says Alvi, taking a sheaf of papers from the American and sitting on the couch. "Have some Turkish Delight."

"Sure," says Alec. "I love this stuff."

"No thanks," says Karen, and takes a small modern calculator from her purse. Mafaz has heard of these devices, but has never seen one. He marvels at the way it displays glowing digits, which change as if by magic.

But when Mafaz gets back to his car, the cold which began in his chest grows great and monstrous. Now he feels it even in his arms and his legs, which he can barely move. He starts the engine, but he cannot drive, and for a time he just sits there with the engine running. He reviews the three loves of his life, along with other losses. He looks down the street, where the heat hangs dank in his headlights. It's still not raining, but beauty has entirely departed from the dusty white road—for alas, within beauty must live honesty. Finally, he puts the car in gear. It's two in the morning, a time between times, and as he drives, he tries to write more of his poem:

Do not stand here forever,
Uncertainly at the threshold of your home.
Either enter and kiss your wife,
Or fly with her to the mountains
Where neither God nor man can find you.

He has not gone far, however, when he becomes too much overcome with emotion to drive. He pulls off beside a shuttered tea stand, cuts the engine, and lets his head bow forward. Exhausted, he falls directly into the dream state, where another voice, his own, breaks in:

"General, I'd like you to meet Miss Elizabeth of U.C. Santa Barbara, our hostess for the evening."

General Ul-Farooq bows slightly, but Mafaz grows confused—how did he and the General get to the Governor's Luncheon so quickly? Have they dressed properly? Clearly, the California Girl hasn't had time to dress, for she stands stark naked, looking a great deal like a pornographic magazine picture he saw as a teenager. Strangely, Mafaz had not noticed her nakedness until he introduced the General. Now he sputters: "I am so sorry, General, that in my dream there appears a naked woman."

But the General says nothing. He merely stands shapeless in his *salwar-kameez,* staring.

Suddenly the scene shifts, and the whole crowd has reconvened on the deck of an ocean liner. Here Mafaz guides the General among foreign ambassadors and tittering Western women in formal gowns. But now Elizabeth has disappeared and in her place Karen Armstrong, with her blond hair and blue eyes, stands with a drink in her hand and absolutely not a stitch on her body. Perhaps that's okay, as she's no doubt the hostess here on the ship, and can do as she pleases. Indeed, Mafaz is getting the idea that Western women simply do not wear clothing in dreams. The General shakes her hand, modestly taking just the fingers. Mafaz hopes the General has not noticed this woman's nakedness either, and he begins to guide the General gently away, before someone makes a scene.

Unfortunately, however, Karen Armstrong pounces on the General with some conversation about California:

"I just love to walk along the beach with all the villas being opened up for the summer. The servants are sweeping out the redwood decks and tending to the surfboards. It's lonely and expectant at the same time—and not entirely safe, for after all, I'm the only woman on the beach with breasts."

Several guests have gathered around by now, and some laughter breaks out at this last remark. Mafaz, mortified that Miss Armstrong has mentioned a subject as inappropriate as a beach, can nevertheless think of no way to draw the General away. The General, meanwhile, smiles a smile as if for a child, and says: "I've never been to California myself."

"Never been? Well, we'll have to remedy that situation," cries Miss Armstrong, and applause erupts from the guests.

She signals a waiter.

From a lower deck of the ocean liner comes the sound of automatic rifle fire, of shouting, of grenades. But no one stirs. They are too polite.

"Of course, your duties must prevent you from making extended trips abroad," puts in the Ambassador from France, who has been conjured up by the word "Villa."

"More than just my duties, I'm afraid," says the General, with great dignity, and Mafaz gets teary with pride at his probity, his piety.

Just then a soldier breaks into the ballroom, and everyone breathes a sigh of relief to see he's one of their own: not an Afghan or a Russian, but a son of the Land of the Pure. It's young Khalid Al-Shiraz, Alvi's brother, in full battledress. Relief passes to embarrassment, however, for the soldier pants with exhaustion. He is filthy and desperate, with blood and sweat on the chest of his uniform. His beard has gone awry.

"Excuse me sir, but I have an important message," cries Khalid, and shoots the General point blank in the forehead.

Mafaz rushes forward to take the message from the boy and hurry him out the door. The reception has turned from bad to worse, and his embarrassment becomes excruciating. How to maneuver the General's body out of the room with some dignity? Mafaz feels absurd and foolish before these people. How can the General can be so calm and collected, even in death? At last he looks at the paper the soldier has handed him:

"Allah Akbar," it reads.

T he dream ends and Mafaz awakens to the sound of rain pounding on the roof and windows of his car, violent and unrelenting. He feels surprisingly calm and rested, his mind clear. In reviewing the curious dream, he believes he finally understands the mission of a man in the world.

Strangely, he finds that a man's mission is not to find and follow a great love, for unlike in the movies or the mosques or the words of poets, all love leads to disappointment, even terror. *Indeed,* he thinks, *I have dallied too long with mighty forces, each of which will bring storms into the world over the remaining years of my life. None of these forces must triumph.*

Let us begin with the love of God, he continues, in his heightened state. *In His heart, God knows that He must not fully triumph or He will leave us no room to breathe or progress or enjoy one another: the complete triumph of God will eventually come, but only at the death of mankind. God knows that better than anyone. Meanwhile, it is our job to be grateful to God, pray to God, praise God, even submit to God— but love of God, well, no thank you, for such a love will in the end prove too dangerous.*

And what of the Nation? The Nation is, after all, nothing but a tool which can be used for good or evil. The Nation must also not be truly loved or it will destroy us one by one with its demands and its cruelties.

And then, yes, a man may accidentally fall in love with the beauties and amazements of the world, such as women or friends or paintings or the freedoms created in the West. These beauties and amazements must similarly not be allowed to dominate our affections, for like God and the Nation, beauties and amazements will not, ultimately, love us back. No, they will ultimately leave each of us alone in the darkness, such as when we fall into the black pit of sadness after we depart the manufactured wonders of a movie house.

He put the car into gear before reaching his conclusion.

No, our only reliable course as human beings must be to balance each of these potent forces, one against another without falling prey to any single force. We must attempt to live in the center of this balance, with dignity, as long as we can. Why? Because in the end, a man has control over nothing but his dignity, and in the dignity of man lies the whole of his greatness. Perhaps I have, in my heart of hearts, always known this—and probably, in this previously-unrealized knowledge has always lain the special greatness of Mohammed Mafaz Karim. As I leave the Kashmir Victory, I must leave with head held high. I must reconcile with my wife. I must placate my father-in-law. I must pray at the mosque to keep God satisfied. And I must accept the job with my dearest wonderful old friend Alvi. I must not, however, love Alvi, for he must not own my soul. It will be my fate to take bribes, but I must take as few as necessary. And when I someday visit the West, I must not let the sad disillusionment of what I find in Paris or San Francisco or London or New York destroy my happiness or throw me into the arms of other, equally unreliable forces.

I shall be Mohammed Mafaz Karim and live ever at the balance point, in the only place where I can truly be a man.

This seemed a solid plan for the next five decades or so he had in this world, and *in sh'Allah*, despite the terrors and wonders to come, it might just work.

Saturday morning arrives at the Kashmir Victory, and at ten o'clock Athar is still eyeing the tray with the teapot and the imported biscuits. He tried to wake Mohammed Karim at six, but was sent away with a grumble. At seven he went down for more tea, but it too became cold. At eight a fine envelope for Karim arrived by private messenger, an envelope emblazoned with the seal of the Governor, but Athar was unable to deliver it with a flourish—instead he was forced to slide it under the door. Now, down in the tea shop, his brother's good friends, the cloth merchant and the tailor, have gathered beneath the ceiling fans to finish their breakfasts. At eleven, they will head back to the bazaar to check the accounts kept by their sons. By the window, sipping tea as if it were a precious honey, a shepherd sits with his rifle across his lap. The shepherd appears ageless, sunburnt, and scraggle-bearded. He's on the way from God-knows-what-mountain to do God-knows-what terrible deed. The shepherd takes out his little leather purse and pays for each cup as he orders it, as if they might not trust him for the money. All morning the shepherd has been a matter of some amusement to the merchant and the tailor. The tailor has been making thinly veiled comments about mountain men, and the merchant, slightly embarrassed, laughs with reserve and strokes his own beard to indicate that despite his prejudices, he considers all Pakistanis his brothers. The shepherd, whose Urdu is imperfect, understands almost nothing of what they say.

"But look, here's Mohammad Karim," says the Merchant suddenly, and stands. "Take my seat, sir, here under the fan."

Mafaz takes the seat with a smile, and arranges his jacket around himself. Athar is all long arms and feet as he runs into the hallway and calls to a small boy to fetch more tea. "Tea for everyone," Mafaz calls after him, "...and British biscuits!" He looks around magnanimously. The fine envelope, torn open, resides in his left hand. Mafaz shows it to his fellows: an invitation to the Governor's Luncheon. The tailor and the merchant glance at one another, impressed.

Ali fetches Mafaz's newspaper and spreads it out on the table with the imported biscuits and a box of matches. They all watch as Mafaz lights a cigarette and glances over the headlines. War and rumors of war, of course. But then, a headline announces the death of General Nasir Ul-Farooq. They have been waiting all morning for Mafaz to read this headline, but the ex-staffer of Ul-Farooq glances at it only briefly.

"A good egg," he says. "As the President says, he will be missed." Then, he asks the merchant, not missing a beat, "And how goes the cloth trade?" He pointedly folds away the paper without reading the article, taking in the whole of the cloth merchant's affection with a friendly glance. And then, in English: "We soon arrive at the season for tourists."

"I expect very few this year, Mohammed Karim," smiles the merchant, switching back to Urdu, and stroking his beard. "In fact, thanks to the war, I would say none at all. Did you see that General Ul-Farooq leaves a widow and three sons?"

"Indeed. He was a very good man," smiles Mafaz. His nonchalance amazes them.

"Actually, the Afghans have brought in a good deal of excellent fabric this year," chimes in the tailor, enlivened by the evident good will and rising fortunes of Karim. He knows that the man has a wife in Paddi who likes the latest materials.

The boy returns, juggling four teapots and a full plate of biscuits. The shepherd eats his biscuit with good will for Mafaz, His eyes are burned by the elegance of the man's suit, by his movements, which are graceful and civilized, and by his measured tones. This must be a man of the world, he thinks, and imagines how he will relate this scene to his brothers back home. "But was this a *man*?" they will ask, and how will he answer?

"You see that I stick with my British biscuits, even though they are baked by colonialists and heathens. And even though our President has encouraged us to buy national goods. I eat them because they contain full butter instead of poor quality oil, gentlemen, and they are far better for my digestion." Mafaz finishes yet another biscuit, and smiles at the astonished looks of the tailor and the merchant. Ali fills in his accounts book, and Athar has taken up his usual position leaning against the doorframe.

"That's fine for you to say, Mafaz Karim," replies the tailor, self-consciously shining in the light of this intimacy regarding biscuits and digestion. "But we are poor men."

"Only poor for a time, my friend. The Nation looks forward to the day when every man and his brother will be able to buy British biscuits, and then to bake them just as well. The secret is not to lower our standards to our income, but God willing, to raise our income to our standards. I am a poor man myself, at the moment, and yet I still buy these excellent biscuits. We can have it all, if we keep our wits about us."

He went on, and his words were like music, like the speeches of the politicians on the radio. The tailor allowed his hands to drop to his knees, the shepherd lit a cigarette, and the merchant helped himself again. Later, Mafaz wrote:

> *I know that you would*
> *Take me to the mountains,*
> *Across the deserts,*
> *Or out upon the sea,*
> *To look upon...what exactly?*
> *I will not go with you.*
> *If I went, who would keep the inn*
> *Here at the crossroads,*
> *Entertaining*
> *The beautiful women*
> *And dangerous men?*

FICTION
Part II

From "The Birds," by Aristophanes,
circa 400 BCE. The birds are speaking:

*"At the beginning there was only Chaos, Night,
dark Erebus, and deep Tartarus. Earth, the air and
heaven had no existence.*

*"Firstly, blackwinged Night laid a germless egg in
the bosom of the infinite deeps of Erebus, and from
this, after the revolution of long ages, sprang the graceful Eros with his glittering golden wings, swift as the
whirlwinds of the tempest. He mated in deep Tartarus with dark Chaos, winged like himself, and thus
hatched forth our race, which was the first to see the
light. That of the Immortals did not exist until Eros
had brought together all the ingredients of the world,
and from their marriage Heaven, Ocean, Earth and
the imperishable race of blessed gods sprang into being.*

*"Thus our origin (the birds) is very much older than
that of the dwellers in Olympus. We are the offspring
of Eros; there are a thousand proofs to show it. We have
wings and we lend assistance to lovers. How many
handsome youths, who had sworn to remain insensi-*

*ble, have opened their thighs because of our power and
have yielded themselves to their lovers when almost at
the end of their youth, being led away by the gift of a
quail, a waterfowl, a goose, or a cock."*

– Translated by Eugene O'Neill

It was Jack who woke Jessica each morning. Not an alarm. He
wouldn't have an alarm wake her. He tried to do it gently: the smell
of brewing coffee, a little Mozart in the hall. Today he cradled a tray
in a heavily muscled arm, sleeves as always rolled up to show his tats.
"Jess, Jess, I'm running late." And when he saw no response: "Jess,
seriously."

Seven months had passed since the tragedy, but still each morning
she did not want to wake up. No energy, she said. Thank God she *had*
to get up for work. Thank God the store had kept her on, no matter
how shitty a job she was probably doing.

The tragedy had been a car accident which had killed their first
and only child, Angelo, at the age of eight weeks—just old enough
for his first real smile.

Unlike mere death, tragedy can go on forever. Certainly seven
months later, "tragedy" was alive and well in the cautious faces and
speech of everyone they knew. At work. In the apartment building.
And somehow, on the streets of Chicago itself, showing as a kind of
grayness, a lack of color. Surely, they would have to move. That was
Jack's only plan: as soon as they could put together a little money,
they'd move to a new city for a fresh start.

Meanwhile: "Jess, Jess."

Truth passes away much more quickly than fiction, but fiction too
can pass. And so it came to be that today, when Jack stood and looked
down at the once-magnificent Jessica, he looked with love, but with
no palpable memory of the erotic tale which brought them together
three years ago—that famous exaggeration of cantaloupe in the produce aisle, the penthouse at the luxury hotel, the departure from reality which had defined their first weeks and led, by many unrecorded
twists, to the present and excessive reality.

Like Angelo, that sweet tale, with its impossible spontaneity, was gone. A border wall separated the Country of Then from the Nation of Now. *Then* was happy Jessica with a thing for buff white men with blue eyes and tattoos. *Now* was sad Jessica, and many deep silences.

She turned over and looked at him, hair beautifully all over her face, large sudden breasts falling loose from her shirt. The slight pink of them. But he knew that look in her eye. It was the blank look. It presaged exactly nothing. It offered no invitation to touch her, and certainly not her breasts. How inappropriate would *that* be!

"Hey sweet pea," said Jack, offering a chaste kiss on Jessica's forehead. "Good morning. Time to rise and shine. Almost seven-fifteen. Give me a smile." She did try to smile, actually. And she promised again to take his call at noon, as she did every day, just to be sure she was okay in her tiny booth at Discount Everything!, sitting up straight and cheerfully in her red "It's a Great Day to Save!" t-shirt. She hated the place, but, "Sit at home? Fuck, no."

This morning, Jack dropped silent Jessica at her job just two minutes late, giving her a second chaste kiss, and making her give him another smile before he headed off to feel alone on the expressway. Credit Jack with this: he did not feel any relief to be alone, to be headed to the plant alone where he could escape the shadow of their failed nest and the shadow in the heart of Jessica. For Jack was a true lover, a lover of women, and a lover of Jessica. He put on loud music in the car, and thought about sex. This is, after all, the same Jack we met three years ago in the produce section, who at that time pretty much lived for sex, and used it as his poetry against the world.

The problem with thinking about sex these days, however, was the inevitable mental progression from "sex" to "Angelo" to "death," and round and round in a circle in his head. No doubt in her head also. Jack turned off the loud music as he headed into the parking lot.

The guys said, "Yo, Jack" with false enthusiasm.

Here are the actual details of the tragedy, just so you know: On the day of *the one first smile of Baby Angelo,* Jessica had been driving with extreme care in a sensible compact car. Angelo had been properly buckled into his certified and approved car seat. Although the seat was placed next to her in the front, the airbag had been properly disabled. It was only Angelo's third or fourth ride out into the world, and she had to have him next to her, to speak to him, to comfort him, to nudge the pacifier back into his mouth.

Then out of nowhere, a sixteen-year-old male in a midsize appeared, having failed to notice a stop sign. The midsize T-boned Jessica's compact on the passenger side. Metal and glass were projected at high speed. That's the whole story. Jessica herself was only minimally hurt, and she had of course seen a therapist to talk it all through, and yes after a time, she had escaped the great and terrifying possibility of guilt: *What if she'd put the car seat in the back, as recommended by the manufacturer? Was Angelo simply too young even to ride in a car? What if she'd had a midsize too?* Such questions she had at last overcome. But she had not overcome the more basic question of *chaos.* She had not escaped her new understanding of the universe as a place where even if you at first have random sex with a white guy you meet in a grocery store, and then are surprised to find him not a jerk at all, and then have a screaming fight with your mother, and soon afterwards run out to marry the guy and build a real life and rent an apartment and buy a sensible compact car and decide to have a beautiful mocha-colored baby together, *nevertheless* that baby can be killed just a few hours after his first real smile. Just one smile that very morning: both she and Jack had seen it. He had reached up a hand and smiled.

Now, here's another thing about the universe, and for that matter, the God whose movements we are trying so hard to track: the universe gives and the universe takes away, but the taking is sudden, while the giving is slow. Creation requires birth, and birth always takes time. God moves upon the dark chaos of the waters, but all things appear from that water in stages, each birthed slowly and painfully from the egg of what came before: plants from light and soil, animals from the plants to feed them, people from the beasts, civilization from the people, ethics from civilization, love from ethics.

A baby takes *at least* nine months...much more if actual romance is required. But death, well! Death can happen in an instant, without warning, in the blink of an eye, and then hey, we find ourselves right back at chaos.

Again today Jessica sat expressionless in her little glass shift super-visor's booth, situated on a cement platform above the vast reach-es of Discount Everything! and accessed by a short stairway above the kitchenware aisle. The booth somewhat resembled a prison guard tower, but at the bottom of the stair was a friendly sign that read, in old-fashioned type: "Come up and ask me something!" Her job included watching the staff and customers on six ever-panning mon-itors, and by directly "eyeballin'em" as her boss liked to say, and occa-sionally "givin'em the stinkeye." He was the one who had the booth constructed with eyeballin'em in mind, though to his credit, he had also had a tiny window cut through the cinderblock wall, so that the shift super might enjoy a little daylight. Well, okay, the window was too high for the super to get distracted by actually *looking outside*—still, the window faced south and let in the only sun to a place other-wise entirely lacking poetry.

Under normal circumstances, of course, neither poetry nor joy can exist in a place like Discount Everything!—not among the pots and bottle openers of the kitchenware aisle, nor among the cables and adapters of the electronics aisle, nor even in the sporting goods section. The fluorescent lighting actively prevents poetry. Dismisses beauty. So does the physical weight of the goods, the colorful pack-aging, the hapless, poorly dressed humanity, and the shine on the floor—in short, the excessive reality of the place.

Only through that little window might something actually valu-able arrive.

At 12:00 sharp, Jack made his call.

"How you doin' today, baby?"

"I'm fine."

"Where you goin' for lunch?"

"You don't have to call me every single day, you know."

"Yes I do."

During their conversation, and even afterward, the world spun on its axis at the rate of 1670 kilometers/hour, promising change to all liv-ing creatures. Remarkably, however, even deep into the afternoon, no change occurred in the life of Jack and Jessica—even into the evening.

So do leading spiritual authorities often picture death. Death, they maintain, *is the state of no change.*

Although he had not read any leading spiritual authorities, Jack understood this principle perfectly. That's why he saw his mission as somehow introducing change into the equation—hence life. Indeed, he saw change as "the man's job." Just as it had been the "he" in the relationship who had made the first move in the produce aisle three years earlier, the "he" who had proposed, and the "he" whose body generally made the first move in the act of sex. And so it was that come nine p.m. that evening, he started in again about leaving town. For the tenth time, he suggested Texas, where he had a brother, but allowed that maybe they should try to live even closer to the ocean than they did now. Galveston wasn't expensive, he'd heard. He discussed a road trip to Texas with loud music in the car and fun in cheap hotels. He painted a picture of a new life. He put his arm around her shoulders, gently and unthreateningly, not as Eros but as Husband. Or at least as Road Buddy.

"What's keeping us here?" he asked.

"My mother. My job. Your job. Sally and Leroy. Monica and Davis." She recited more names of friends and relatives, pulling a pillow against her stomach. By now it had become a ritual response. "It wouldn't do me any good to leave town. I'd just take it all with me. We'd just spend a lot of money and have to scramble for new work. You know that." She did, however, make the effort to turn to him with her small, dutiful smile: "But thanks for trying, Jack. You're a good guy."

Such is death, thought Jack's subconscious, ready to make another effort at motion, and in fairness, his subconscious did take a few tiny steps toward the future before it came to rest again.

Jack had not read Aristophanes, so he did not know that the universe was birthed when Eros mated with Chaos, or that the gift of birds could re-open closed thighs. But in a vague, male way he knew that *some* level of chaos, *something* beyond "good guy," and *certainly sex* was required to begin the cycle again. Jessica did not see this great and male truth. Her reaction to tragedy was to close down, to numb up, to stop everything, and with this strategy to avoid chaos as best she could. Hers was, one must admit, the obvious approach.

Which brings us back next morning to the super's cubicle within the great obviousness of Discount Everything!. You would think that within such a space, being so very huge, you would find some kind of local climate: huge mountains, after all, generate their own winds and clouds, so why doesn't a megastore have its own gusts down the aisles? High pressure systems in lingerie? But alas again, inside Discount Everything!, where even the music did not change from hour to hour, we need not discuss the weather. We need only note that this morning, outside its cinderblock walls, the sun had risen with a June blaze.

At 9:35 a.m., the store manager passed through the cookware aisle and looked up to note, as expected, Jessica's grim expression—not actually sour, but certainly unworthy of a shift super. It might yet require months of patience, he reminded himself, before he could get rid of her in a seemly way. Call it another kind of stasis introduced by tragedy.

At 12:00, Jack called, and said, "Hi baby."

At 12:07, a customer walked up the stairs to complain about the usual mess in the shoe section, but was effectively put off by Jessica's complete lack of interest.

Then, at 12:08, the world began again.

Now, we have already noted that the birth of anything, at least anything valuable, requires time and effort—but we left something out of the equation. Unlike death, which requires neither spark nor invitation, warning nor effort—*birth requires a seed. An egg. Something* to begin the cycle, for only nothing comes from nothing. On their own, neither Jack nor Jessica could have overcome the tragedy, or for that matter, the little booth in the megastore. So often we are told that if we just made the effort, we could climb out of anything... but it's not true. Sometimes, help really must come from outside.

In this case, help arrived at 12:08, just before Jessica's morning coffee wore off, just two minutes after she put away her phone after demonstrating false cheer to Jack, and just thirty seconds after ignoring her customer.

For at precisely 12:08, a bird passed rapidly by the tiny, too-high window foolishly cut through the cinderblock by her boss. This bird threw a shadow briefly across Jessica's ever-panning security monitors. We do not know what kind of bird: most likely a pigeon, but possibly a Glaucous Gull, as the bird was fairy large and Lake Michigan not far away. In any case, Jessica did not consciously register "bird" at all, for the shadow passed only for a thousandth of a second, truly like the blink of an eye.

Still, that shadow was enough to trigger a chain of subconscious events in Jessica's mind. The sequence went something like the following, but much faster than you can read it, such being the forward urge of life: *Bird > wing > angel > Angelo > angel-child > Cupid > that Renaissance painting of Cupid I saw in school as a child, when the teacher gave a slide show > the nude, buxom women in those old paintings that drew me, embarrassed me > Cupid as a later Roman devolution from the Greek Eros > In the next slide, Eros as a young Greek man of beauty and muscle and wings standing beside a buxom nude woman > The first smile of Jack in the produce aisle > The first smile of Angelo > The blue eyes of Jack > an arrow in flight! > birds! > winged sex! > life! > the possibility of joy.*

After that, Jessica went early to lunch, where she uncharacteristically ordered a strawberry milkshake. After lunch, she went to the manager of Discount Everything! and told him that she was feeling sick—maybe the milkshake— and could she have the afternoon off?

He was only too happy to say yes so he could make another dark mark in her employee record.

Now, it's one thing to have an inspiration, but it's quite another to act on it. After all, inspirations come cheap. Most of us probably have an inspiration every day: triggered by a movie, a song, a sunset, a bird flying by a window. Really, inspiration runs out of control. But inspiration alone is nothing: really no story to tell, like loud music playing in an empty car.

In this case, Jessica stood in the parking lot of Discount Everything! and called her husband.

"Hi sweet pea," said Jack, with his usual excessive cheer. "What's up?"

"I have something I want to do."

"Okay," he said.

"Any way you can take the afternoon off?"

"Uh...no."

"It's important."

"How important?"

"Well, after I do this, I will likely be ready to leave town."

When they arrived at the gate of the cemetery, Jack had to ask at the office where baby Angelo was buried, as they had not returned since the funeral. They drove slowly along the little roads on cemetery hills crowded with the dead until at last he parked the car and gave Jessica an expectant look. She touched his arm and got out. They walked over to the grave. It was on a grassy slope, in full sun. How well he remembered the spot when they finally arrived: The sun. The tense words. The stone of Jessica's face on that day.

But this time Jessica knelt. And lo, this time she cried. And lo again, this time she kissed the small brass plaque set in the ground, the one with the absurd set of dates. Then she stood upright and opened her arms to the chaos of the heavens.

She addressed the chaos of the heavens and said:

"Thank you for that one smile."

And then she looked up at Jack and saw his beauty and desired him again.

And fiction returned.

AFTERLIVES

One MORE
Second CHANCE

*"In poker there aren't good cards and bad cards,
there are good bets and bad bets. The game
simply reveals who can tell the difference."*

—A poker expert, heard speaking in an interview

Izzy Samuels heard the Incantation just four times in his life, even
though his life was pretty long. The first time he was seven years
old and coming back to consciousness in a hospital bed on the south
side of Chicago. The year was 1933, and the Incantation was hardly a
whisper, though it had a kind of melody behind it—a sing-song melody from some antique place, not America. The words were almost in
Yiddish, he thought, but not quite. *Shpilare? Kholishi? Boratey?* Not
Yiddish. But not Hebrew either. He did know the voice, certainly
after the Incantation had been repeated forty-nine or fifty times. The
voice was strange, but it was the voice of his mother—a woman then
beautiful, with red hair and a serious look in her eye.

Why had it taken him so long to recognize the voice of his own
mother? *Well fine,* he had thought. *I might as well wake up.*

When he opened his eyes, a collective gasp issued from the people in the room and he became aware of the crowded smell of too
many human beings gathered for too long in a tiny space. Here were

his mother, his father, his uncle Pinchas, his older brother Oscar, his bitter maiden aunt Leah, and some others he couldn't remember, all looking unkempt. Just behind his mother, his shriveled grandmother, Bubbie Chava, could be seen mouthing along with her words, silently and encouragingly.

Why were they watching me sleep? he thought.

Izzy's eyes first caught those of his father, Jacob Samuels. For the rest of his life, he recalled that his father, then thirty-eight, had looked surprisingly dashing at that moment, a man with magnificent black hair, lengthy black sideburns, unlimited self-confidence, and a pinstripe vest. He was the only person in the room who didn't look sleepy and rumpled, and Izzy remembered his father's eyes widening strangely. With pride. The pride seemed undeserved—after all, what had Izzy done to make him proud but wake up? His father winked at him, and at that moment a special bond was formed with his father, as if they shared some private understanding about the universe.

Soon Izzy learned that he had awoken from a six-day coma—a coma brought on by falling four floors from an apartment balcony. Being a child, he thought only, *"Wow,* I bet this has something to do with the singsong words I heard. Not to mention the collective gasp." He didn't understand the full implications of his father's wink until he was in his mid-teens.

Izzy's mother had broken off the mumbled chant soon after his eyes had opened, and the next few minutes he ever remembered as a series of stop-action movie frames. Everyone seemed to take a step forward and then stop in their tracks. Several people spoke his name and then said nothing. He remembered how his mother, eyes shining, red hair loose and wild, rushed forward tearfully, but did not, for some reason, dare to touch him. His head had begun to hurt, along with his left arm, his left leg, and his entire rib cage. The left leg, it must be admitted—Incantation or no Incantation—would never be quite the same.

The first one to break the silence was his Bubbie Chava, who said in her strong accent and poor English, *"Baruch HaShem.* He's been come back for some big purpose, to do some greatness thing in the world!"

"Shush, mother," said bitter Aunt Leah. "Shush with the Voice of Fate crap. You're always putting things on people. Do not, I repeat, do not put that on the boy. How can he ever live up to that?"

"Yes," said Izzy's own mother hastily, "it's not right to say things like that."

Everyone mumbled agreement, and after that, the tale of the way young Israel Samuels had recovered from not a two-story or a three-story, but a *four-story fall* to a sidewalk on the South Side of Chicago, actually bending a rail on a second-floor fire escape and tearing six branches from a tall elm on the way down, was a tale told only in a whisper. No one called the newspapers to report the miracle, so as not to jinx it. As for the Incantation, it was not mentioned, nor his mother's role in the matter explained. The whole incident was simply referred to as "the blessing." Young Izzy at first felt he had been let in on a huge family secret: a magical Incantation passed from mother to daughter for generations, a secret which could actually save a life. But after a while, when everyone refused to discuss it, he began to wonder if he had simply dreamt the whole thing. His brother Oscar assured him that his mother had, as usual, "Been praying a lot, probably in Aramaic or something stupid. But there's no such thing as an incantation. Don't be an idiot."

After "The Blessing," Izzy's father Jacob paid a lot more attention to his second son: often smiling at him and often winking, and always calling him "the lucky boy." By the time he was a teenager, Izzy realized how that first wink beside the hospital bed, as with all subsequent winks, acknowledged the concrete presence of the "Samuels Luck," a family asset Jacob Samuels held dear. Jacob had always depended upon the family luck to get him through life, and it had now obviously been passed down, full-force, to his second son. Without his even trying, Izzy's proven ownership of the Samuels Luck moved the boy very near to his father's heart. Even though Izzy never made much of himself, while his brother Oscar went on to be a successful attorney and even a state assemblyman, it was always Izzy who brought his father actual joy. His father spent hours teaching him important life skills like playing low-ball poker, bargaining down the price of a sport coat, and how to disappear into the bathroom when it was time to clean up after dinner.

Once he grew up and left home, Izzy became less shy about telling the tale of the Four-Story Fall. During the war, he would tell it to his army buddies, while adding the disturbing joke: "Maybe I have some great mission to accomplish, or maybe I really shouldn't be here at all."

It was a thing he should not have said, for words like that, once spoken, are hard to unsay.

Anytime anyone heard the tale, of course, they were annoyed that Izzy could not recall any of the actual *words* of the Incantation. He did try to tease some of them out of his memory, now and then, as a boy and a teenager. Even as a grown man, he tried to nag them out of his mother—but to no avail. Like everyone in his extended family, his mother refused even to discuss the subject.

World War II was the great event in Izzy's life. He held a rifle in France and killed several men while fighting for a great cause. He made buddies. He played the role of a patriot and a "regular guy." Like every Jew, he was devastated to learn the awful truth about Europe, and for a time it meant something that he had fought. Later, it meant less. After the war, he had a hard time adjusting to civilian life, and he stopped being a regular guy altogether. Like many men, he experienced a crisis of "now what?" that never entirely left him. At twenty-six, after a year of living with his parents and "looking around for something," Izzy deeply feared that that the greatest moments of his life had already passed. Hadn't he saved his friend Lenny on a dark night a week after Normandy? Scenes of fog and mud replayed in his mind, like a tremendous movie matinée from which he had emerged into a dull afternoon. So strong grew his feeling of life "already being over," that he failed to look for a real job when the other GIs were looking for real jobs, and failed to develop a social life with his peers.

More and more, as the rest of the world moved forward, he became obsessed with the idea that he "shouldn't be here at all." It was unhealthy and debilitating.

But Izzy always had his father Jacob. And always he was the apple of his father's eye.

Jacob's latest business gambit was a liquor store unprofitably located in the heart of a Jewish neighborhood. Izzy began to hang out there and help behind the counter, where every afternoon, the remarkable and ever-dashing Jacob held court. It was always a spectacular performance. The neighborhood men who had nothing better to do gathered to talk sports, spin phonograph records, drink a little liquor (unfortunately, very little), play poker, and listen to Jacob tell bad jokes and play memory games. No one much noticed Izzy, Jacob's "unsuccessful son."

The remarkable Jacob never forgot a joke, good or bad, and he never forgot the little hopes, adventures, and relatives of his friends, so he was never without charm or company.

He'd lean back, and lead with his trademark, "So....." to get everyone's attention. Then he'd tell a joke as if it were a true story from his own life. For the first few lines people were often fooled. "Remember Shlomey? No? He was an amazing guy, a natural businessman in the old country. And in America too. When he emigrated from Russia to America, he came over on a ship, naturally. But the second day, a huge storm erupted. People screamed and chairs went flying. Yet Shlomey just sat and casually read a book."

And here Jacob demonstrated Shlomey's nonchalance, flipping through a book and looking around at the chaos as if through thick spectacles, such that even before the punchline Jacob got a laugh.

" 'Shlomey!' yelled a fellow passenger. 'How can you sit there when the ship may be sinking?!'

" 'What's to get excited?' answered Shlomey. 'The ship belongs to me?' "

Big laugh. No one else could get such a laugh with such a joke. Then people would quiz Jacob's incredible memory:

"What's the name of my cousin in New York...you met her at my wedding."

"Oh, that's easy." And Jacob would reach up into the air, as if plucking a fact floating by. He was the king of memory.

"Flora. She had nice eyes and sexy black hair. Too bad I was already hitched to a redhead. That proved to be trouble. And your third daughter, Shoshi? How's she doing in Frisco? Do you send her enough dough to attract a Jewish boy? Or only enough to attract a goy?"

It was nonstop...at least as long as the liquor store lasted, which was not that long.

Late at night, when everyone was gone, Jacob and Izzy would clean up together—on and off they could afford help, but near the end, it was just them. Jacob would pinch his son's cheeks as if he were still a kid.

"Izzy, what a handsome face! Not as handsome as when I was your age, but good enough. Let me give you some advice: Don't get old. Or at least, make sure to look into the alternatives."

Near the end, the store was sustained mostly by the Thursday afternoon poker games—because Jacob, having such a terrific memory for counting cards, often enough came out ahead. Well, maybe not quite often enough. Sometimes the Samuels Luck also held at the track or on a jag to Vegas, but you have to say, like most luck, it was touch and go.

"It's all in the numbers," said Jacob. "The secret is to just keep dealing the cards, *just keep dealing the goddam cards,* and odds are, eventually the cards *will* fall your way." His wife, the once-beautiful Rachel of the Red Hair, disliked most of his sayings, but this one she hated with a special passion. Especially since it appeared to be Jacob's basic understanding of earning a living. Or rather, why he never seemed to earn a living. "He's a loser," she would say to her bitter sister. "A charming loser, but a loser." Izzy's father was, however, the only thing Izzy really had to keep him attached to the earth. Indeed, Jacob's unflinching rejection of the idea that a man had a mission in life, that he had any responsibility to nurture his talents, or go on a great quest, was the only thing that kept Izzy sane.

When he was in his early thirties, Izzy heard the Incantation for the second time. His Bubbie Chava, now ninety-eight, lay tiny and dying in a hospital in St. Paul, Minnesota, where his father had briefly moved the whole family to take a job in housewares at a department store where he also managed to get Izzy a job. Izzy worked in bedding.

Bubbie Chava was angrier about dying in St. Paul, away from most of the family, than she was about dying, but Izzy's mother was entirely inconsolable. This did not surprise Izzy, as he knew his mother was more attached to Bubbie Chava, to places gone forever, to special opportunities missed, and to certain people departed for many years, than she was to the here and now. What he hated about his mother was that she saw him not as "Izzy," but as the last hope that all those lost items would someday be found. As a kind of repository for those lost items.

Here I am again in a little down-market hospital, thought Izzy. *And I can feel it coming.* Meaning, of course, the famous family Incantation. His grandmother's head, withered, was bent way back on the pillow, and her breathing was more than a struggle; it included a *death rattle.* This did not particularly shake Izzy, as the sound of his grandmother's breathing had for some years held within it the sound of death. *She's old,* he thought. *It's time, for God's sake.*

Suddenly, his mother tried to chase him from the room, saying, "Leave me for a while. Give me two hours alone with Bubbie."

"Mother, I am no stranger to death," he had said with the lingering pomposity of youth.

"I want you to leave the goddam room," his mother had said, more clearly. But just then she had to give up the argument, for when she pulled up the wrinkled eyelids, she could see that Bubbie Chava's eyes were rolling back in her head. It was now or never. So Rachel forgot Izzy, wiped the inconsolable tears from her own eyes, and began the Incantation in earnest: *Baruyen, Aten, Adonian, Shloyme, Rofey, Rofey, Chukkah*—or something like that. The rest, of course, Izzy could not recall. The Incantation was repeated forty-nine or fifty times, his mother falling into a kind of fierce and womanly concentration, until actual sweat broke out on her forehead. Izzy was beside himself. *Is this right? Is this proper?* he wondered, even though he was not a religious man—or perhaps because he had just enough religion to be afraid.

Soon it felt as if they were the only three people in the entire universe, and a long, long time seemed to pass, a kind of whole epoch created just for them. A weird quiet entered the room. Bubbie Chava's breath grew increasingly regular and calm. Even the hospital equipment seemed to exude a gentler susurration.

Sure enough, after two hours, his grandmother's wrinkled eyelids fluttered open. Izzy's mother broke off, and they waited. At last, Bubbie Chava swallowed a couple times, then cried out in a strong, but horrible voice: "Why did you call me back? It was my time! It was my time!"

"Mother, I couldn't just let you die."

"Yes, you could! Stupid!"

And truth be told, the old lady suffered a lot over the next five or six years. She did, however, eventually manage to die in Chicago.

After the department store let him go—too much talk, too few sales—Jacob lured Izzy into a business selling pre-packaged deli sandwiches to local markets. By now Izzy was almost thirty-five, and desperate to make a go of something. He put in a lot of money and time, but the venture was doomed when it failed to get a nod for effective distribution in the greater Chicago area from either the mob or from that very near relation of "Samuels' Sandwiches," Izzy's brother, State Assemblyman Oscar Samuels.

On the same day the would-be prepackaged empire officially collapsed, Rachel walked out on Jacob. Among the things yelled loudly in the final hour, was something she directed across the living room to Izzy. She said, "Luck is for losers, Izzy. Get away from your father and work your ass off at something. It really doesn't matter what."

He had to admit her advice had a lot of potential, and indeed Izzy moved across town and had the best ten years of his life. Having learned something profound about food containers from the prepackaged sandwich disaster, he found a man whom he considered to be an honest partner and entered the packaging business (only cardboard at first, then more profitably, protective foam inserts). The business prospered.

He also found a good woman whose name was Joyce. Usually he called her Joy: "Joy of the beautiful smile." He could see that she had sense. For example, the fifth or sixth time Izzy told the story of the Four-Story Fall and the family Incantation, and made the fey and uncomfortable joke, "Maybe I have some great mission I have to complete, or maybe I shouldn't be here at all," Joy became angry and told him to shut up and never to make the joke again.

"If you can't help saying that stupid thing about, 'maybe I shouldn't be here at all,' you should stop telling the whole damn story. And as for the Incantation, it's all just coincidence. Some old mumbo jumbo and selective observation. Your mother dismissed the whole topic when I was stupid enough to raise it. Anyway, I don't like the boys hearing any of that crap. Like religion, it confuses them. And it makes them think there's like, some way out of things, when there's not. There's no way out of things."

Yes, Izzy now had two boys. By the time they hit seven and nine, they were bright-eyed, crew-cut, and trying hard to understand the world. Izzy tried to explain it to them a few times, but mostly he let Joy do the parenting, and during those best years, he just focused on earning a living. He felt his job was just not to tell them they were destined for some great mission in the world. Unfortunately, the boys did not read this as wisdom and focus, but as disconnection. Why did their father always seem so confused and distracted? Was he a weakling?

Ten years into the marriage, two bad things happened to Izzy. First, he wrote a check to his suppliers on the company account for $132,567 when in fact the company account held only $12.36. It only held $12.36 because his partner had taken out a loan from said account without telling him. And second, when he told this news to his wife, she said to him, "Who the hell are you, Izzy? What are you? Who did I marry?"

These two events caused Izzy to feel again the vast undertow of uncertainty which moves, sometimes unseen, beneath all human life. He had to tell himself, "Joy is not an illusion. The boys are not an illusion. This is real. It is intended. I am really here." But sadly, he could not convince himself—and as a result of his uncertainty, his old angst returned, and probably as a result, his luck continued to change for the worse. Soon, for example, he discovered that Joy (no longer of The

Wonderful Smile) was having an affair with Arnold Kornbluth, the nice bachelor lawyer who lived just down the street.

Apparently, it all *had* been an illusion.

Still, rather than falling into honest despair, or socking Kornbluth a good one, he felt with renewed force that the events of his own life seemed in some way not to touch him, as if he were watching them from a slight distance, or as if those events did not, somehow, actually matter. He began to drink. Again and again he said to himself, "Damn that fucking Incantation. Bubbie Chava was right. It was unnatural. She should have died. I should have died. But if I had died at seven...then what of my boys? They would not even exist."

It was a paradox, for sure.

After Joy left him for the fucking lawyer, Izzy began to have nightmares about his father's wink: the terrible wink which promised luck without meaning. The wink he still got from his father every time he visited the old bastard, who was now earning his living entirely from card games with other old guys in his retirement condo complex on the outskirts of Sarasota, Florida. Of course.

Izzy knew his current thoughts about the meaning of life were unhealthy thoughts, and he thought about going to a therapist, but then he thought, "A therapist will just make me think even more."

The third time Izzy heard the Incantation was 1973. By now, he was forty-seven, had been divorced four years, was thirty-five-plus pounds overweight, and he had come to Sarasota to say goodbye to his father, who was dying of heart disease. The idealism of the 1960s, which he had celebrated from a respectful distance, had passed without his participation. And now it seemed that he was also too late for his father, who had slipped into unconsciousness just a few hours before Izzy arrived.

Tears were in Izzy's eyes as he recalled that Jacob, now seventy-eight, had failed as a husband, a father, as a housewares department salesman, a prepackaged sandwich king, a liquor store owner, a candy store owner, a car salesman, a fruit importer, and probably lots of other things too. He had only done semi-okay as a gambler— spending his last decade hanging out in card rooms first in Atlantic

City, and then Miami. The day before, when he heard he was dying, Jacob had called Izzy in Chicago and said, in the way he used to say as a joke:

"Izzy, tell the doctors I need just one more second chance. I just want one more roll of the dice."

As usual, he didn't say what the second chance was *for*, but no doubt he was confident he would get that chance, right up until he lost consciousness that same evening, cradled in the arms of a hospice nurse as she gave him a sponge bath.

Just now it was close to dawn. Izzy had taken the red-eye, so he was in a heightened and philosophical state of mind as he stood on the blue shag carpeting of his father's condo. In this state, the phrase "one more second chance" seemed more than a joke, it seemed laden with pointless irony. But as often happens at the bedside of death, Izzy began to feel guilty about neglecting and judging Jacob.

"In nature," thought Izzy to himself (not wanting to trouble the hospice nurse with this kind of thing), "there are no second chances. No one rushes to the aid of a dying wildebeest. If a firefly falls into a pool of water, no one plucks it out. If a lioness fails at the hunt, no one brings her dinner. Only human beings give each other second chances. And who knows? Maybe the big guy does too."

Naturally, he thought of the Incantation.

Finally, at 8:02 a.m., Izzy stepped out onto the balcony of the fifth-floor condo and slid the glass door closed on the telephone wire so that neither his father, lying in the hospital bed set up a few feet away, nor the hospice nurse, a pleasant Filipina woman named Alma Fernandez, would be able to hear. Outside, in the full glare of the Florida morning, he dialed his mother's number in California, and waited while she was called to the phone by her ever more bitter sister, Aunt Leah, who had defended him from unnecessary expectations decades earlier.

As he waited, he stared at the view from the balcony, but he at first saw nothing much worth looking at: just the parking lot of his father's condo building, which included three wheelchair-equipped vans.

"Hi momma," he said. "I hope you're doing okay. You know dad's dying, only it's fast now—he's got, like twenty percent function or something. They've given him just days maybe. He's unconscious."

"Izzy, it's five a.m. here, and I know all that—but what the hell, I never sleep anyway. Is everything okay with the boys?"

"I want your help," said Izzy, recalling how her hair had gone all white, except for just the slightest memory of red. Ever the realist, she hadn't dyed it. The seriousness and religion had gone too, replaced with an irritating humor.

"Help? How could I possibly help?"

"You know perfectly well what I mean," said Izzy.

"Izzy, listen up: *que sera, sera.* He's almost eighty. He didn't take care of himself; even when he lived in Philly he never took care of himself. He always thought he was immortal. Always thought he could smile his way through anything. Sometimes he did. Mostly he didn't. This time, not likely."

"Heart disease is not his fault. And these days, seventy-eight is pretty young."

"Of course the heart disease is his fault. He smoked and ate red meat his whole life. And he's not that young. Your Aunt Linda is only seventy, and look at her."

"Mother, please. If you don't want to do it, you could teach it to me, and I'll do it."

"Are you taking care of *yourself,* Izzy, through all this? You sound terrible. Have you been trying to lose weight?"

"Mother, don't try to change the subject. You know what I'm talking about."

There followed a long silence during which things never broached might at last be broached, or might, on the other hand, not. To Izzy, it seemed like the whole world beyond the parking lot (which he saw, with increasing interest, actually included a distant blue lake and low, blue-green hills, half-hidden behind a bank of clouds) was waiting for the decision as if for a spring rain. Would someone finally speak openly about the damn Incantation? Or would the *only genuine magic* he could recall in his entire life slip away like youth, like Italy, like love, like Joy, like his sons, like his relationship with his father, like the friendship of his brother, like the sweet afternoons at the liquor store, like the happy sound of Big Band music, like the old neighborhood in Chicago?

It was the most sincere prayer of his life, and who knows, maybe it worked, for suddenly Izzy's mother said:

"You can't teach the Incantation to a *man*. Only a *woman* can do it."

Izzy was stunned. She had used the actual word! She had admitted that the Incantation existed, and that it *was* an Incantation. If Izzy had been living in a movie, the orchestra would have sounded a fanfare. A flashback would have played. A light would have arisen like strange fire above the blue-green mountain.

"So you remember it!"

"Using that *particular technique* just now would be wrong. Just wrong."

"What *wrong*? I'm talking about life and death! I know you haven't gotten along with dad since—"

"Izzy you were there that night with Bubbie Chava, when we used the Incantation. What? Fifteen years ago? I'm sure you *remember*. I shouldn't have used it then, and I shouldn't use it now. Your father is old, and besides the heart, I hear his kidneys aren't so great. Plus he hasn't been financially okay for fifty-plus years. It's different when you're talking about a little seven-year-old boy who takes a fall. Or your cousin Abby, just back from college. That's okay. That makes sense. But not..."

"Cousin Abby? Do I know her?"

"Of course you do—Linda's second granddaughter. Wears those sweaters?"

"What happened to her?"

"Izzy, chapters close, life goes on." And with that unintentionally ironic comment, she said a quick goodbye, and hung up.

If there *had* appeared a strange fire above the blue-green hills, it was fading now into the prosaic sunshine of another Florida day— just like the life of his family, like hope, like what little religion he still had left. Which wasn't much.

Izzy stepped back, defeated, through the sliding glass door and into the living room of the condo, where his father breathed now with considerable effort (read: rattling) even though he had an oxygen tube taped into his left nostril. Izzy took Jacob's hand while meeting the dark, but sympathetic eyes of the Filipina nurse. He recalled her name, Alma, and he was pretty sure Alma meant "soul."

She gave him a serious nod.

"I do appreciate all your work, Alma—"

But before he could get any further, the phone rang.

"Hello?" said Izzy.

For a moment, he heard only silence on the other end of the line.

"Hello?" he repeated.

At last, a grim and flat voice responded, sounding a lot like a Voice of Fate: "It's your Aunt Leah."

At age sixty-six, ever-more bitter Aunt Leah was a bit of a cipher—a strange mix of depressing words and family loyalty. Yelled at everyone and called them fools, but phoned on special occasions and sent them candies out of the blue. Come to think of it, she had been a bit of a cipher as long as Izzy could remember. It was part of what always made it uncomfortable for him even to sit in the same room with her.

"Uh, hello Aunt Leah. Can I call you back? It's not a good time."

But Leah persisted in her trademark grim and flat voice: "You forget that Bubbie Chava would have taught *me* the Incantation, too."

This time Izzy provided the silence.

"Well?" prompted the spinster.

"Can you fly out here?" asked Izzy.

"Are you paying?"

"You mean...the flight?"

"Of course, the flight. What did you think I meant?"

"Yes, yes, of course," mumbled Izzy. "Of course. That's terrific, but—"

"You know I never liked your father."

"Of course."

"Just so you know."

"Doesn't matter," said Izzy. "That's okay. That will be fine."

Thirty or so hours later, around six p.m. on a remarkably bright spring evening, Aunt Leah sat next to the rented hospital bed in Jacob's fifth-floor condo. Her large body overwhelmed a straight-backed chair. She had taken her shoes and socks off and her shapeless feet massaged the blue shag carpeting as she drank a glass of hot tea. Izzy noted, as he had in the past, that she resembled Winston Churchill with Einstein hair. His father had not awoken. Alma (which does in fact mean "soul" in Spanish, but also "nourishing" in Latin and "learned" in Arabic...I'm just pointing this out) busied herself at the back of the room.

The air, as they say, grew thick with expectation.

"Do you want the lights up or down?" asked Izzy, and turned off the bulb by the bed so it would not shine in Aunt Leah's eyes. Light continued to stream in from the blinding late sun setting through the sliding glass doors, making a kind of corona behind her gray and wild coiffure.

The woman was in no hurry. She said:

"I figure there are just five possible reasons for staying alive when you get old and sick."

"Really?" asked Izzy, uncertainly. Now he remembered that Aunt Leah said things like that.

"Yes," said Aunt Leah.

"Oh," said Izzy.

Silence fell again. They watched Jacob breathe.

"Uh...What reasons?" asked Izzy after a time.

"I've made a lifelong study of the question. But you may not care."

"Of course I care."

Aunt Leah took a sip of her tea. "Do you have any cookies?"

"I don't think so."

"Oh sure, sure we do," offered Alma brightly. She was thirty-six, but in her innocence and crisp white outfit, seemed much younger. She found a box of vanilla wafers, which she opened onto a plate.

Aunt Leah smiled. "I like this kind, especially the lemony ones."

"I'm afraid these aren't lemony," said Alma, with concern.

"Nothing's perfect," noted the aunt. "Trust me, I know." Then she explained the five possible reasons for staying alive when you are sick and old. "Believe me when I say that I've given this a lot of thought," she said again, settling her bulk, and holding up a finger. "Because I'm always thinking about checking out. *Right* out."

"Right."

And so finally began the second or perhaps third or fourth defining moment of Izzy's life. Fate likes to play games like that.

"Number One," said Aunt Leah. "It may be that each of us has the potential to save the world—to make it come out, if not okay, then with some kind of clever and meaningful twist. Under this theory, all the billions of us get our chance, and eventually one of us will actually succeed. Trouble is, once it's clear you've blown your chance, you may as well die—like in a chess game, where you do everyone a favor and resign instead of dragging out the game for another pointless hour of pussy-footing around the board." She took a sip of her hot tea from her left hand, and a bit of unlemony cookie from her right.

"Wow," said Izzy, who could not think of anything else to say.

After brushing away some crumbs, she held up two fingers. "Number Two." Then after a dramatic pause, "We may, like all the artsy Aquarius types think, each have 'our own individual mission' that we have to find and fulfill—you know, something nice like raise brilliant kids, rescue a concert violinist from a burning car, start a hospital, write an amazing play, give five bucks to someone who as a result becomes Mother Theresa, whatever. And once we accomplish that singular mission, we may as well die. Under Possibility Number Two, you can never be absolutely *sure* if you've already fulfilled your purpose—so staying alive does have *some* excuse, even in old age, despite arthritis and incontinence—both of which, by the way, I have." She paused. "I wear diapers."

"Ah," offered Izzy, thinking for the thousandth time about the time he saved his friend Lenny, almost forty years earlier, during the war. Lenny had become an accountant and probably saved a number of families and businesses from bankruptcy over the years. Surely, that had been some kind of—

"Of course," returned Aunt Leah, "the chances keep getting smaller and smaller and smaller, but you can see some *slight* odds that you'll luck out, and after all your screw-ups, after all the idiot things you've done, all the dumb-ass failures and false starts, you'll still pull off your Individual Life's Mission, even though you may not know it. In fact, maybe better not to know, because then you'll be sure it's all over."

"Interesting," said Izzy, glancing at his watch. "But still pretty damn depressing."

"Then there's Possibility Number Three: Instead of *one* mission, we may all have hundreds of missions to complete throughout our lives. You know: help one another, procreate, give to the March of Dimes, bake bread. They *all add up* to making God happy. Under this possibility, it's okay to hang on, but only so long as you're *doing something useful.*"

"That's probably it," said Izzy, brightening. "I'm pretty sure I heard a rabbi say something like that once. You get lots of chances to do good, not just one," he said. "So keep at it."

"The problem with Possibility Number Three," continued Aunt Leah, ignoring his hint, "is that after a certain point we all become merely a *burden* to others...just a bundle of complaints. By the time we're seriously old, we know we're not going to help anyone at all. I figure once you're a wreck, you can forget Number Three."

"Mmmm," said Izzy.

"That's my own personal situation," said Aunt Leah. She took another sip. "It's one reason people don't like me."

"I can see you've really thought this through," said Izzy, and checked to see if the nurse was becoming upset. He was glad to find that she was looking at a magazine in the back of the room. No doubt in her job, she'd heard it all. Okay, maybe not *this,* but everything else.

"Number four would be reincarnation," continued Aunt Leah.

"I don't believe in reincarnation," said Izzy.

"A lot of Buddhists believe in reincarnation."

"Okay," said Izzy.

"These Buddhists claim that the purpose of life is *to learn something,*" she scowled. "That life's all about learning some great lesson, and then taking that lesson with you somehow into your *next* life. They don't explain the physics, since no one remembers *any* of the wonderful lessons from their previous life, but it's a clever approach, because then there's always some point to staying alive right up to the worst, nastiest end. I mean even if you can't raise a toe anymore, or talk, or eat; even if you're nothing but an annoying, self-centered burden, you still might still *learn something*. You gotta hand it to the Orientals. They are plenty smart."

"I was wondering."

"About reincarnation?"

"Where you were headed with all this," he said. "I think dad sounds worse. Maybe we should get started."

"Just sit still. I'm getting to Possibility Five, and it's the big *Numero Cinco*. The most popular theory of all."

"Yes?"

"Number Five says that the purpose of life is to just stay alive as long as you can—*just to stay alive. Just to do it. Just to keep going.* And the longer you stay alive, well, *the longer you damn well stay alive!* Get it? No other purpose whatsoever. And guess what? Even though it makes no sense, most people you meet subscribe to Possibility Number Five."

"Really?"

"Sure. Think of all the movies about staying alive. And how people love to see people escape death. And tell each other when they've like, just missed getting hit by a car. Or survived a horrible accident. And why not? There's plenty of evidence that just staying alive is the actual point of life. Don't the plants and the animals all just try to stay alive? Do *they* have some great mission they have to fulfill? Some universal goal? Some clear purpose? No. They just get up and do it *over and over again, day after day. Just because they can.* What makes us so different? Why should we think we're so special that we need a *reason* to go on?"

She let her eyes blaze briefly, picked up another cookie, and repeated the strangely delicate motion of taking a bite of cookie from one hand and a sip of tea from the other. Then she said, with finality:

"That's it. That's all five possibilities."

"Excellent," said Izzy. "I think that all makes amazing sense." He hadn't quite followed everything she said, but he realized that the sun had set and evening had entered the room. She looked more grim in the half-light from the kitchen than she had ever looked before. A terrible feeling crept over him, and for the millionth time he forced himself to deal with the angry words of Bubbie Chava when his mother had revived her with the Incantation, lo those many years ago. The exact look on her face returned fully and horribly to his memory.

What if it really *was* his father's time, *right now?* What if his mother was right? What if the Incantation was some dark, illicit power that should not exist—not a "prayer," just a "technique," as his mother had called it. But something dark. A dark technique. And then he recalled those words which he should never have allowed to escape his own lips, but which had escaped them so many times, shorn of the opening phrase about his life's mission. Joy was not now here to prevent him from asking one more fucking time: *What if I'm not really meant to be here at all?*

Fortunately, at that moment, an entirely different thought arrived to distract Izzy from his old obsession, and he did some counting on his fingers. Surprised, he counted again.

"Are you sure?" he asked, at length.

"Sure of what?" replied Aunt Leah.

"Sure that's what life is about? I mean, 'just to stay alive'?"

She laughed: "Not at all. I didn't say I knew *which* of the five possibilities is true. Just that *one* of them must be true."

"Right." Izzy did some further counting. And for the first time, maybe ever, he truly met his aunt's eyes.

"You know, if you think about it, in *three out of those five possibilities,* it makes sense to...to..."

"To stay alive as long as you can? Yes, in three out of five," she nodded with approval. "You're cleverer than I thought, to have come to that on your own. Even your father might not have picked it up so fast."

"Not bad, those odds."

"No, not bad."

"Not bad at all!" he echoed, but loudly. "Three out of five. Maybe the old man was right. Maybe the main thing is to *just play the odds.*"

She shrugged. "Sure. It's what's kept *me* going, all these years."

Izzy smiled in growing understanding. "Then you'll do it? You'll recite the Incantation and save my father even though he's old and you don't like him?"

"Even though he's a loser and a jerk and always treated me like dirt." And she shrugged again: "He's family."

Izzy found he hated Aunt Leah less. In fact, as she began the impossibly ancient, sing-song chant, he saw her as a kind of ageless philosopher, even perhaps like old unhappy Moses, who tried really hard to understand the will of God, but never quite did, and through some misunderstanding, never deserved to see the Promised Land. Surely, neither she nor Izzy nor Jacob for that matter deserved to see any fucking Promised Land.

Izzy slipped his hand into his pocket and flipped on the small recorder he had hidden there. This time, he wouldn't depend on anyone else to hand the sucker down.

Atenu, Atnu, Shloyme, Rofey, Rofey, mumbled Aunt Leah —or something to that effect. It went on for a long time.

Now that they had lost themselves in the Incantation, both Leah and Izzy forgot about the nurse. They didn't at first notice when she stood up and crossed through the half-light to the sliding glass door, where her figure was silhouetted dramatically against the glow remaining in the western sky. With her white shawl drawn across her shoulders, Alma resembled an angel, and when he did finally look up, Izzy caught his breath. In his excitement, and in the half-trance of listening to the Incantation, he thought: *What does this mean? Is it right that Alma hear these words? Shouldn't we keep the Incantation secret from her?*

In truth, the nurse had lost interest in their doings. She had listened to Aunt Leah's theories for a few minutes, and then stopped paying much attention, being herself staunchly religious in an obscure sect we won't bother to detail. And when the Incantation had finally started, she tuned in to a strange verse or two, then stopped listening to that as well. After all, she had heard thousands of prayers, had heard them in dozens of languages, and because she generally maintained a much closer relationship to God than did any of her patients, she already knew all about the five possibilities, and the three-out-of-five odds, and had discussed the issue directly with the Almighty.

In fact, Alma liked to share little jokes with God from time to time, so now she offered: "All prayers are really the same prayer, right? There's only one prayer. So why do they make it so complicated?" She offered this with a tiny smile.

"They all want to live," God replied in a friendly way, for He and Alma were chummy like that. "I make sure of that. Otherwise, nothing would happen, and no one would be here to see a thing."

"Right, right," said Alma with a sigh.

God then suggested what He always suggests to human beings. He suggested she open the sliding glass door and take a look outside. Alma, of course, did this immediately. On the balcony, she breathed in the rapidly cooling air, and looked beyond the parking lot and the wheelchair-equipped vans, past even the lake toward the now very dark, blue-green hills. Here she noticed that a large number of castellated clouds had begun to gather, lit beautifully red, then purple by the sun. Great lights and shadows shot across the sky. In minutes the clouds multiplied, and soon the sound of a wind crossed the parking lot to merge with the sing-song chanting of the Incantation. This wind ruffled Alma's hair and lifted her shawl, causing her almost to laugh—though she was too professional to make any sound at so solemn a moment. She had become acquainted not merely with God, but the way He sent life and death apparently at random, according to His will—the whole "I Will Be Whatever I Want to Be Whenever I Want to Be It" thing being the operating factor in most of His doings. In this case, death had seemed pretty inevitable, so she was mildly surprised to hear life gathering itself for another storm.

"Goodness," said Alma to God. "What *are* You thinking?" But she knew already. He had already said it. He had just mentioned *a sixth reason* to live a long life, and possibly the most important anyone had mentioned that evening. People often continued to live so that they might look out the window. So that they could see the things of the world. *That's it,* she thought. *That's the secret.* People died only when the time came for fresh, young eyes to see the world anew. In the morning, when he awoke, she would wheel Jacob to the window so he could see outside. That was her job. Maybe he'd even want some time on the balcony. If so, she should probably wait until the day had warmed.

Through all this, Izzy continued to watch Alma with growing interest. No doubt aided by the vision of her silhouette against the glowing sky, and prompted by the strange atmosphere conjured by the reciting of the Incantation, he began to think that Alma was indeed a supernatural being, quite possibly an angel, secretly sent to help the Incantation along, and just now calling up grace from the balcony. Certainly he could feel some kind of unidentified meaning slowly accumulating in the room, along with the many words of the Incantation. It made him dizzy and lightheaded.

He began to feel what? *Lucky.* That was it. *Did luck have meaning?* He was sick of asking that question, and decided to ask it no more.

Never again.

Next morning, Izzy would call up his ex-wife. "Sweet Joy," he would begin before she could answer in anger. "Joy," he would say. "Joy, my lost love. Joy." He would tell her he was sending her the recording of the Incantation, and beg her to learn it. Maybe even chant it for him someday, if she found him on some unnecessary deathbed. Give him another roll of the dice and grant him a fresh opportunity to...well, he'd figure that out when the time came. Meanwhile, he was only forty-seven.

The sky faded completely and the only light came from the partly open kitchen door. Aunt Leah droned on. And soon it seemed to him that the four people locked together in the fifth-floor condo were the only people who existed in the universe. As time slowed in a strangely familiar way, he leaned down to whisper in his father's ear. He said, "Dad, dad. One more second chance." A weird quiet entered the room. Even the medical equipment seemed to exude a gentler susurration. Old man Jacob's breath grew regular and calm.

The FREEDOM
of the DEAD

"One life is not long enough to understand life."

—The LevTov, circa 1861, in conversation

Later on, everyone agreed that something more than academics had been afoot that night. Dr. Abigail Becker was an established scholar of comparative religion, so when she said to a handful of grad students that "life is the mask of death," it shook them. They had gathered in her shabby townhome on a fall evening and were drinking mint tea. "Think about it," she said, leaning back into her shawl in a thin, gray, and virginal manner. "The thoughts of the dead are so much more with us than the thoughts of the living—Plato, Kant, Jefferson, the authors of the Bible. And when you consider the big picture, our short time alive really just hides our much more important, and long-term role as one of the dead—our role as member of a generation, our place in a mode of thought, in a culture, a historic moment, a religion. We wear our life-mask to hide, ever so briefly, the enormity of eternity." *Surely,* her tone implied, *this is obvious.* In the pause, she smiled her tight little smile. "Though I quote Handelman by way of Feigelson, I am not, of course, speaking of the supernatural." They had, of course, all read Feigelson at the beginning of the term. The name Handelman they had to write down.

"But it only matters what we do when we're *alive*," protested Mary Beth Reagan, a perky twenty-year-old pursuing a masters in public health. She was taking Philosophy of Religion 36B to fulfill a humanities requirement—others in the group, she knew, were more serious. "I mean, we don't actually *do* anything after we're dead."

"Is that true?" replied Dr. Becker. "If you think about it, you will see that the dead actually *do* a great deal more than the living. Think how often the influence of the dead grows after their deaths. How they themselves change and evolve, communicating different things at different times to different people: Van Gogh. St. Paul. Nietzsche. And I don't just mean famous philosophers and artists, but everyone: mothers, fathers, friends, lovers. Most of the other people in our lives reach their full potential only after they pass on. Often many years later. Like ripples in a pond. When you think about it, you realize that the dead constitute a much larger and more active world than the living."

"It seems rather exhausting, an active death," said Granger Atkins, a student serious enough to say clever things. But Dr. Becker had plans for Atkins, and she would not allow him to shift the moment into levity.

"Why do we only reach our full potential after our deaths, you may ask. Because the dead have *greater freedom to act than the living.* You know the saying that a watched pot never boils? Well, as Feigelson argues, it may actually be true that watching the pot *limits it, circumscribes* its true potential, just as in those physics experiments where scientists change the nature of particles by observing them. Maybe *only when the teapot is unobserved and unmonitored* does it come to a boil as quickly as possible: There's no way to know. Now consider a person. When a person is alive, he or she is watched *constantly*— Right? Most everything we do, every word we speak is judged, commented upon, criticized by others—hence circumscribed. Only the dead can move unseen, as it were, and hence take action, as it were, in an unlimited manner. They move in our emotions, in our thoughts, in our literature, in our art, in everything we do." And she put down her teacup decisively: "Again, nothing supernatural in the whole idea. Just the way things work."

Here Dr. Becker gave Atkins a private smile, for they had once discussed important things after class. She had been disappointed when he had missed her office hour earlier in the week, and it must be said that she searched his now-quizzical look for that dedicated loyalty which might identify him as a budding protégé, and she as his mentor. Someone who might, *well it had to be said,* continue her work. To her disappointment, no such moment transpired, but she soldiered on by lifting a heavy tome from her coffee table.

"Lately I have been re-reading the *Ohr LevTov,* the writings of a hassidic rabbi who died in 1863. The LevTov (an honorific for a much longer name you needn't remember) led a small group of devoted hassidim in the Ukraine, and maybe two hundred people ever heard of him in his lifetime—mostly in his teeny tiny little village. But his words were collected by one of his followers into this remarkable book, the *Ohr LevTov,* translated from Yiddish into Hebrew and published only some twenty years after his death. The name LevTov translates as "The good heart" or perhaps "The heart of the good," and *Ohr* means "light," so the book could be called "Light of the Good Heart." Over the last 150-odd years, you will find him quoted here and there—but his influence has only really blossomed over the last decade or so, so that now you hear him in occasional colloquia. And no doubt sermons. In short, he has never rested on his laurels: he takes action, and most efficiently. Lately, I seem to encounter him everywhere. Most of his writings are merely pietistic, but here's one of my favorite sayings from the *Ohr LevTov:*

"Truth is not found at the end of a path. Truth hovers above all paths, and one must look up from the path to see it."

Everyone smiled. It was just the kind of saying they most enjoyed: mildly iconoclastic, nondenominational, and widely applicable. It was enough. Indeed, they were more than ready to move on from the subject of death—and young Atkins, disappointing Dr. Becker again, obliged by wiping his glasses on this vest and starting yet another tedious discussion about free will.

The LevTov, however, did not move on. As a spectacularly old man with an enormous gray beard, a fearfully shapeless coat, a black fur hat, and penetrating black eyes—he did not like to be ignored. He was given to aphorisms, and just now, from the grave, he prodded Dr. Becker with one of his favorites: "Argument is the beautiful ship we use to navigate the ocean of God. But we must never forget that the ocean is greater than the ship, and God is greater than the ocean."

Dr. Becker rather took this remark as a personal criticism, and she lost the thread of the whole free will discussion when it popped into her mind.

"Well," she said privately to the LevTov, "I'm a rational theist, so I am doing the best I can."

"You do not do the best you can. You evade the real issues of these students' lives," replied the dead rabbi, and harshly. "Perhaps out of cowardice. Or maybe just long habit. You make the *Ohr LevTov* harmless for your students. Yes, the truth may transcend all paths, it may very well hover above all paths, but it cannot be glimpsed overhead without diligently following *some* path. Truth is fleet and elusive and cannot be hunted down by a mere individual; indeed truth cannot be found at all without carefully following in the footsteps of those who came before. You must look up, but you must stay on the path. You left out *that* entire section of my quotation. Hence, you mislead these children into thinking that nothing really matters but their own cleverness. There's a Latin word for "the belief that nothing matters" which you know, but which I will not repeat, as to speak of evil is to empower that evil. Perhaps worst of all, you make these children think they are alone in the world, when they are not." Then he added something he often added: "Remember, my *hassidim*, I do not speak for myself. I speak for those who came before."

By hassidim, he meant his followers, which of course Dr. Becker was not. You see, the LevTov wrote this last line late after his sabbath, closed up in the only bedroom of a pitifully small and drafty row house in the tiny miserable village of Vlabisk in February, 1861, where outside, the muddy street had frozen solid and snow had begun to fall. Three meager candles guttered on his worn desk and a grimy bottle of wine stood open at his side. Just outside his door, in a crowded sitting room warm and redolent with men and fire, he could hear his hassidim drink and sing, drink and sing, banging on the table to coax him back out of his room for more words of wisdom. His wife had just joined them, crying out: "Feivel, stop being rude!" For the LevTov had left the gathering abruptly, and without a word. Only he knew that he had left the party in deep shame. Why in shame? Because he had been expounding on an exquisite point with great eloquence when he suddenly felt shame at his own vanity, at the way he had been enjoying the power of his own voice, his own cleverness. Indeed, he could hear that his words were *merely* clever, and in fact unhelpful to the real lives of his followers. They were words "without echoes." At this realization, he had suddenly stood up, and with only a grunt to the gathering, he had brushed the crumbs off his coat, and locked himself in his room. There he intended to write about this shame, perhaps thereby to mitigate it. "You must look up from the path to see the truth," he wrote, meaning not what everyone thought later, but his own path that very night, his path of vanity. The wine on his little desk was very bad, almost vinegar, but it reduced the guilt and it allowed him to pray: pray, write, pray, write, that was the way. Were his prayers getting through? Sweat was on his aged forehead and he felt the darkness outside his home like a wall: a wall against prayer that God Himself may have erected. This vision terrified him, and he wrote: "On which side of that wall waits the dark Latin word? That dark Latin word for 'belief in nothingness' which I will not speak? That terrible word which I hear arriving with a thud, like our fate, like a sword into the chest of the world? Do I keep myself and my hassidim safe from that word *inside* this wall, or am *I myself* bringing this ugly word into the world through my vanity, through the cleverness of my words, through the way I love to watch the hassidim *appreciate* my words?" And here he ran fingers crooked with age through his spectacular gray beard and took a long sip of the awful wine. "Remember," he wrote feverishly, "I do not speak for myself. I speak for those who came before." It was, as we mentioned, something he said quite often.

"Trust me, I never quote *that* particular line of yours," returned Dr. Becker, back in the twenty-first century, speaking peevishly, but not aloud, and no doubt believing that because she lived in the future, she would get the last word. "It puts everyone off, as it's laden with false modesty, and it's old hat. Of course you speak for yourself, mister. You've no right to speak for anyone else. None of us do. All of us understand that now."

"One life is not long enough to understand life," replied the Lev-Tov to Dr. Becker, expertly using the freedom of the dead and the curious power of time to bend words. "It's that simple. When you say that the dead are more active than the living, here is what you really mean, minus the clever wording: you mean that the purposes of the dead persist among the living. That you work together with the dead. *That truth, however, constitutes the dignity, and not the humiliation of the living.* The living are *not less* than the dead, and the dead are *not less* than the living, because we are all bound together by a single purpose. *That is the true dignity of man, living or dead.* Me, I try to acknowledge as primary my role in that purpose. I try to align myself with the only genuine purpose among all possibilities, which is to move us all toward God." And back in the mid-nineteenth century he finished off the grimy bottle of wine. "But you, Dr. Becker, who were once an idealist, you have grown, like so many of your colleagues, into a mere intellectual provocateur. Over the years you have learned to count yourself out of the *essential argument,* and to become a mere observer. Hence, *alone.* That makes you clever, but unimportant. And it limits your so-called freedom to a far more limited path than mine."

This insult particularly disturbed Dr. Becker. She had always thought of the LevTov quite warmly, even as a kind of friend. After all, she quoted him frequently. Would he really have thought so little of her, were he alive today? Would he have criticized her so harshly?

Briefly, but efficiently, as her students continued to drone in aimless speculation, Dr. Becker re-evaluated her life. Like most of us in the early twenty-first century, she was really good at re-evaluating her life. Indeed, to stay in practice, most of us re-evaluated our lives several times a day, even without prompting by dead thinkers. Socrates may have said that the unexamined life was not worth living, but in our time, most of us would call the unexamined life "a nice break." As the grad students wandered down dead-ends concerning free will, Dr. Becker managed to relive her early years of precocity under the watchful eye of her father, himself the dean of a small liberal arts college on the East Coast—and along the way, re-evaluated him too. Then she moved smoothly into memories of her lack of friends as a teen, when she began to show her intellect and had dresses from the five-and-dime. As the free-will conversation slouched inevitably toward Dostoevsky, she recalled in detail that horrible teenage day in a park in St. Louis when she cried and was seen to be crying by the others. She went on to recall her flirtation with faith at twenty. And then, for the ten-thousandth time, she recalled her year-long affair with the beautiful Caleb when they were both twenty-four, an affair which might have led to much more, even to a great love, even to children, but did not: a false start. Caleb went west for his studies, completing his Ph.D. at Berkeley, then a post-doc at USC, where their paths crossed again at midlife only in sterile discomfort. As Atkins stepped up his game with Kant, she even took the time to go back to the evening she and Caleb broke up, and again paused at the moment when, after her and Caleb's final conversation in the main library, she walked out and saw an old-fashioned lamppost, standing above an intersection of several campus sidewalks. Again, she recalled its ancient shine in the darkness as an inspiration for her coming academic life.

That's the way inspiration operates, you may recall from our discussion of birds, in a momentary way like that, sometimes becoming more important than persons.

As for false starts...well, it has to be said that you never can be really sure which are false, and which are merely lying back, waiting for their consequences to arrive. Did young Atkins resemble the Caleb of Dr. Becker's lost days? Perhaps, in a certain light: the same eyes, the same hair, and of course, Atkins was the same age.

As for Dr. Becker, she let her eyes pass above Atkins to see the framed degrees and accolades crowding the walls of her townhouse. The years among the Jews at the Jewish Theological Seminary stood out, the near-decade among the Catholics at Notre Dame. The photographs with the presidents of universities should have resonated deeply—but like most of us, she recalled all her best times as the early times, the times of *becoming,* the times of *discovering,* the times of *not-knowing,* of *investigating, of her intellect being born in uncertain-*

ty. Once one *knew anything for certain,* she reflected grimly, the fun seemed to go out of that thing. On the shelf just above Atkins's head she found the neat row of eight books she had authored, perhaps a million words exposing misguided notions, suggesting new historical frameworks, demonstrating metaphorical relationships, overturning scholarly contradictions, and unearthing previously unnoticed trends. She had done okay by her sixty-six years—and if she died tonight, she would die content. She protested that if she had once lived as an idealist, *she damn well still lived as an idealist.* She was a warrior in the service of scholarship, a maintainer of the lamplight, and scholarship was the ideal to which she continued to adhere: for only scholarship explored *the truth that hovered above all paths,* all histories, all time. Truth did not pursue *purpose,* she re-asserted. Truth pursued only *truth.*

Still, an unexplained bitterness took her heart, and into her mint tea, unheard by the students, she mumbled, "Fuck you too, LevTov."

The evening ended somewhat early, as Dr. Becker had spoken little after her words about the dead, and the free-will discussion had petered out into predictable conundrums. The students departed in a noisy group, leaving Abby (from here on, as we have become her intimate, we shall use the nickname she reserved for friends) feeling tired, and the house feeling cold. The "fuck you" had taken a good deal of effort, and was probably insincere. After all, she did *like* the LevTov—she considered him a kind of poet, particularly in his later parables—and she felt that she might have misrepresented him to her students.

Well, that could be remedied later.

Irritated at herself for again rehearsing her self-doubts, and for *once again re-evaluating her whole damn life,* Abby tidied the tea things with a clatter and hurried upstairs to bed, where the God greater than oceans sent her dreams. Deep dreams of great agitation, causing her proud gray hair to fall this way and that in a spectacular and wavelike fashion. Herself become a Noah sailing across a pillow soaked in sweat.

In the first dream, she wandered through an enormous amusement park packed with a great crowd of people—men, women, and children in the loud and ugly clothing of her time. She had always hated amusement parks, as well as crowds, and now that it was getting toward evening, she had no coat, and she was looking desperately for the members of her family, whom she needed to save. It was they who were lost. She could smell the sickly smell of the popcorn and cotton candy, hear the music from the rides closing in. The lights were coming on and everyone was smiling except for her. Beyond the lights rose a great wall of darkness which she feared. She needed to ask for help to find her family, but for some reason, she was unable to speak. Why couldn't she ask? Then she realized she could not ask because she could not remember what her family looked like. Were they tall or short? Young or old? What were their names? Unless she could remember her family and how many and how they were dressed, how could she ask for help in finding them? Panic set in, and she began to run through the crowd, bumping into people and grabbing them, but unable even to scream.

If she loved her family, why could she not remember their names?

Then at long last, perhaps after multiple hours, and realizing she ran only in a dream, she willed herself to wake. For a time she just lay in bed, looking at the digital numbers on her clock and breathing hard. Finally, in order to fully shake the disturbing vision, she went downstairs in her gown to make herself some hot chocolate and sit in the front room, again in her big chair, and listen to the cold outside.

Only when she started back upstairs did she glance at the heavy tome on the coffee table. This glance apparently allowed the LevTov to speak again. He was nodding over the paper on his desk in 1861. The clock had moved well past two and the sound of the hassidim faded from the other room as one after another departed. He wrote: "As small children, we try to see the magic. As young men and women, we try to see the joke. As adults, we try to see the advantage. Only when we become old, do we try to see the important." This statement sounded strange coming from a nineteenth-century rabbi—somehow very modern. Indeed, Abby had analyzed the full quotation as part of a well-received paper called "Attitudes on Aging in Eastern Europe before the First World War."

"You are crossing the boundary, Abby my dear," laughed Reb Lev-Tov in his long sleep. Ever the self-promoter, he said: "You are becoming old. Surely that means you should read my book again, just once more before you die. It will do you good."

Abby snorted in amusement, but when she went back to her bed, she dreamt once more. This time she found herself deep under the ground, wandering through a kind of coal mine. The mine was very dark, the air was filling with dust, and she found it difficult to breathe. Again she found herself running. She ran from tunnel to tunnel, with no clue on how to locate the exit. Again she panicked— not so much because she felt she was lost, but because she was alone, and she could not find her way back to others in the land of the living, where something important had been left undone.

"No, not yet," she cried. "I never had a chance to— " and a thousand uncompleted desires crowded into her dream. But then the oxygen in the mine was all used up, her breath stopped entirely, and she did die, as she had always feared, with no one to hold her hand on her narrow path.

In the land of the living, they identified the cause of death as a brain aneurism and the university authorities comforted everyone with the news that "Dr. Becker passed peacefully in her sleep." The president of the university spoke at Abby's funeral, where her grad students crowded together to recount the strange way in which she had discussed the "freedom of the dead" just before her own death. A visiting teacher completed the last few weeks of her courses; he was quite good, and certainly better organized. In short, life offered its customary crowd of events, and by the time the term ended, both students and faculty had already forgotten about Abby, except at the occasional dinner party where the subject of spirits might arise. At such moments, they laughed about the likelihood that Dr. Becker would haunt them all. Indeed, the story of the fateful evening grew over time. After a few months, for example, a stormy wind was added, along with an odd, faraway look in her eye. "Of course, I've seen no evidence of activity by her since," joked Mary Beth Reagan. "So perhaps she was wrong after all."

Sadly, nobody much read Abby's books, and after five years, each one went out of print, and her million words exposing misguided notions, suggesting new historical frameworks, and demonstrating metaphorical relationships, were forgotten.

Follow numerous delays, however, Granger Atkins did finally complete his dissertation toward his Ph.D. in comparative religion. His title: "Ideas of Immortality in Post-Modern Exegesis." For the most part, he too had forgotten Abby, who he had after all known for only a half-semester—except that after he reviewed some of his old notebooks, he added footnote 372 to his 414-page paper. It read,

> [372]Dr. Abigail Becker, in conversation, expanded on this idea with the following remark, drawing on a line from Rabbi Dr. Mimi Feigelson (see note 147), herself expanding on Handelman (see notes 243, 244, and 271): "Life is the mask of death...Our time alive hides our more important, and certainly longer-lasting role as one of the dead—our role as member of a generation, a mode of thought, an historic moment, a religion, a culture. We wear our life-mask to obscure the enormity of eternity." Although this idea need not be related to religious faith, as such, Dr. Becker did connect it to the "many pathways" concepts in the *Ohr LevTov* (see notes 566 and 633). Strangely, Dr. Becker passed away on the very night of her remark.

Exactly six people ever read Granger Atkins' dissertation in whole or in part. Three of these people were on his Ph.D. review committee, but they didn't read it very carefully, and they skipped over most of the footnotes. Granger's mother read her son's work cover to cover over the course of several months, but entirely ignored the footnotes, and despite her best efforts, never really grasped his passionately defended thesis, which had something to do with "Moebius thinking." Granger's brother Peter, a practical man, skimmed the first chapter before a family Thanksgiving, so he could make a clever remark. But that was it. Granger's dissertation earned him no notice, and he could never quite build an academic career. When he reached his mid-thirties, he felt no regret when he joined his practical brother in real estate.

Back in one of Granger's numerous grad school classes, however, a fellow student named Sarah Goldsmith had taken a brief liking to him. They dated six months, during which Sarah dutifully reviewed the first few chapters of his dissertation in draft form. She grasped his Moebius thesis, but it did not impress her, and she eventually abandoned the read, along with Granger himself, as pompous and insincere. She did, however, get as far as the footnote cited above, which struck her deeply. And although she was literally the only person on earth ever to read this footnote, it caused her to find and study the *Ohr LevTov* in its entirety.

Later, she taught the work during her tenure at Northwestern.

When she turned fifty-six, Sarah Goldsmith wrote a short paper called "Five Paths Out of Postmodernism," based partly on the LevTov's thinking.

At fifty-eight, she turned her paper into what would become a popular book. She completed the first draft of this book while sitting in Chicago's Millennium Park on a crisp autumn afternoon, her mind remarkably clear while all around her red leaves fell ceaselessly. She finished just before the afternoon grew too cold to continue.

As it turned out, within just nine months after publication, *Finding the Heart of the Good* enabled at least 122,000 people to escape nihilism completely.

FIRST WATER

"*And the earth was without form, and void; and darkness was upon the face of the deep: and the Spirit of God moved upon the face of the waters.*"

—Genesis

Of smells, Shunu loved deerhide drying in the sun, smoky cooking fish, men in the sweathouse, and the distant sea. Of sights, he loved the muted colors of face paint, his mother's ochre skirt, morning light filtering into their bulrush hut, and fires scattered in the night: especially the sparks rising like bright little birds, then disappearing forever. Of sounds, he loved the call of old men before the hunt and the harvest. He loved the wailing, high-pitched songs of old women, imitating the wind. He even loved their long slow song of death, the lullaby for the hopelessly sick called the "Bridge Over the Sea," which he knew by heart before he was five.

All these smells and sights and sounds were smells and sights and sounds of his village. For in his youth, Shunu was entirely in his village and of his village: the village was himself and everyone he knew.

Except, not his father.

When he was about six, Shunu realized that something was very wrong with his father—almost as if, shockingly, his father was not of the village and did not love the things of the village. His father, Alysehu, had a vague and far-off look which was a wrong look. He had his own hut, and did not sleep with Shunu and Shunu's mother.

And though his father tousled his hair and tried sometimes to teach him the bow and the spear, Shunu could see that the man's heart was not in it. He saw that his father was perpetually impatient, and often disappeared—not like the other men, on the days-long group hunts, but by himself, for weeks at a time. By the time Shunu was seven, he realized that his gaunt, uncertain father was not much liked and certainly not much respected in the village. He heard his father called "Alysehu of the thin arms," a phrase which meant not strong, not reliable, and not to be trusted.

On the mornings of his father's departures, Shunu would stand unhappily outside his mother's hut, watching the man walk down among the smoking embers of the evening fires, then alone down toward the sea with his spear and his bag. At these moments, others would pity Shunu—at least, up until he was about eight. Pity was short-lived within the village, for the village was all. By the time he had grown into his teens, and his own arms became important, Shunu realized that his father's reputation had tarnished him as well. People did not trust Shunu. They figured a son of Alysehu would eventually prove to be another Alysehu. They remembered that Alysehu had refused to take a bear at sixteen, and they wondered if Shunu would take his own bear at sixteen. And though Shunu did take his bear, and everyone smiled the right smiles, he could see in their eyes and glances, "well enough, but blood will out." And though Shunu brought his strong arms to each and every harvest, people reminded him that his father had disappeared just when he was most needed. It grew worse when Shunu's mother died. People said, "She died young because she received too little marital pleasure;" and though at seventeen, Shunu found his own woman of strength and valor, she was not, of course, high born, and he had to pleasure her loudly, for all to hear. When she bore him two boys in rapid succession, he was sure these births would end the curse—but they did not. He could see the gnarled medicine woman fingering the boys' arms and legs, looking for weakness.

And so it came to pass that when he was a man of nineteen, with a wife and two infant sons, Shunu was glad to learn that his father was dying. Shunu had been in the mountains, hunting deer with the men, when on his return he found three old women already sitting outside his father's hut, singing the Bridge. They told Shunu he must sit inside the hut while his father died—but the hut stank, and Shunu refused. Strangely, the old women nodded their approval. Although it was clearly his obligation, they knew Shunu must break with his father now, and begin a life fully within the embrace of the village.

At sunset on the day his father died, however, strange things happened. First, a hot, dry, demon wind came down from Red Mountain, causing the gnarled medicine woman to confirm that it would be Alysehu's last night on land. By morning, she said, his spirit would head west across the ocean, blown by the wind. Quietly, she owned to the three singing women her surprise that Alysehu had been granted a sign as important as a demon wind. Then she was downright shocked when a large raven came to circle the village three times, and three times only, just as the sun dropped. This was closely followed by the cry of a mountain lion.

"Go in," she said to Shunu, alarmed. "Go in quickly."

Nineteen-year-old Shunu accepted a talisman and went into the stinking hut. There he knelt beside his father, bowing his head, as was the custom. At that moment, a curious feeling came over him, as if much were about to change. He was aware that the moon hung fully waxed and yellow-huge above the oaks outside, and as he waited for his father's breath to stop, he was aware of the breath of the demon wind as it whispered, "Alysehu, Alysehu"—as if his father were important. Just as he placed a damp, scented rag on his father's dying forehead, the high, keening chant of the Bridge rose above the wind, and his father's eyes opened wide.

"Shunu, Shunu," said the old man of forty-seven, reaching up to grab his son's arm with surprising strength.

"I am here, father." This too was correct ritual.

"Shunu, I do not die in peace."

"Yes, father," said Shunu. "Sleep. You will need your strength for the journey."

A desperate breath, then: "I know where it is!"

"Yes, father."

"I know! I've known for years, but I could not find it."

"Of course, father."

"No, listen to me, Shunu. She told me before she got away...the spirit."

"Yes, father."

"No, listen Shunu. She was dressed like a villager from Red Mountain, but it was just a disguise. We met by the sea, and she admitted she was really a spirit."

"When was this, father?"

"I was young, younger than you. But it doesn't matter, surely the pure water is still there. It has always been there."

"Rest, father."

"Oh, the regret. The regret! You know I always lacked...the true courage. I went...but never far enough, never tried hard enough. I could not get it out of my head. Now I'm about dead, and it is still in my head. You will be ashamed—"

"Hush, father. Hush."

"No, listen to me, Shunu. I know where the pure water rises. It's in a ravine of the fourth mountain, northeast along a stream that drops a waterfall directly into the ocean. Directly into the ocean! She told me! Follow the coast for twenty days, find the waterfall, and follow its river up into the mountains, where this river branches into muddy streams. The larger branches mislead you. You must follow the muddiest, smallest, most unimportant-looking branches. That's why no one ever followed the right one to its source. In the third ravine of the fourth mountain...I never even found..."

"You mean the First Water, father, but no one knows where the First Water rises." But as he said this, the wind rose again.

"You will have to bring weapons! It will be guarded by demons! That's how you will know you're on the right path. Go alone! I don't want anyone else to get the credit. When you find the pure water, everyone will remember both you and me. They will sing us songs."

This kind of personal ambition, however fanciful, was shameful in the village. "Father—"

Now his father let his head fall back, staring at the shadows of fires dancing on the bulrushes. "She was beautiful, the girl. She had long,

long, black, black hair. Long, long, black, black hair. Oh, oh! She made love with me. I recall the smell of her! I stood tall like a pine! It was the greatest moment of my poor sad life and I did not want to let her go. I held her arm tight when she tried to go. That's when she revealed that she was a guardian of the pure water! If I would let her go, she said, she would tell me the path—though she warned me it was dangerous even for a warrior, and I was no warrior. Oh, oh! I tried. But I regret. I regret. I regret all the life not lived. I do not go peacefully, Shunu. I regret!" Then he shouted incoherently, the wind lifted to a frenzied peak, the lion spoke again, and he was dead.

As was the custom, Shunu sat naked outside the hut, covered in ashes all the rest of the night, but all the while thinking, "What if it's true?" At the burial, he felt his wife watching him. She had said nothing about the tale, which of course she had overheard while listening outside the hut—but he could see her agitation. Finally, she said, "Now your father sleeps without dreams."

He knew she said this as a warning.

The First Water bubbled beneath all the village tales. The First Water had not only fed creation, it had preceded creation. The First Water was the source of all life, just as life was the source of all land, all ocean, all sky—for in this village's understanding of the universe, earth and heaven did not precede animate life; life preceded earth and heaven. Raven, Turtle, Eagle, Coyote, and even Man preceded mountain, rock, and field. Only the First Water preceded life, for without water, no life can exist. It was sometimes called the only pure water, the water which fed all water, and of which all other water was the muddied offspring. The apparently solid earth on which the village sat floated in the lake of pure water, which bubbled through in one place as a spring. Tradition had it that the man who found the hidden spring and drank of the First Water would not only be granted eternal youth, he would become a shaman and understand everything. Everything: the before and after, as well as that within the village and that beyond the village.

As far as anyone knew, of course, no one had ever found the spring.

Throughout the three days waiting for his father's soul to depart—the three tedious, actionless days sitting now in his own hut, but still naked and covered in ashes—Shunu brooded. He saw the lifelong, slightly lost look in his father's eye, and he wondered if that look were coming to his own eye. Most strangely of all, he felt himself moving outside the embrace of the village, losing his love of its smells and sights and sounds. Still..."Father! Father!" he cried from time to time, to the great satisfaction of the still-keening women, who always appreciated serious grief, even for a man of thin arms.

When the three days were up, Shunu emerged in a specially painted loincloth, properly bowed to dismiss the old women, properly knelt to kiss the dust of the earth, then properly reached both his hands up to the sun. Strangely, however, the ceremony seemed to mean nothing to him. "I must go on a long journey," he told his wife. "I must go while I am young and I have the strength."

"You have two infant sons," she replied sharply. "One is not yet weaned."

"You take wonderful care of them."

"Don't be a fool," she said, and slapped him hard across the face. This brought tears to Shunu's eyes. He hung his head and made himself go out into the potato fields, where the others greeted his work especially warmly. Come evening, he brought his family three rabbits. But that night, he slept badly, and when his wife approached him with her touch, he at first refused. Just before dawn, however, she woke him, saying, "Here is the First Water," and opened her clothing. Touching her sweet water, life occurred again. This time, twin daughters with laughing eyes and strong hands.

With their birth, Shunu fell entirely back into the dream of the village. For the first time in his life, he found himself becoming a completely happy man: free of his father's curse, back in love with the lights of morning and the lights of night, the scent of his wife, the noise of his children, the sound of the old women and the old men. His wife's well-timed slap was followed by fifteen years of hunt and harvest, joy and ceremony, pain and beauty, dust and sunlight—years which made Shunu entirely forget his foolish father's words.

These years were not, of course, without suffering. One year, Shunu fell and hurt his left leg so that it was twisted badly; but he limped on, undaunted. His younger son drowned in the ocean; but children were frequently lost, and this death did not change Shunu's spirit the way all the later deaths would. The life of the village continued, and it was the village that mattered; indeed, over time, the village began to respect Shunu deeply. The village began to see him as a resilient and reliable man, and it forgave, even if it did not forget, the weakness of his father. Shunu's words were considered carefully in council, and on the evening his older son dragged his own bear into the village, Shunu's entire family was rewarded with full-throated shouting and singing.

Unfortunately for Shunu, just two weeks after his son's bear, an epoch lasting ten thousand years came to an abrupt end—as epochs often do. Rumors of gigantic ships resembling winged birds reached the village. White men appeared with outrageous beards and terrifying weapons. Red spots appeared on nearly all the villagers, and about half died, including Shunu's wife and twin daughters, one of whom was pregnant. The keening of the Bridge was heard nonstop—until no one was strong enough to sing it, or care.

Like all song, all custom fell away, from face paint to drying deer-hides. The white men gathered the young and strong among the survivors, told them to work in gigantic fields, and everyone began to eat a new harvest. In the dead of night, after a single desperate moment of goodbye, Shunu's sixteen-year-old son ran away northward, scandalously holding the hand of a girl he had not married—ignoring all decent practice, and leaving Shunu alone. Within a year or two, the village itself largely disappeared. As the white men's towns grew along the coast, most of the remaining villagers moved down to the adobe dormitories being built beside the fields. Soon, only the old, the sick, and the lame like Shunu still lived in the ridiculous, drafty bulrush huts. As one by one his joys ceased, Shunu became vacant and gray before his years, as well as nearly speechless with despair.

But of course, no epoch ends without another epoch beginning. Even Shunu knew this, not least from the varied tales told in the village, where one age often overturned another. There was the age before the Flood and after the Flood. The age of Lizard or perhaps Raven, followed by the Sun God and his daughters, the Coyote of the Sky, or perhaps Mankind. Like most, Shunu had never bothered to get it all quite straight. He did know that his own youth had ended. His family life had ended. His village had ended. The smells, sights, and sounds he loved had ended. But the world was not filled with nothingness; it was filled with white men. Through his vacant eyes, Shunu saw the young begin to wear the white men's clothing. Speak their language. Sing their songs. Even adopt their gods.

The next age had clearly dawned, so Shunu at last moved down with the others, down to the white settlement and into a hot, un-comfortable adobe building with many rooms. There he was given a nickname, Lame Sheep, and made to sit in long lines with others under the hot sun (recently stripped of its divinity) to hear tales of the new gods. Lame Sheep attempted to learn the new language as well, but failed. With gestures, he was told to clean up each day af-ter the workmen building a new and enormous structure of magnif-icent lines. Each day Lame Sheep shuffled with a broom and dustpan among the workers making adobe bricks, then down along the walls and corridors where the bricks were laid. The bricks were mixed from clay and straw and dung and water, pressed into wooden frames, then laid out in long rows to dry. The work was not pleasant, but Lame Sheep understood that as long as he did this work, and as long as he went on sitting in the sun to hear new tales, he would eat. Just as im-portantly, he learned to drink a new liquid called wine. Wine made one forget, at least briefly, the end of one's ten-thousand-year epoch.

In short, Shunu became an old drunk Indian, shuffling around the construction site of a Spanish mission in what was already called California. The mission symbolized an epoch which ended up lasting only about sixty years.

All these events, however, led to a remarkable moment, which ar-rived late one June afternoon in the year 1786. At the end of a day limping around the mission, eyes averted, broom in hand, Shunu (for when he was alone, he was not Lame Sheep) often crept into the big and ornate, if uncompleted, chapel, which he found generally cool and quiet. Here he could hide in a corner and drink in peace as he looked up at the white gods. One by one, these gods had begun to stand in the chapel. They were built of stone and perfect in their stillness—a stillness entirely unlike the ceaseless noise and motion of Eagle, Raven, or Coyote of the Sky. It was perhaps best that these white gods were housed indoors, for male and female alike, their stone noses and eyes and ears seemed unsuited to the smells and sights and sounds of the world outside. Their eyes focused instead on the painted walls of the chapel—as if those walls were a form of forever.

On this particular afternoon, Shunu arrived particularly drunk, and his stupor was enhanced by the day's last sunbeams, which streamed spectacularly through openings in the partially installed stained glass, apparently straining to pick out scarlet draperies and silver monstrances in beauty. But as he found his usual dark corner and pulled out his bottle, Shunu saw that he was not alone. A master painter stood on a scaffold, mixing pigments and working on a huge mural in the fading light: one of several murals slowly filling the great chapel's walls. This mural showed a white friar, decked out in his brown robe and strangely fringed bald head. Shunu marveled that the friar was standing above a village very much like his old village. Here were the same happy bulrush huts and cheerful cook fires, the women in their painted skirts, and the men in their painted loincloths. In the distance stood his village's own lofty mountains, and in the foreground, he could see the big new fields and the mission—here shown entirely complete. The friar held up his hand in the same way as the white gods, ready to lead the villagers away from their huts, down to the fields, and into the sparkling new epoch.

For a time, Shunu simply watched in awe as the master painter did his work. His motions with the brush were miraculous, and Shunu could see another villager begin to take shape—a woman who could have been his own mother from long ago.

But then something odd happened. The artist made a mistake— Shunu could not quite see what it was—and the man took up a rag to wipe at the mural with some water. The rag was too wet, and the colors suddenly ran badly, causing the artist to curse aloud. In his haste, and as he wiped at the drips, the artist made large and terrible smudges, dissolving part of the village and a corner of the fields.

At that moment, and in his drunken state, Shunu had a new thought.

Any man who has seen his entire world dismantled in a short time might have had this thought. Especially a man who had lived his whole life outdoors, then suddenly found himself living in enormous buildings with hallways. Even more especially if he were at that moment sitting in the ornate chapel of an enormous building with many rooms and hallways, staring at a smudged mural.

"All beings live in painted rooms," thought Shunu. "All beings live in painted rooms, but most never know it: coyote, sparrow, or man. Indeed, a man may live his entire life in a painted room without realizing that outside are doors and hallways leading to other rooms. Why? Because a room is like a dream, and a man moves unconsciously in a dream, not seeing outside while he sleeps. The village and the potato fields, my family, the mountains, the raven and the bear, only appeared to exist outdoors—in truth we all lived in a very large dream-room. The walls were painted by our fathers and mothers and gods. All the things I loved as a child—the smell of drying deer-hide, the light through the weave of the bulrush hut, the sound of the women singing—each were painted by master painters, long dead. Gods or forebears, these artists were truly masters, because neither I nor the other villagers ever knew that other rooms existed just down the hall, or that someday we ourselves might accidentally wander into a new room and find the old room gone."

Then he paused.

"No one, except perhaps my father."

As Shunu watched, the master painter slowly began to repair his error, and Shunu thought, "White people have learned to construct rooms and paintings at will, and to their own liking. It is a remarkable trick. They then fill them with their apparently still and perfect gods. These gods are made of stone in the hope that they will not change, nor attempt to leave these rooms. Both rooms and gods are meant to exist forever—unlike the smells and sights and sounds of the village, all of which existed only for a season, and had to be recreated with effort by each generation."

For a moment, even through the wine, the sadness of his loss returned: each and every smell, sight, and sound. Songs, especially. Then he pulled himself together to complete the next part of his thought:

"Nevertheless, even though the white people have learned the trick of imitating forever, they too are human. Sometimes, like us, they forget they have fallen into a dream they constructed for themselves." At this point, and for perhaps ten minutes, Shunu considered suicide. You and I have to admit that, just as it did for Red Peters a couple hundred years later, suicide represented a reasonable option for Shunu, given his deep despair, coupled with his new understanding of the universe.

Instead, just like Red, he took out his bottle for another pull.

"Of what is a room constructed?" continued Shunu, his mind fighting its intoxicated haze. "A room is built of bulrushes grown in a river, or it is built of adobe, which is merely water and straw and sand and clay and dung mixed together. Murals are painted by artists, who use nothing but pigments mixed with water and egg whites."

At that, he suddenly remembered the white men's story of the creation of the world, a story he had by now heard many times, usually while sitting in those long rows out in the hot sun:

And God moved across the face of the waters...

"When the chief white god built the first rooms of the universe," ruminated Shunu, "he had to build them *somewhere* and out of *something*. And, as both friars and shamans say, the only thing that first existed was water, the First Water, which existed prior to adobe, prior to pigments, prior to bulrushes, prior to the village, and prior to all the gods of every age. Like our gods, the chief white god built *from the water and upon the water*."

Interestingly, unlike Plato, Shunu did not that afternoon conclude that everything we see is but the shadow of a finer world. Unlike the Buddha, he did not conclude that everything we see in our painted rooms represents a false construct of our own minds. Shunu had not read either of these gentlemen, so in his cups, and sitting in the ornate chapel, he took quite a different path. Rising at last fully above the alcohol, he said to himself:

"A room is not an illusion. A room actually exists. And each room is necessary, for each room nourishes and sustains the creatures which dwell within it during their proper epoch. Thank the gods and ancestors for the rooms they built, the rooms in which we may dwell. Their work was all well and good. But alas... *every room eventually pretends to be a forever room*, like this master painter's beautiful mural, which pretends to be perfect and unchanging. The village was tricked by our ancestors into believing that its smells and sights and sounds would go on forever. The white people trick each other with their statues and murals. I doubt they successfully trick their gods.

"Coyote and Eagle knew that no room lasts forever—and most likely, the white gods know that as well. Surely, even the white gods know that however still they have been asked to stand as statues in this magnificent room, if they walked down the hallway, they would find a different room. Surely, even the white gods know that each room is brief, and will eventually be lost: paintings being so easily smudged, statues so easily smashed, adobe bricks so easily melted in a rain..." And here he remembered the white men's story of the Flood, so like the villagers' stories of the Flood.

"Wise gods know that only the First Water is forever. Only the First Water builds and only the First Water destroys, just as the Flood took everything back to its original elements. The wise gods know that only the pure water can grow bulrushes, make new adobe bricks, and mix new pigments. Wise gods—and, just maybe, a few wise men—know they must perpetually go back to the First Water if they wish to create new things: new smells, new sights and new sounds. Wise gods—and, just maybe, a few wise men—know they must perpetually build new rooms to house new epochs, even if those rooms will eventually be dissolved.

"Only fools do not build. And only fools believe they are building forever."

As the capper to Shunu's thought, he posed this question: "I have heard many tales, in the village and among the whites. But what if the only tales truly worth telling are tales of men and women searching for the First Water?" From his dark corner, Shunu again opened his eyes to the chapel. As he did, he imagined first the mural, then the village, then all the rooms of the mission, then the adobe of the mission itself, each smudging like the artist's pigments, breaking into their underlying elements, and running down into the earth to dissolve in a pool of H_2O.

Aloud, he said, "No wonder the gods have hidden away the spring."

At this point, of course, time collapsed, and Shunu again found himself kneeling in the bulrush hut where his father lay dying. Again, the raven circled the village three times. Again, the mountain lion spoke. Again, the moon hung yellow-huge above the oak grove. But this time, when the demon wind blew hot and wild, it did not speak the name "Aliseyu, Aliseyu," it spoke the name "Shunu, Shunu." And this time, when he looked out the door of the hut, Shunu saw the spirit with the long, long, black, black hair standing outside the village, imitating the wind. Like the wind, she sang "Shunu, Shunu," as inside the hut, his father again recited the directions to the spring. The waterfall into the sea. The lesser paths.

This time around, Shunu saw that his father had not been a mere weakling; *he had been a man who had accidentally stepped outside his room.* Once outside, his father had seen that his village was not everything. He had seen that the village and its joyous smells and sights and sounds might at any moment pass away. Naturally, his father had tried to find the one true source of all things. Naturally, that had led to suffering.

This time, when his father died, Shunu did not stay and mourn. This time, he arose and walked out of the bulrush hut. Around a turn of the path, just beyond the village, he found the spirit with the long, long, black, black hair and tried to speak with her. But she was looking away, toward the journey.

It took Lame Sheep a full week to prepare. He had to steal food and make new shoes, sew a leather bag, and file down sticks for a staff and a spear. When he told the others he was leaving to go north and look for his remaining son, they laughed. But on the third day after the beginning of spring, like his father before him, and without say-

ing goodbye to anyone, he limped down past the great adobe structures of the white men (which had not yet dissolved into their baser
elements, though of course, eventually they would) toward the sea.
The path was green with spring grass and run across with wildflow-
ers. And when the sea at last appeared below the hills, the saltwater
glittered blue and white as if with a song he had not yet heard. A
flock of a thousand seabirds rose as he approached, and shedding his
clothes and supplies, he dove straight into the waves to cleanse himself of everything that had happened to him.

As he emerged from the waves, Shunu cut his left toe on a sharp
stone, which made him laugh. "And so it begins," he said as he bound
the wound with a little cloth, and begin limping all the worse up
along the beach to the north, leaning heavily on his stick. After a
week of careful use, he ran out of wine, and for two whole days he
went through shakes and terrors; then another three days of despair
until the terrible desire finally passed.

In the beginning, Shunu mostly walked on the wet sand, but often he had to climb up rocks or walk along a bluff. He slept in the
little groves of stunted pine which began to appear along the shore,
or he went further up to find shelter in a ravine—but he was careful
never to lose sight of the sea. Three times he found villages of fishing peoples. Each had suffered from the red spots, along with priests
and soldiers. In every face, he could see that the life they knew was
ending, ending, ending—dissolving right before their eyes. He en-
quired about his son, but of course, no one could help him, and soon
he passed beyond the land of his own tongue and could no longer
speak with the people he met.

At length, the shore became rougher and wilder, with no more
villages. Enormous waves crashed against enormous rocks. The bluffs
became high cliffs, and the coastal oaks and grasses he had known
his whole life gave way to larger trees and unfamiliar bushes. Because
of clefts and trees, it became a struggle to see all the shoreline, and he
worried that he would miss the waterfall completely. Many times he
found a creek that dropped into the folds of a ravine, and he'd follow
it eagerly to a beach; but always these creeks grew gentle before reaching the waves.

Then, at last, three weeks after leaving his home, having travelled further than anyone from his village had ever travelled, and standing on a thousand-foot cliff, Shunu spotted it far in the distance: a waterfall that dropped off a rocky shelf directly into a small wild bay.

The waterfall was as beautiful as a thing out of a white man's tale of forever, and for a long time he just stood and watched it tumble. He realized that behind his back arose many mountains. He tried to count four mountains, but he could make no sense of the peaks or the ravines. In any case, how could he actually be in this place? Didn't it exist only in tales? And if it did exist in reality, would not both the gods of the white men and the gods of his own people conspire to stop him from going further? Shunu could see no immediate way that led directly down the cliff to the waterfall or its bay, so he backtracked far south along to a ravine he had explored a day or two before, and followed it again down to a narrow ocean beach, loud with crashing waves in a sea filled with great rocks. He would have to go by way of the sea, bay by bay.

Shunu tied his clothes and belongings in a bundle that he strapped to his back, and he entered the waves with a shout of courage—a shout to honor the lifelong, uncompleted journey of his father. He fought his way out to the true ocean, evading the rocks and swimming to round a terrifying point to another beach, and then another. A day passed, and he slept tucked into a forest above a third bay. He was not a strong swimmer, and it occurred to him that he might die among the rocks and currents.

In the afternoon of the second day out in the surf, he lost the bundle of his clothes and belongings. Even the clumsy spear.

"Fine," he said to his father, who had surely awoken in the land of the dead to watch him. "See me! See that I am not afraid! I seek Fourth Mountain and Third Ravine, and who knows? Unlike you, I may find them by pure luck." Indeed, at that very moment he rounded the last point and saw the waterfall again sparkling in the sun, the waterfall that fell directly into the sea from a height at least ten times that of a man. For a time he lolled in the churning surf while above him, like a sign, the waterfall roared. He swam directly beneath it and stood up to wash himself, for it was shallow here, and very close to shore. Wiping his eyes, the exhausted, half-starving Shunu was sure for a moment that he saw the girl with the long, long, black, black hair standing in the tree shadows just above the narrow shore.

"Like the birth of a child," he said of himself as he struggled onto the pebbles naked, holding nothing, nothing at all. "Father, father." he said. "I am sorry, but I have lost the weapon I brought to fight the demons." After warming in the sun, he parted the small bushes where the woman had stood, and wanted to shout, but did not dare: for here was a path that wound up the cliff next to the waterfall, easy and well-trodden. How was that possible? Soon he found himself up in the full green of the forest once again, the stones and dirt and grasses cool on his bare feet. It smelt damp with moss and fungus and recent rain. He inhaled deeply and thought the smell like his wife, and remembered for the first time in years how she had parted her clothing.

Almost at once, the path crossed the small clear stream that fed the waterfall. Then the stream divided, the right branch bright and clean, and the left small and muddy and overgrown. The well-used path, of course, followed the more promising branch, but Shunu did not hesitate in following the darker way, his feet squishing into the streambed as he pushed through the brambles that scratched his unprotected body.

The muddy rivulet branched a second time, into two more ravines, but this time the choice was less certain. Both branches seemed putrid and forbidding, each barely a trickle through the mud, but Shunu chose what seemed the slightly smaller and less impressive branch, continuing to push his way through the ferns and vines and brush, mostly walking in the stream bed. Pine trees grew tall and straight and towered far overhead. The forest grew greener. Bats flashed through the slight, jagged patches of sky, and squirrels ran in the branches. He knew he must look for a new weapon, and at last he located a heavy stick and a sharp rock. He found these just in time, for at the next division of the waters, he saw a demon, sent by unknown gods to protect the First Water from human beings, just as all gods protected the secret of life, and just as the white god had set the flaming swords to protect his Tree. The demon had taken the form of a mountain lion, which stood directly over the third branching point.

Shunu raised the heavy stick in his left hand and kept the sharp rock in his right.

The lion had startlingly yellow eyes, and for a moment Shunu saw himself as he must look to those eyes: a thin, naked, lame human being with scraggled gray hair and scraggled gray beard, his body covered in mud and cuts. In short, appearing to be nothing but his desire. Then he forced himself to see himself as he must see himself: timelessly young, muscular, beardless, fearless, with his own long, long, black, black hair tied back in a knot. The mud became war paint on his chest; he drew himself up and summoned a snarl. The mountain lion leapt, and Shunu, now a warrior, struck first with the stick, and then, as the lion reached him, brought the sharp rock up beneath its neck. Blood spurted, and a horribly surprised and mangled cry came from the lion before it scrambled to its feet and ran away to die.

In his native tongue, Shunu shouted, "Fuck you, fuck you, fuck you."

After the demon disappeared, Shunu stood breathing hard and letting his heart calm. Only as he began to move, did he notice a long bleeding scratch torn along his right arm—and he laughed to think he might die before the lion. He looked down at the two streams, and washed his arm in the stronger current. Still the stream on the left seemed smaller, darker, less promising; so he pushed on that way, leaving a trail of blood on the leaves and in the little ponds of stagnant water.

He began to hear music: a pipe as from the village, when the shaman played at the lost ceremonies. He thought he heard a chant, as of the choir in the chapel. He began to think it was raining, though when he looked up he could see the sun through the trees. He began to imagine a mist in the forest, though when he looked hard, it was gone. He realized he was probably losing his wits with his blood, and stopped for a while to tie leaves on his arm with vines. The little stream began to climb up through steep rock, and he climbed with it, only to find another level of forest.

At last the stream petered out into a little swampy clearing filled with tall grasses and silent bulrushes. He circled the swampy clearing, but found no further stream. He was at the source of the stream, but it appeared dank and filled with rot, not creation.

"I am young!" he shouted to the spirits, and his voice was delirious and angry. "Strong! Forever young! I have come at my father's bidding, at the bidding of the First Water! I live! I wish to begin again!" At that, the forest came alive: The spirits of owls few among the trees, the spirits of raccoon and coyote and raven and deer whirled in the woods. He saw the sad-eyed spirit of his father fighting the fierce, yellow-eyed spirit of the mountain lion in the shadows. Here danced the spirits of his dead wife and daughters. And his dead son, wandering lost. Shunu did not try to approach these spirits, which he knew to be an old man's distractions, sent to protect the spring. Instead, as the music rose, he turned his attention to the middle of the swampy clearing, where the woman with the black, black, long, long hair gestured him forward. He pushed his way through the grasses, which cut at him. He slogged through the deepening mud, up to his knees. And yes, as he pushed back the last of the foliage, he saw it: in the very center of the queasy muck and weeds and flotsam, a welling of pure water. Coming up directly out of the ground, a powerful gusher of pure water rose with such force that it pushed back a beautiful clear blue circle in the larger, muddy pool; continuously filling it, and by extension, the whole world. How wide was the blue circle? As wide as a hut or an ocean—one could not say, since it existed before the description of all things. The sun yet shone directly overhead, and as he stared, Shunu realized that though it seemed half an epoch, little time had actually passed since he emerged from the surf. Indeed, time had stopped, along with the music and the dance of spirits. In the midst of this sudden quiet, Shunu dropped his rock and his stick and waded yet entirely naked through the mud into the First Water, there to kneel in its beauty. He let it envelope both his good and his bad leg. His feet found the force of the welling, and as he bent forward, he forgot about rooms and murals and epochs. Instead, he thought of the first and the last, the prior and the subsequent, the beginning and the end, his father and his father's fathers, his wife and all women and the white people and the Red Mountain people and his own people and the demons and the demon wind and the endless mountains and the ceaseless lands unfolding. His wife was right and his father was right and the old stories of all men and women were right, and all arose from the First Water. He lowered his head and he drank deeply. He drank for a long, long time. Until, at last, he raised his head and saw everything anew.

The BIRTH of NOAH
Part II

"And Jesus was a sailor when he walked upon the water....And when he knew for certain only drowning men could see him, he said all men will be sailors then, until the sea shall free them."

—Leonard Cohen, 1966

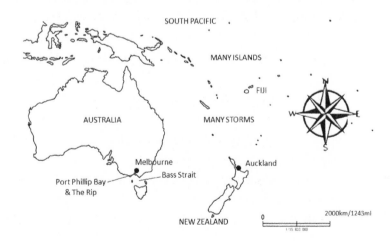

Finding himself penniless in Melbourne, Noah Caldwell became a sailor. It was just after the turn of the year 1980, and here's how it happened. For starters, Noah never located his Uncle Thomas of the many letters to America—how could he? The last forwarding address was a hotel, and a hotel before that. But he felt it didn't matter, as he'd already learned everything his uncle had to teach.

In the beginning, Noah was no sailor, not even a pilgrim on a voyage of self-discovery. Instead he was just another young American drifter, male like most, and largely occupying the inland hostels or shabby areas down among the great shipping docks. Here he would sometimes find work carrying crates or moving fruit around dark warehouses smelling of diesel. He was never aboard the big ships when they departed, and often he only caught glimpses of their mighty hulls through warehouse doors and windows, or walking up ramps into their cavernous holds.

Still, like his uncle, the ships excited him. The way they headed out. And he was beginning his life anew. And he had broken from sadness. And he was still young.

Sometimes, Noah would use his small funds to take a bus and join the tourists along the coastal walks beyond Port Phillip Bay. Here he would try not to slouch like a worthless drifter as he strolled on a beach or climbed rocks to see tidal pools. Or he would stand ankle-deep, watching the breakers and ships move across the horizon. Like the tourists, he would consider the infinite without the infinite actually sweeping him away.

At least, that was the plan.

Here's the thing about the infinite, toward which Noah has been moving since his story began—toward which all our characters seem to be moving: At the same time we fear the infinite, we find ourselves drawn toward it. We are as small children standing on the edge of an empty street, daring one another to run onto the vast asphalt. Some children do run into the street; but even the bold know they can handle its enormity only in limited doses.

Like Noah, go and climb on the black rocks of a seashore where the coastal creatures live. Notice how the barnacles and urchins, mussels and lichen, crabs and gulls and sea lions await the sea to bathe them, threaten them, encourage them, and feed them—all while they cling to their black rock homes. These creatures love the sea for its infinity, for its never-ceasing newness, for the way the surge washes everything to them and washes everything away again. Some swim far out each day. The gulls range great distances. But before long, they want to return safely home. Why? Because they rightly fear the sea, as well as love it. Probably they even hate the sea, because even as it feeds them, they know it might at any moment tear them away from the shore.

And someday, of course, it will.

So do most humans go and stand for a few hours in a desert beneath night skies, climb briefly up hills above great forests, or take tourist strolls along seashores. Like coastal creatures, most of us only want to experience the infinite for a few minutes or hours or days. Briefly, daringly, we imagine the thrill of losing ourselves in it forever. Briefly, we dream of obliteration. Then, like the mussels at low tide, we are relieved to be free of the infinite again. We run back into our cars. We close up our tents or RVs or shutter our seaside hotels, imagining ourselves safe until we can handle the unlimited, just one more time.

We should never feel ashamed of this rhythm. Even the greatest among us can only survive by being part of, but separate and protected from unlimited things—keeping ourselves to ourselves as long as we can.

Or as long as we wish.

Never mind philosophers or clergy. Missionaries or drunken Indians. No doubt the greatest human dance with the infinite occurs on ships at sea. As a sailor, you are safe as long as you keep your little boat sealed and secure. As long as you check her rigging and polish the rust out of her steel. As long as you diligently read the weather and check your supplies. If you take loving care of your boat, the boat will take loving care of you. By day she will carry you among restless white-flecked waves while keeping you and the waves separate. By night her berths will cradle you safe within the darkest bowels of unlimited things, until one day you are not safe at all.

Believe me, sailors think about this every fucking day.

One night, about four months after he arrived, and recovering from a warehouse gig, Noah loitered uncertainly in a crap bar back behind the Melbourne docks. As you may have gathered, Noah often loitered uncertainly: seashores, docks, bars. Indeed, loitering uncertainly had pretty much become his profession. He had successfully left America, but he had not yet entered into anything new. This night, however, right around ten, the bar suddenly filled with loud and happy young men. He saw they were dressed in clean whites and expensive boating shoes. He saw they were sunburnt and unafraid. And the loudest, happiest, most sunburnt, and least afraid was a redhead named Riley Killian.

When Noah ordered a well whiskey, Killian heard his accent.

"Just what Melbourne needed, another fucking Yank," cried the man.

At that moment, things might have gone one of two ways. Noah might have smiled uncertainly and continued to loiter, or he might match Killian's tone.

"Fucking sorry, mate," replied Noah just as loudly. "I'll try not to let it rub off on your fucking whites."

"Fuck no," said Killian. "I just got these clean."

And just like that, Noah's life as a sailor began.

He learned that the happy young men were not rich, they were crew for the rich men who owned yachts on the bay. Owners like the retired sheep herder, the retired bank president, the retired shithead American fucking entrepreneur you've probably fucking heard of, mate. The owners were all rich but mostly old and rheumy-eyed, their yachts worth millions. As a young crewman with a good arm you could help them live out their final fucking dreams, and make a decent fucking dollar doing it. The yachts were laden with heavy chain, enormous sails, and endless friggin' teak that never friggin' stopped needing friggin' oil, mate.

So youth was in unlimited demand.

"Never crew commercial," intimated the spectacularly sunburnt Riley Killian. "Fuck the smelly thousand-footers. Pay's ripper, but they have a million rules, and hauling shit's a bore. Plus, the commercial ships want, like, training and certificates and shit."

The old men with the well-kept yachts were essentially fools, explained Killian's bully mates. "In ten minutes you'll know more about their boats than they ever will. You'll learn the fucking ropes," they said, knocking back their pints. "You just need to look clean. They really like clean."

"Worst case," leaned in Killian, whose red hair crowned many freckles and a particularly effortless good humor, "you can mix their martinis." He paused for effect. "Don't look so glum, mate, you're just handsome enough to mix martinis."

Then they all laughed again with the joy of youth, of the sea, of knowing more than old rich men, of beating the sea at its game, of the memory of wind in sails, of the frothy mouth of Port Phillip Bay, of immortality.

At twenty-three, Noah was indeed handsome in an olive-skinned, curly-haired, middle-eastern sort of way. He had all his uncle's letters in a suitcase back at the shabby room he'd rented, and from those letters he now reminded himself that all men were sailors anyway—no matter what they might pretend. It was a fact of life hidden in plain view. Every man was a sailor, and he had been told to visit many islands. So why not make a living of it? The next day he bought a sailing book. He did pushups on the carpet of the shabby room.

Within three days, Noah and Riley became pretty close, and why not? At thirty-one, Riley was remarkably alive, and seemed to have perfected the art of drifting—he'd figured out how to live cheap and flash plenty of the ready at the right moment. He had a long, lean face, bleached blue eyes, and red brows flecked whitish-blond. The freckles offered a misleading innocence. Riley talked a mile a minute as he took Noah on a tour of the posh little marina at St. Kilda, crowded with old men's yachts. "The buggers keep these babies spotless, and they're always adding the latest doo-dad. Radio direction finders. Night fucking scopes. The hard part is getting them to take their little darlings out to the real ocean."

On day three, he taught Noah to fake an Australian accent—as American lads were rightly suspect as bums.

On day four, they whored together.

On day five, Riley slipped Noah in among the crew of a forty-four foot sailboat for the annual St. Kilda Rum Run inside the bay. And run they did: high winds with Killian as race skipper for an old man, rail down, close in on the buoys, laughing as he watched the terror on young Noah's face. He pushed to a win by cutting off the nearest rival—the other boat forced to fall off the wind to avoid a collision. The owner of Killian's boat, now briefly a happy old man, laughed as he saw a now unhappy old man, owner of the second place boat, flushed and shouting, raise up a protest flag. The losing skipper, a young buck Noah knew from the crap bar, laughed across the water to his mate Riley, acknowledging "the master." To Noah, Riley said, "Yes, yes, yes, fucking yes. This is what a man *does*. He *flames on*, mate. He *flames big* on the water." And in the sun, his red hair did seem to flame. Magnanimously, on the leisurely run back to port, he made time to show the American one or two of the ropes.

By day six, Noah had become Riley's disciple. Apparently, just like his Uncle Thomas, Riley had grasped the infinite. The sailor seemed to hold it in his strong right hand, and Noah could almost see it too: after all, the sun radiated wonder nearly every morning over the ocean, and when it did not, the morning brought a mix of soulful grays, the gray of cloud and the gray of sea turned into spray and low-hung stratus so you could hardly tell the difference. The amazing Riley Killian sailed upon that sea. He conquered the sea on behalf of old men.

By day seven, Noah believed he himself was finally becoming truly free of a tedious past, and like his new mates full of uncaring manhood. He developed his own sailor's laugh, a laugh which would have been unrecognizable to his unknown father and unfathomable mother.

Noah's father, who you may recall died in Vietnam when Noah was just five, existed for Noah only in photographs. But on the night of day seven, drunk in his room, Noah said to his father, "See me old dad! I really *will* fucking escape!" And as he crawled into bed, he thought anew about his once-seeking, but now dead mother, who, as he had read in her letters to Thomas, "wanted to find something." Well, he would find it.

By day ten, Noah was headed into the infinite.

John Rogers, owner of sailing yacht *Far Horizon*, was seventy-six, American, weathered, and deep in his final dream. He had become a sailor just a couple years before, if sailor he could be called. Certainly he had not yet reached a far horizon. Rogers was not a retired sheepherder, he was a retired CFO of a capital management firm located on the twenty-first floor of a high rise with a view of the bay in Baltimore, Maryland.

A series of dark events had brought Rogers to Melbourne.

First, while still a CFO, Rogers had made the mistake of going to visit his boss, the chief executive of his firm and an icon of capital management, after this boss suffered a massive stroke. It was hardly standard procedure for members of the firm to visit one another as they lay in hospitals—and for good reason. The CEO, who had always appeared ruddy and sharp, and in this guise had been Rogers' mentor for decades, looked like hell in the bed at Baltimore General. His gray hair was strewn, and he was unable to form complete sentences. Sure enough, next day, Rogers got the call telling him that the CEO had died.

Shaken, Rogers had decided to retire, giving just one month's notice. He said to himself, "Somewhere along the line, I made a mistake."

At one month and three days, Rogers' wife of forty-one years left him. Maybe because she couldn't stand the thought of having him around, or maybe because he'd diligently spent his last month cashing out stock options into more liquid assets. By way of explanation, the suddenly cold Alice Rogers had said only, "I never loved you, shithole. Who could love a shithole like you?"

His wife had, perhaps, been one of his mistakes.

The final blow came a year later, during the second divorce-related countersuit. At 10:16 a.m. on a lovely June day, Rogers' two adult children, Faye, forty-six, and Julian, forty-nine, had stood up in a courtroom, renouncing him as their father and vowing never to speak to him again, due to his shocking treatment of their mother. At two that same afternoon, Rogers had sat on a folding chair in his tony Baltimore home, emptied of furniture by the first countersuit. As he sat, he recalled how, as he had sat on the twenty-first floor of the high rise for thirty-plus years, he had enjoyed watching sailboats tack across Patapsco Bay.

John Rogers had never been the child who ran into streets. But now he wanted to be that child. He did not, of course, use that metaphor. Instead, he said to himself, "All men are actually sailors—whatever they may pretend. Some recognize it and some do not. Some find their courage and some do not. Some rot in cities trying to make those fucking cities work. Either way, we are nothing but lonely sailors all." Within days, a broker found him *Far Horizon,* a forty-four foot cutter-rig, low slung, with a bow sprit and old-fashioned teak decks. Better yet, the boat lay far away from his family, in Melbourne, Australia. A photo showed *Far Horizon* carving a white bow wave through Port Phillip Bay against an azul sky: a sailboat as out of a movie. Inspired, and eager to escape entirely, Rogers made the long flight and bought the boat within two days, using a goodly chunk of what he had left.

Far Horizon immediately became the sole joy of the old man's existence. He lived aboard her in St. Kilda, loved her, diligently kept her deck waxed, steel polished, and teak oiled among the final dreams of the other rich old men. For a couple of years, this was enough. He purchased expensive yachting whites and puttered around the club. He stood rounds. He hired crew for lively day sails and club races. He exalted in his adopted country, which he praised to the other old men as, "Truly a younger America, not yet ruined by fear and lawyers."

This joy held until Rogers realized that his companions were, in fact, *all old men.* Until he began to see the cluster of magnificent yachts in the harbor as mere coastal creatures, clinging to the black rocks of the shore. Until he saw that even though these yachts had been built for ruddy sea voyages, with sturdy rigging and deep keels; even though they had been designed for sailing ecstatically to places like Raiatea and Tonga; most left their slips but rarely. And only for short whiles. And usually just on Port Phillip Bay. And then, like all the other shore creatures, like himself and all sailors lacking true manly courage, the sturdy yachts scurried home, there to be hosed and oiled and put to sleep again.

Rogers did, of course, see real men leaving or arriving from the infinite. These real men appeared across the bar, casually confident and magnificently sunburnt. But they did not speak to John Rogers. He saw their boats, ragged and scarred from great journeys, while his own *Far Horizon* remained spotless.

Then he learned he was dying of pancreatic cancer.

Surprisingly, this news did not cause Rogers to panic. In fact, even though the sight of his dying and speechless CEO flashed grimly across his mind, he welcomed his coming change of fortune. His training as CFO had taught him to capitalize on all change, even death.

Immediately, he began to plan for his new future, and he called his plan "The Grand Voyage."

The Grand Voyage would be John Rogers' last great undertaking. It would be his final repudiation of all lies. He would hire a couple crew, stock up, and brave the notorious cross-currents of Bass Strait, raging outside St. Phillip Bay. Breaking free to the southern ocean, he would ride the westerlies across the Tasman Sea to Auckland to re-stock, then right up to Fiji, and using Fiji as a base, he would spend his last five or six months drifting among obscure Pacific islands. Among these islands he would die, preferably while offshore. Storm or cancer, it didn't much matter.

He had a plan. It was a grand plan. He could see the whole plan in his mind...right up to the end. He could imagine his crew bringing him coconut water and morphine, and then, when the time came, unceremoniously dumping his body overboard. He said to himself: *Fuck all doctors. Fuck all hospitals. Fuck all shameful suffering. And most of all, fuck Alice and Faye and Julian.*

But even though his wife and daughter and son had renounced him, Rogers did not actually plan to disappear entirely trackless from the earth.

No, no, not entirely.

And that's where Riley Killian came in.

For Rogers could see that Killian was the most sunburnt and casually confident of the true voyagers who sometimes wandered into the bar at the St. Kilda Yacht Club. A man of loud and uncaring conversation. A true and unabashed sailor. He appeared to be magnificently unattached to anything.

Killian represented the secret denouement of the Grand Voyage, the subplot which would make his entire life make sense. Rogers would hire Killian as first mate—at a price the man could not refuse. He'd ask Killian to locate a clean second mate, and the three of them would take *Far Horizon* out of fucking Port Phillip Bay, which now also sickened him. Then, somewhere on the way to Fiji, if Killian proved all he seemed, Rogers would dramatically reveal his illness.

Once he told Killian he was dying, and dying soon, *he would offer Killian his boat,* along with the small remainder of his fortune. With that act, he would enable a true, but no doubt perpetually broke sailor to cruise the great oceans in his place, forever. It would be a different kind of immortality. Just as importantly, he would keep both boat and fortune out of the hands of Alice and Faye and Julian. And lo, his long years as CFO would somehow achieve a total and complete logic—far and away into a wonderfully unknown future.

What more could a man ask? Well one more thing. In return for the boat and the small remainder of his fortune, Rogers would ask Killian only one great favor. He would ask Killian to sail him for a couple months in secret among many Pacific islands, and ensure an easy death, thanks to the copious coconut water and morphine. Rogers would write Killian into his last will and goddam testament right on deck. He had the papers already prepared, and just in case something happened, he had pre-signed them, leaving a blank for "heir." The second mate would serve as witness. Rogers had already purchased plenty of morphine.

Never mind that the old man hardly knew Riley Killian.

Never mind that he had spoken to Killian perhaps three times in his life and had hired him as skipper only once.

Such are the glorious illusions of humans: We construct one another from small hints and ideals. We see each other as types and metaphors...so long as we never get to know each other too damn

well. Indeed, as the great departure loomed, Rogers was more convinced than ever...*for damn if Killian hadn't skippered* Far Horizon *to
her first win under his ownership! First place in the Rum Run! Damn if
under Killian's hand, his boat hadn't danced across the Bay! And fucking flamed Dougie Wilder's boat twenty meters from the finish!*

Riley told Noah about The Grand Voyage by night. They were
standing together with beers in Riley's apartment, looking out
toward the bay, where the big harbor lights shone between rooftops.
The spectacularly sunburnt redhead raised his white-flecked eyebrows and said to his new disciple, in his exquisitely offhand way:
"Forgot to mention, mate...I'm leaving early a.m. for three months on
the bounding main. Same boat you raced Sunday. Nice bucket, hey?
Remember the old Yank? He's way overpaying."

"No shit?" replied Noah, hiding his disappointment as best he
could. His new life, after all, had only just begun. Without Riley Killian, what would he have in Melbourne?

"Auckland. New Caledonia. Fiji." smiled Riley, with a look. "The
bounding blue main."

"Sounds ripper," said Noah.

"But the second mate—you know that shithead, Peter? They call
him Saltpeter? Mate who never talks?"

"No."

"Well, Saltpeter scrubbed."

"No shit."

"At the last fucking minute." Riley took a pull and raised his flecked eyebrows a second time. "Want the gig?"

As Noah stood speechless, Riley put down has beer and plucked a
few island notes on a small guitar, painted a gaudy red and gold.

Later that night, as Noah stood before the mirror in his shabby
room, you could see his father and his mother and his uncle gathered
behind his eyes, burning with desire to leave shore at long last.

And sure enough, just after dawn next day, Riley and Noah
showed up on the dock beside *Far Horizon* to join the Grand Voyage of John Rogers. The morning was gray and queasy with heat and
clouds, but each man had a large sea bag slung jauntily over his left

shoulder. Noah sported a couple days' fetching stubble, and his dark ringlets fell across his forehead, making him look like a prince of the sea. Although he appeared very clean, the stubble helped establish his credentials.

Along with his name, of course.

"Where's Saltpeter?" asked Cap'n Rogers, squinting up from the deck.

"His mum died," said Killian. "Or something like that. Anyway, I've done you one better. Here's Noah. Much finer choice. The lad's in from a two months' roundabout to Jakarta, fighting off fucking pirates. He's had a whole week's beauty rest, so he's ready to rock'n roll. Right, Noah? And of course, Cap'n, you'll remember he was part of my kickass crew for the Rum Run."

Noah smiled and nodded amiably. Like Saltpeter, Killian had told him not to talk.

Separating Melbourne from the southern ocean is the notorious Bass Strait, and separating the Strait from Port Phillip Bay is The Rip. The Rip opens just three kilometers wide from headland to headland, but the whole tides and currents of the enormous bay must pass through it, along with any boats heading to or from the world. Tides run up to fifteen km/hr, pushing great ships and pleasure craft alike among reefs and eddies and confused waves.

In short, as Riley Killian remarked on the day of their approach, "The Rip is like a fucking birth canal."

Cap'n Rogers had never taken *Far Horizon* through The Rip, though others had, before he owned her. But First Mate Riley loved the passage as his own, and on the second morning after they departed Melbourne, gear stowed, rigging checked, wind up, face to it, he stood at the wheel for the moment of rebirth to the sea.

The night before, as they lay at anchor within sight of the lighthouse at the mouth of the Rip, ready for a morning passage, Noah had read his little sailing book by flashlight. Now he crouched in storm gear on the dipping leeward of the cockpit, ready by the jib sheet as *Far Horizon* pounded into crested rollers under full sail and seabirds heralded the great world. The great world! He felt nauseous, but secretly laughed at Cap'n Rogers' attempt to match the steely grace of his first mate.

"All we ever ask are new beginnings," Noah quoted to himself from his uncle's letters. And truly, as they emerged from the bay, it did seem like the violent birth from a womb. As in his imagination, the day of crossing was bright and rough and the first mate cried out "yes, baby" every time a wave crested over a forward rail. Clearly, for her part, *Far Horizon* was ecstatic that her days as a shore creature had ended. It was one more second chance for her, too.

"It's okay," thought Noah, who did realize, just for a moment, that he was heading to sea with two men he hardly knew. "Everything that needs to happen is finally happening."

Going out full sail was a bit of a statement by Riley Killian, though the others were too ignorant to notice. The wind blew twenty-two to twenty-four knots, and by rights he should have reduced sail. But when he was young, Riley was the kind of child who *always* ran into streets, and now he was the kind of man who always entered The Rip at speed. Several times he had to fight against round-ups in a big swell—though again, the others did not notice.

The spray was in his face. And in all their faces. And "hey baby, baby," Riley decided again that he loved *Far Horizon,* as he always loved a new woman.

"Well done," shouted Cap'n Rogers, by way of establishing his authority.

Killian ignored the compliment, by way of establishing his own. "Harden up the jib, there," he cried to Noah, who gave him a quizzical stare. When the Cap'n looked away, Killian winked at Noah and made a motion as of cranking a winch, to give him the fucking idea.

On night four, the three mariners sat in the cockpit as wind and waves blew hard, but invisibly around them. The only light came from a small electric lantern lashed to the backstay, and the first mate had an easy hand on the wheel. A thoughtful mood came upon the captain and first mate, just as two weeks later a thoughtful mood would come upon their ghosts.

Despite their rebirth, the past had come along with them, at least this far. How long can the past survive at sea? We shall find out soon enough.

The captain spoke first:

"I was always a fool, but I didn't know I was a fool. I thought I was born to build some kind of *dynasty*. Really. I was born a poor man—well, 'lower middle-class,' we'd say in America. My father sold paint his whole life. Not artist-type paint...house paint. He never even owned a goddam paint store. He just knew paint, and he sold it, and in retrospect, I suppose that was an honorable profession, but I despised him for it at the time. My mother worked as a checkout lady, stock clerk, sometimes a shift manager. You know: the overweight checkout lady at Discount Everything!, that sort of thing. I despised her for that too, I suppose. But my parents dreamt a dream, and that dream was *me*. All their energy went into *me*. I was the golden boy, winning the math competitions, debating club. That sort of thing. When I won the scholarship to Cornell it was a fulfillment of their lives. Greatest day of their lives. Nothing more for them to do, almost. My mother kissed me on the top of the head, and I suppose it was the greatest day of my life too."

"Cornell?" asked Killian politely. "That's in America?"

"I saw my future clearly. I would work at one of the Big Four, I would have children, and I would found a *dynasty* going way, way into the future." As he said that vaguely offensive word *dynasty* again, you could hear that it still resonated with him, despite everything. "The *Rogers Dynasty*, started by the famous John Rogers and continuing down through history—wealthy, powerful, admired. 'He came from humble stock,' the bio would read, 'but he founded a *dynasty* known worldwide.' That would be my *legacy*."

He paused to let the irony sink in, but no one spoke. To them, it was rich man crap.

"I chose my wife carefully from the girls at Cornell. I chose her with great seriousness of intent. Alice was not beautiful, but I thought her wise and practical. And I suppose, in a way, she *was* wise and practical—just not in the way I imagined. Foolishly, I thought she loved me, and when she married me, I thought we were really, you know, *married.* I learned that wasn't true only at the end, when she called me a shithole. *Called me a shithole."*

"So she was a bitch," shrugged Riley.

"There was Alice and there was Carl Frederick Sands. Those were the two important people in my life. Maybe you've heard the name? No? In America, he was known as a guru of both venture capital and long-term capital management. He's dead now. Four years. I saw him in the hospital just a day before he passed. That was when I realized I'd made some kind of basic mistake. You know, *all along."*

"Right," nodded Killian, pretending interest. How many old men had told him that having become rich, they'd tossed it all in for sailing? That is, *after* becoming rich.

Cap'n Rogers pressed on. He was dying, and he wanted this man, *his presumed heir,* to know at least a little of his story. Even if the bastard... But only Noah heard something, already, in the words of the captain. He wasn't sure what it was. Some echo of the others he would meet on the sea. A sailor's song, of a kind.

"I was sure I wanted to work for one of the Big Four. Know what those are?" Both men shook their heads, but he didn't explain. "Instead, Carl Frederick Sands talked me into joining his startup. He wasn't famous yet, so I was taking a chance. But Sands Capital did eventually go public."

It was strange to Rogers, hearing how thin these words seemed now, in the windy night. How important they once were to him, spoken in the highrise in Baltimore. And among his friends. The parties in his friends' homes. Standing with a drink saying those kinds of words. But now in the wind.

"Right," repeated Killian.

"Carl was a new father to me, truly a great man. Eventually, I became CFO of Sands Capital." And here he paused again, in case that would impress them. But of course, it did not. He heard a stupidity and desperation in his own voice.

"Alice and I had two beautiful and intelligent children. A boy and a girl. When they were young, they were so happy! Truly beautiful, I'm telling you. Blonds, both of them. They played with the toys all children want. I got them all the toys young children want. I took them to parks and once to the Appalachian Trail... I wasn't an absentee dad... I don't think so anyway." He got a little confused here. "I mean, obviously... Later, they turned out to be *neither happy nor kind.*"

When he said this, the faces of Faye and Julian appeared briefly to Noah: intelligent, pampered. Faces oddly *arranged* for him. *And now, too old.*

"Well, their mother was a bitch, right?" put in Killian.

Rogers looked at him quizzically in the lantern light, as if this had never occurred to him before. "Maybe. At the time, like I said, I fooled myself. She did all the right things. Read them books. You know... Took them to museums. They'd hug me. They really loved me, I think. When they grew up and didn't... I made excuses for them. I forgave them too often."

"Too *fucking* often," corrected Killian, trying to teach the old man to be a sailor.

The sound of the ocean increased. For a moment, they all looked to windward.

"But I get ahead of myself."

"Take'r time, Captain," said Noah, in his sketchy Australian sailing accent. "We've nothin' else to do."

"True enough," added Killian. On the bench beside him lay the small red and gold guitar. With his free hand he touched the strings. Again, a few island notes sounded in the wind.

Tears came to the old man's eyes.

"But now I can't even speak my kids' names. I saw my own children say I was no longer their father, even though they knew that *I would write them out of my will.* Which, of course, I did. Which I did even though Alice's lawyer managed to..."

Now Alice flickered before Noah's eyes. Preternaturally thin. Dyed redhead. Seventy-five. Not beautiful. Never beautiful. Pinched nose. Her face in the night.

Rogers had drifted off for a moment. Now he returned, reinforcing the vision: "I actually saw that happen, gentlemen. I mean, I was standing right there."

"What's that, Cap'n?" asked Riley, hand still gentle on the wheel.

"In court, when they renounced me." And again, the carefully arranged faces of Rogers' children appeared briefly to Noah. *Carefully arranged.* There was no other way of putting it. Of course, it was very odd that Noah could see their faces at all.

Riley Killian shrugged. He was thirty-one and had no children he knew of. He was a sailor without expectations. Things happened on many islands. Different things. Different cultures. Men. Women. Then came the next island. At this point, just as the wind rose further and *Far Horizon* heeled lower in the night, the first mate spoke his piece.

"Your mistake, Captain," said Killian, "was in thinking that anyone gave a shit about you."

He steered out of a trough, then continued.

"The last thing in the world I would ever do is try to found a fucking *dynasty.* That's completely random, a *dynasty.* Just *luck.* And who cares once you're gone? We're all in this thing alone. Some mate once said this to me: 'Think of life like a flower blooming in the middle of a deserted island, all alone and unseen—beautiful even if no one else sees. The bigger the flower, the better its colors, that's the best it can do. That's all it can do. Then the flower's fucking gone.' A mate once said that to me, and I think it's true," Killian repeated. It was important to have a philosophy, to get you along. He smiled at his present brief companions. "Me, I can only be the best goddam sailor I can be. That's it. That's all. I'll bet you were a goddam *amazing* CFO, Captain." Here he laughed at an old man's confusion, and slapped the melancholy Rogers across the back. "That should be enough, whatever the fuck else happens."

But he was not done speaking.

"In Bangkok I had this girl named Daunphen. That means 'full moon.' I looked it up. Daunphen was a great girl. In fact, she gave me this guitar. Good old Daunphen told me she loved me. But I would never have actually *believed* her. I mean ... I took her out to bars and really nice restaurants ... cheap, but good. You been to Bangkok? Try the Tom Yum Gung, like anywhere. We had some great times, Daunphen and me. But I never believed she *loved* me, even though she said it like fifty times." He caught the captain's eye as best he could in the half-light. "She liked the good times and she liked the cash. And that was enough, captain. *Plenty enough.*"

Duanphen appeared before Noah, exactly like the full moon. A sad, beautiful young woman. Almost a child. He saw her face in the neon of a Bangkok night, a pale moon hanging low along a crowded street, barely visible in the glare. A sweet full moon, still shining for Riley.

The first mate had one more thing to say, and it was about the fucking sea.

"I love the fucking sea because out here a man *knows* he's on his own. He *knows* he depends only on his own fucking skills and a good fucking boat. A boat is better than a person, because you can really *know* its weaknesses and its strengths, know what I mean? And seriously: everything has a place, and you can *put* everything in its place. If a thing's not in its place – a rope tangled, a winch handle not there when you reach for it—well mate, you may just die, *but it won't be the boat's fault.* It will be your fault or God's fault, and that's all. I mean, it may be just be the hand of God, you know? But you can't blame God either, he's just...you know...*like that.*" Here Killian could not help adding a deep philosophic aside: "You know, the thing you have to watch out for with God is the fucking *ironic twist.* The old bastard just loves to grab you with an ironic twist. Just when you think you're safe... boom!" And he shrugged. "In any case, it's no one *else's* goddam fault. Governments don't matter out here. Taxes. Crap like that. Not out here. And the sea? *The sea?* Well, like every woman she's both your lover and your sworn fucking enemy... But she's dead honest about the deal. *No pretending.* You may love the sea, but you know she never loves you back. Not even on a sunny day, on a firehose reach with a steady breeze, when she *still* might pluck you right off the deck, God or no God. You ride her hard and sometimes she rides you hard. And sometimes she just takes you down. You just have to say, fuck it all, I'm sailing fast and free for now, so fuck it."

The captain asked a question with a shaky voice: "And your shipmates, mister? What about them? Don't you depend on *them?*"

Riley smiled. "We do depend on each other Cap'n, you and me and Noah here. During the run we'll depend on each other totally.

But that's why it's best when the crew's all men. We know we'll have each other's backs all the way, but then we can say *goodbye and good luck mate* at the next port and no hard feelings. And on to the next fucking kip."

This made the old man tremble with inner exultation. He had chosen well.

"You ever get afraid out here, Riley?" asked Noah.

Killian laughed fully at this question, and shook his head in warning to the second mate. Such a question would hardly come from a man who was just off a two months' roundabout to Jakarta, fighting off fucking pirates. Plus, the boy had forgotten his fucking Aussie accent. In any case, it did not merit an answer.

Somehow a beer appeared in Killian's hand, though his companions had no beers. Two watches later, toward dawn, they passed the reefs and islands that guard the eastern borders of the strait. Killian stood in the cockpit against the sky, sighting along a west of wispy clouds, until at last he headed below.

As he watched the first mate descend, confident and calm, Noah thought: "We survived The Rip. We survived Bass Strait. All is well." It was the thinking of a child who did not understand past and future. And sure enough, in time, the wispy clouds would build.

After listening to Killian the night before, the old man woke for his watch still excited. Riley Killian had spoken well. He was vulgar and uncivilized, but Rogers was sick of civilized men. Here was clearly *a man beholden to no one. He would make none of the mistakes made by Rogers. He would follow no goddam mentor. Commit to no traitorous wife. Depend on no worthless children. Seek no immortal dynasty.* After Rogers' death, Killian would sail on, free across the oceans, full canvas to the fucking wind, thumbing his nose at women, children, governments, ledgers, old men, straits, tides, black rocky shores, and the entire universe— until the universe fucking took him too. Until that moment, Rogers' own spirit, or what little was left of it, would sail with Killian on the foredeck of *Far Horizon*.

They arrived at the northern tip of New Zealand after six days, coming in under the great Harbor Bridge of Auckland by night, at full sail, the enormous lights on the span making Greek columns across the water. Rogers stood on the foredeck, marveling, happy. Killian docked the boat *right ho*. Then he disappeared for a night of whoring.

When he'd gone, John Rogers said to Noah: "The accent's fake, isn't it mister? Actually, crappy as hell. I think you're from the Midwest. Maybe Chicago?" When Noah startled, the ex-CFO continued indulgently: "You're a nice enough boy, and I'm sure you've learned a lot about sailing over the last week."

Rogers did not care much that he'd been deceived, since the deception had been hatched by Killian. Not knowing Noah's mother's ambitious plan for her son, he thought Noah unimportant. Now, alone together for a few nights, and in a fatherly way, he did his best to express to the lad his own love of the sea. Like many of the other old men at the club, this love had developed late in life, though in his case first formed on the twenty-first floor of a Baltimore high rise. Since he could not adequately express the poetry of the sea, its extension of the sky, its ceaselessness, the way its waves formed and unformed inexplicably and without mercy, all he could say was: "Here's the thing about boats. We don't really own 'em. As sailors we just take care of 'em for a time and ask 'em to carry us safely across the ocean for a few years. Then we pass our boats on to others."

The storm caught *Far Horizon* in the place of many storms which lies about halfway from Auckland to Fiji. It came late at night, when Riley Killian was on watch and the others were sleeping. The wind had been playing games for an hour, shifting around the compass, and when it rose at last to a joyous pitch, Killian grinned his famous grin. As at The Rip, he knew he should shorten sail right away, but as we have learned, he was not a man of caution. And the voyage so far had been dull. He thought, "Just a bit of push before I wake the others. Just a taste of bone in the old girl's teeth." For a time it was glorious. *Far Horizon* rode at her very best, leaping up the sudden frothy swells with élan.

"Good girl," said Killian.

A swift knock to port finally woke both Noah and Rogers, throwing them near out of their bunks and bringing them rushing up into the cockpit half-clothed. The lantern swung. Wind howled in the ropes. Spray made cold white flights. An army of waves marched from the darkness.

"I was about to wake you lads," said Killian lightly, pulling out of another deep trough. "Take the wheel, one of you, hey? I've got to furl the jenny a bit more, down to a goddam handkerchief, in fact. Then we'll reef. Oh...fuck." For just as he spoke, the furling line snapped and the big foresail unwound fully into the storm, dragging the bow down into an oncoming swell. The swell coursed blackly right down the deck, momentarily filling the cockpit. Killian hesitated before he handed the helm to the now wet and shivering old man. Then he sprang to the top of the cabin, working his way forward against the spray. "When I give the word, bring her up into the wind for ten seconds while I drop the rig, then back to port. But not until I say," he shouted. Then immediately, "Now!" Rogers turned *Far Horizon* into the wind so Killian could drop the whole foresail rig, but the portside sheet tangled and caught, and as the sail began to come down, the whole thing billowed backwind, taking them through the eye and heeling the boat horribly to starboard. Killian crawled up the now steep wet foredeck to port. He struggled with the tangle. As he struggled, the boat kept turning, all the way downwind, uncontrollably. The mainsail gybed violently, and Killian was pinned against the rigging as the angry jenny swung back over him, his strong left arm and mighty sunburnt chest caught in the growing tangle of ropes. Old man Rogers handed the wheel to Noah and grabbed a knife. He was usually cautious, but this time, like Killian, he wore neither life jacket nor tether. He climbed forward. He breasted the spray to save his intended heir. In fact, this climb to the foredeck was surely the greatest moment of his life. Reaching Killian, he began to cut desperately through the ropes. Briefly, Rogers and Killian worked together like father and son. Noah tried to steer back into the wind, but could not.

At last, the rope parted, and Riley Killian was free.

A smile crossed both men's faces, father and son alike.

Then a wave overtook the bow, and they were gone.

For two full seconds, Noah Caldwell stared blankly at the foredeck, unable to understand what had just happened. If he had had more time to reflect, he would have recognized how, like his Biblical namesake, or maybe like all of us—maybe, as Killian might put it, *like every fucking human who ever lived*—he had suddenly been made skipper of a boat without sufficient training.

Give him this: after three seconds, Noah threw the wheel around to circle through the wind, now possible because the sheets were cut and the jenny flapped free, already beginning to tear itself to shreds. Waves caught him abeam and nearly rolled the boat as again and again he circled, shouting into the black waves.

Then dawn arrived, but the storm did not abate.

In the fresh light, and after reading up in his ridiculous little sailing book, the new captain managed to reef down the mainsail, and reading a few pages later, set a staysail. His own cries of the two men's names lessened. He tried the radio, and may or may not have figured out how it worked, but raised no one from the middle of the sea. For another complete day and night he circled. He never heard nor saw either man. Nor did he find any trace of their passage into the waves. And on the radio, only static.

Near sunset of the third day, our hero fell asleep against his will, with the windvane on, and *Far Horizon* continued north through the unrelenting tempest, heading by chance directly toward Fiji.

The ghosts came around two a.m.

Noah was lying in his bunk above four inches of seawater sloshing along the floorboards. The boat was not sinking, but wave after wave had flooded in through the companionway, and the automatic bilge pump had long since jammed. He recalled that when he fell asleep it was still day. Now it was full dark and several disreputable sailors, maybe three, were singing a shanty in the cockpit. Looking up, he could see their shadows against the night, but for a time he dared not move. The words of the song were repetitive, sometimes lost in the cry of the wind.

> *Oh a hundred years is a very long time,*
> *A hundred years ago.*

A hundred years on the Eastern shore,
Oh yes, oh.
Old bully John from Baltimore,
I knew him well, that son of a whore,
A hundred years ago.
Oh yes, oh.
But now he's dead and he's gone to hell,
A hundred years, a hundred years ago.
He's dead and gone forevermore,
Oh yes, oh.
He's dead and gone, that son of a whore,
A hundred years, a hundred years,
A hundred years ago.
A hundred years have passed and gone,
Oh yes, oh.
It's a hundred years since I made this song,
A hundred years or more.

And then with a change of key:

They say the stars are set alight
By a bunch of angels every night.

Had it really been a hundred years, already? It seemed like just a couple days. *Time is collapsing,* he mused, *as time sometimes does.* At last, Noah leapt up and burst into the cockpit, where the wind was howling, but the skies had cleared to crisp stars and angels. Or had it? A cloud passed just as suddenly, obscuring the stars perhaps forever, and causing him to cry like a baby. He took back the rudder from the complaining windvane. No sailors could be seen now, but Noah thought: "Those bully boys weren't steering properly, if they were steering by angels instead of stars."

He stopped crying. The full moon appeared through the clouds. Surely it had not been there before? Then he saw it wasn't really the moon. It was Daunphen, Riley Killian's whore from Bangkok. She sat quietly across from Noah in the pitching cockpit, and she had the same longing, girlish look he remembered from two weeks before, when he'd first heard her name.

"Now that Riley's gone, what will I do?" asked Daunphen.

"Are you a ghost?" asked Noah.

"Does it matter?" she replied. "Either way, it's up to you now."

"What?"

"Riley's gone, so it's up to you to think of me," she said simply. Then she began to relate her hard life's tale. Born in a village high into the Luang Prabang range, her family had moved to find work in the city when she was about ten. Only a few months in, they regretted their decision, but it was too late to go back... the farm had been sold. At fifteen, she had turned to pleasing men for money, mostly western businessmen, but sailors, too. Her family could not at first understand how her English had become so good.

Daunphen's tale continued a long while, but fortunately, Noah had nothing but time.

"I truly did love Riley," she concluded at last, bowing her head. "Perhaps I still do. I am heartsick at his death in the oceans."

"Of course," nodded Noah sympathetically.

Next came Alice, John Rogers' estranged wife. She was ugly, but extremely well kept for seventy-five, dressed sharp and sitting just so in the cockpit. Preternaturally thin. Dyed red hair. Her lawyer perched right above her, rather precariously on the cabin top. *Not to worry,* thought Noah, *he's a ghost too.*

"First off, I was beautiful when we married," began Alice, without introduction. "You can't see it now, but I brought a photo." Indeed, she handed him a photo of herself at nineteen or twenty. More pleasant than now, for sure, but beautiful would be a stretch. She had the same precise look he remembered from her children. *An arranged look, so at odds with the sea.*

"Of course," said Noah, but he was becoming more sympathetic with the departed John Rogers.

"I need to tell you my side of the story."

"Naturally," he replied, and pulled up a cushion for his back. The wind yet cried in the rigging, but the boat was under control now, racing northward even under shortened sail, carving through the surge. He looked up, proud of his seamanlike reef and staysail. Just like in the book's illustration, but disappearing into the sky. *No need to set a light,* he thought, *no one to see it.*

Alice told of their early years, how Rogers had romanced her in an old-fashioned way. Roses in her dorm room. "Then," as she put it, "came the hardening of his heart." Not long after their marriage, *the hardening of his heart, just like Pharoah.* Noah saw Pharoah in a children's book illustration, from a hundred years ago. She told of old Bully John's unlimited demands. How nothing had ever been good enough. *Nothing.* Picking her goddam jewelry for her when they went out at night. The goddam pressure on the children. Like Daunphen, she spoke for some time to the patient young man who had nothing but time and an ark. "I was stupid to be obsessed with John, even stupid to be obsessed with Faye and Julian, for all the good it did them. They both became asses, as you have heard. I was stupid to have no life of my own. I never did anything with my degree."

"Did you *ever* love him?" asked Noah.

"No, I *never* loved him, Noah. How could anyone love a shithole like that?"

"How sad...." replied the new captain of *Far Horizon,* then looked over at Daunphen, who was still there, listening. "But perhaps for the best." This last with a gentle smile for the girl.

Even if time had collapsed, he just had to ask the question that kept nagging him, even in his dream: "By the way, are you still alive, or are you a ghost?

"We're certain it doesn't matter," replied the lawyer, speaking for the first time. "Just so long as you remember her tale. That is, now that Rogers is gone. You see, we're not sure if he confided in anyone but you and the Aussie sailor. The sailor is gone. Dead and gone, along with that other son of a whore. Hence..."

"Right," said Noah, nodding.

"Thank you ever so much," said Alice, softening, and placing a warm hand on his knee. "You are a lovely boy. It's just for another sixty or seventy years."

Next came their fine children, Faye and Julian, standing at the mast, still forty-six and forty-nine, just so. Noah could see they were asses much more clearly now. Julian wore tennis whites, because they seemed right for sailing. Both argued soullessly with the lawyer about something he did not comprehend... But like their faces, he could also see that the scene had been arranged for his benefit. *Arranged so he would remember...*

When Carl Frederick Sands appeared, in a pale blue hospital gown, chiseled features, but unable to speak, Noah began to get uncomfortable. But Sands was quickly joined by the mute Saltpeter, who had never got to tell his story here at all. Meanwhile, Riley Killian's ruddy mates from the pub came jostling along the foredeck. They, of course, chattered and swore, casually clinging to the lifelines in the wind. It gave Noah vertigo to watch them, but he did his best.

The wind lessened, and the sea calmed. Noah, captain of his now quite crowded ark, knew that he would be forced to carry all their tales across the infinite, as long as he was able.

When Riley appeared, he carried the small red and gold guitar. Noah found this suspicious, as he was pretty sure he'd seen the guitar below, tossed on Riley's bunk.

"You turned to port, mate, but if you think about it, we fell from the port side, so you might have fucking run us down. Not that it would have mattered. As it was, we lasted barely ten minutes. Never a breath to shout with..."

"Hello Riley," said Noah, not wanting to hear the next part. "I will remember you too...at least everything you managed to tell me in the short time we knew each other."

Riley laughed. "Glad you know so fucking little about me, mate. If you're not forgotten when you're dead, what's the use of dying?"

Daunphen sobbed, seeing how Riley held the guitar she had given him, perhaps in a way he had never held her.

"You told me enough," said Noah. "Enough for me to, you know... put together a picture."

Riley narrowed his eyes, puzzled.

Looking at the ghost, Noah saw that all men and even women may be sailors, but we are never truly alone on the sea. All men and women may be sailors, but we are the sum of all the people who came before us, and all the people we've known or loved or hated on the many islands we pass. So at least while we are alive, we are never alone on the sea—never a complete starting over. A complete starting over is impossible.

He tried to explain this crucial idea to the puzzled Riley, insisting, "Not just Rogers is part of me now. And not just you. But Rogers' ex-wife and the spoiled children who brought him to this ocean. His mentor at the firm who helped him make his fortune, his mother the checkout lady, his past I know and his past I do not know. *I cannot un-meet you, Riley.* The future Noah will be formed partly by your own unknown past, your Aussie accent, your whores, your many births through The Rip. All that brought me here has become part of me. Don't you see? Rogers was right about founding a dynasty, but he did not understand what that meant. *All men and women found unintentional dynasties."* The words seemed apt. And sufficient. And he no longer needed to speak to Riley, so he turned away. And in his dream, looking for a moment out to sea, Noah began to see all life as a pattern of waves, one moving restlessly into the next, such that *only* the sea truly existed. Even land structures like mountains, forests, and cities became in his mind but wave-motions, sometimes passing quickly and sometimes passing slowly to form the landscape of the earth, each carrying part of the form of its parent, which was never truly lost.

It was enough revelation for a Noah. Certainly better than a fucking flower on a desert island.

John Rogers sat at the stern rail, looking up into the deep, glittered ink of the rapidly clearing sky, thinking of the mistakes that had determined his life. He said, "When I was a child I remember looking up at the stars and thinking how small I was. How small we all were. That scared me, but then I thought how wonderful it would be to disappear among the stars... just be drawn up and disappear forever. I remember spinning around, looking up at the spinning universe, and getting dizzy in the most wonderful way." He looked at Noah and smiled. "How could I have forgotten how wonderful that was to imagine? Or maybe I did remember, and that's what brought us all out here. Who can say?" He paused. "The boat's yours now, Noah. You'll find a will in my luggage—the little brown leather case. Perspicaciously pre-signed by me. You can just write your name right in there. You'll also find copies of notarized letters I sent to my lawyers, confirming my plan to choose a sailor during this voyage..." He spoke as CFO for a time, covering details. Then finally, "I'm sorry to have burdened you."

"No, no it's fine," said Noah, who was righteous in his generation.

Noah's parents stood each side of the mast, holding on as the unfamiliar boat rocked and swayed. They appeared young and handsome, full of life at eighteen and fifteen, as out of the photo Noah had in his battered suitcase, stowed up forward somewhere on the boat. The two of them on her porch.

His father, who he'd never really known, was one of the mute ghosts.

"Death is sweet," said his mother, with her uncertain smile. "Just hang on 'til then."

Her son bowed his head in acquiescence to her words.

Morning dawned bright and serene. The water became full of sun and laughing waves. In the old man's bag, Noah found the will. He wrote his name into the blanks, and forged Killian's signature as witness. When he arrived in Fiji, he renamed *Far Horizon,* and hired a man to paint on the new name: *Ramona.*

Then he turned to face the sea.

The TREMENDOUS
MOUNTAIN
Part II

"I will pour out My Spirit on every kind of people: Your sons will prophesy, also your daughters. Your old men will dream, your young men will see visions. I'll even pour out My Spirit on the servants, men and women both."

—God speaking to the prophet Joel,
about 3,000 years ago

Mickey Kohl sipped a Pernod inside a crowded café not far from Place St. Michel on the left bank in Paris. It was late on a rainy February afternoon, and he was dressed in a black leather jacket. The noise from the bar was joyously deafening. The Pernod was expensive, but it was genuinely French. He could not decide if he deserved a genuinely French drink, just as he could not decide if he were playing the fool. On the table before him lay a small sketch pad on which he was attempting to draw his left hand as part of an assignment from L'Académie St. Germain des Près. A passing art student—and several did pass—would not have been impressed, even though the drawing became increasingly angry and abstract.

Here's the thing about art: it may be the answer or it may not. Mickey could not yet decide. Already, eight months after the vision which God had granted him in Central Park, along with the momentous, uncompleted phone call in the stock room of his brother's deli, it was clear to Mickey that one could not make a simple assertion either way. As for you and me, we can only note that if a person seeks a quest around which to organize existence, nothing is more immediately attractive. At the very least, art offers the chance to rise above the common, the quotidian, the normal. It offers the chance to influence future generations with a work which will perpetuate the small brief flicker of one's soul in the same way that a tiny burst of light reaches the earth many years after it has left a dead star: passing beautiful and intact across the centuries. The master muralist watched by Shunu back in the mission chapel might have argued that art exists only to serve a greater idea, but he did his work too damn well. Centuries later, we discovered that art constituted the idea itself. By the time of Mickey Kohl, every grade school teacher, every other movie, and ninety percent of all talk shows argued that *art, if anything,* must provide an answer.

Certainly for Mickey, who wanted to ride that last wild horse to the top of the Tremendous Mountain, nothing else seemed sufficiently important. He had quit his brother's deli business in bitterness—having found to his surprise that he had no legal claim on any of the assets. He had told his bewildered girlfriend Frances of his outrageous intentions. He had shown her his expensive acceptance to the Académie, squeezed the hand of his aged mother, and packed his leather jacket. He told everyone that the rent from the apartment he owned in Brooklyn could just sustain him, along with whatever he might pick up by working off the books in a Paris deli.

Everyone expected him back in New York within the month, but already he'd made it in Paris nearly six. He and Frances had emailed for a while, but then they had stopped.

And the Tremendous Mountain? He'd had no further visions, but he had dared to begin drawing horses in class. Muscular white horses! Unfortunately, although he formed them in increasingly abstract twists, radiating fear and anger, his teacher remained unimpressed. Along with her general *sang-froid,* she was also French-thin, Paris-humorless, formerly-beautiful, and though the classes were taught in English, he was pretty sure she disliked his work because she disliked Americans. He was only partly wrong. Actually, his teacher was a genuine artist who could see beyond the simple problem of his immature skills. She could see that Mickey's abstract anger was itself false—a pose. She could see that on the whole he was merely "nice," and like many French of the time, she believed that falsely "nice" Americans were ruining the entire world. "Everything," she noted, "is okay with them. It's a bore." Later, of course, like everyone, Americans changed. Either way, his teacher felt that the *Académie* should not accept students who could accomplish nothing more than paying her salary. Or, if true that they were necessary to pay her salary, then such students should be isolated somehow in special classes, taught by lesser lights. Sometimes she took the charcoal out of Mickey's hand and rudely added a bold line to his work, saying, *"Regarde! Regarde!"*

Mickey also knew he did not fit in with the other students. They appeared intense. Well-read. Several sported stringy, unkempt hair, while he remained open and practical in the manner of a Yank. He shaved every day. He went to the American action movies playing in Paris. He bought tourist guidebooks and went to see sights. No doubt many of the others laughed at him, not least because of his advanced age, which they guessed as probably over thirty.

On this particular February afternoon, round about five, when it was starting to get dark outside the loud café, a girl he guessed to be about twenty sat down at Mickey's table and in a curious parallel to the actions of his teacher, grabbed his sketch pad right out from under his pencil. Her name was Nicole.

"Bof," she said, *"C'est assez bonne, ça.* But I am thinking you are only just a student."

"Hey!" said Mickey, who had never seen the girl before. But he did not say "hey" with any anger, since she was so beautiful. Black hair. Dark eyes. Pale skin. French nose. And yes, also very thin.

She smiled. "Don't be angry. I think it is lovely. *Formidable.* But you look so lonely, and I don't have even any money for a wine."

Mickey laughed, charmed, conscious of their age difference, and a little suspicious. "At least you're honest. Well, except perhaps about my drawing."

"If you buy me a wine, I will give you praise to your art as long as you wish. *D'accord? Et bien,* I can practice my English." When she took off her coat, she smelled of the rain outside. Of the rapidly approaching night. Of woman. In bed, Nicole was full of heat and laughter, and for the first month she did not ask him for any money at all. For the first year he often thought himself in love—even though she lied to him constantly. Even though she soon began largely living off his funds, disappeared for days at a time, and left her shit all over his garret. By the second year, the frustrations of his life with Nicole caused him to grow perceptibly more intense, though not well-read. He let his hair grow. He allowed for a slight shadow on his chin. His drawing technique improved even if his soul had not yet found any great subject. These changes helped him find some acceptance among the other students, though largely thanks to Nicole. He drew her breasts, her feet, her lips—and the searching, even desperate look that sometimes came into her eye. Three years in, he held an exhibit with two friends in an abandoned storefront in Pigalle. They propped the canvases up on crates, and called it "Angry Animals." They served whiskey in jars to anyone who wandered in. One of the friends sold a painting, but Mickey did not. In celebration, Nicole had sex with this same friend in the back room of the exhibit. Mickey forgave her, but he did make her get a job as a waitress in an American-style burger place. Not long afterwards, at the age of thirty-five, he quit the Academy, telling the thin teacher it was a *libération,* making her smile in pity. But he did not leave Paris. Part of his prediction had come true: He was working off the books at a Paris Deli, called, ironically, *Épicerie Amsterdam.* He felt old, stupid.

Throughout these years in Paris, Mickey willed the great vision of the Mountain to return, usually as he lay in bed late at night. One sunny Tuesday afternoon at precisely 15:17 he sat on a bench in the Jardin de Luxembourg with a nice view and begged the vision audibly, and in so many words, to "please return to me." It did not. But he could not decide if the non-return of the vision boded well or ill. Did the absence of the vision mean that the last wild horse still circled safely in the meadow? Or did it mean that Mickey was successfully riding the last horse, riding it hard up into the cold escarpments of the Tremendous Mountain? Who could say? Who could sort through all the possible goddam metaphors? As often happens with artists, his self-worth had begun to depend on his art—worse, on the alignment between his art and his soul. If his art had value, so did he. If not, then he had failed as a human being. This does not so frequently happen to people who merely run delis. Such people usually manage to separate their self-image from the products of their labor.

Nicole had enjoyed Mickey's American optimism, his forthright Yankee *naïveté,* but now that he was getting as depressed as any other typical artist, he was not so much fun. Because she was adrift, she could not afford to maintain a *liaison* with someone who was also adrift. So she broke up with Mickey during a shouting match down along the damp of the great Paris river at twilight, and disappeared the next day, even changed her mobile number. After all, she reasoned, as she took a train to meet a girlfriend in Marseille, she was now twenty-seven.

This turn of events left Mickey often walking with his hands in his pockets. He felt like a cartoon, but he tried not to drink too much. In the next two years he called his brother just twice—the day after a hurricane hit New York, and the day after their mother died. The calls were brief, not because Mickey still hated his brother (though he did), but because he was feeling defeated and could not bear to speak through the mouth of a defeated man. "Sure, everything's okay. Plugging along. Making progress. I really love Paris."

But five years had now passed not just for Mickey; it had passed for the entire world. Think of it! Five years of seven billion people pushing forward toward their desires. Some becoming artists, but most not. Not incidentally, this included Mickey's former girlfriend Frances. She had not become an artist. She had left New York and moved to Cuyahoga Falls, Ohio, to take a job as a hospital administrator.

Now, like Nicole, you may have considered Frances just a minor character in these stories. But of course there are no minor characters, not in any story. Such men and women only *appear* to be unimportant, thanks to the limitations of a human author, who can usually focus on the fate of just a single soul. Even a great author, say a Tolstoy, can focus only on a single nation, a people, an idea. The difficult Nicole, for example, was not of course a minor character in her own life: among other important events, she suffered a deep and important tragedy at the age of sixteen which we haven't the space to detail, but which was the source of the searching, almost desperate look which Mickey had tried to capture on his sketchpad. At age forty-six, over twenty years after her appearance in this tale, Nicole inspired true love in a good man—though she never did get a steady job.

It may even be that God offers all characters, at some moment in their lives, and without the knowledge of any human author, a glimpse of the Tremendous Mountain. I'm convinced that everyone gets that glimpse. At some point surely God gives everyone at least a quick look, just to see who will give it a try.

But I was going to bring you up to date on the not unimportant Frances. At thirty-seven, she had green eyes and prematurely gray hair which in a certain light made her look extremely competent. Certainly she was more practical than our hero Mickey. To Frances, Cuyahoga Falls, Ohio, part of the greater Akron area, seemed like an adventure comparable to St. Germain des Prés. For her, renting a small apartment in which to live was as fraught with uncertainty as choosing a crowded café in Paris in which to sip coffee and draw one's left hand. She made sure she always had five good work dresses, and alternated them through the week so that her colleagues at the hospital might not sense her poverty. She limited herself to no more than two hours of television each night, even though she was lonely. She ate sensibly. She spoke to others in an upbeat tone.

During this period, however, the otherwise practical Frances read several novels which featured single mothers in heroic roles, defying their biological clocks at the last moment to raise sprightly children with mops of unruly hair who loved literature, jazz, and tree-climbing while abjuring the general assumptions imposed by a capitalist society. God had chosen this particular way to give Frances at least *a passing glimpse* of the Tremendous Mountain, and one cold December night, this happy vision influenced Frances to make her own momentous decision. She had allowed a nice, good-looking, and certainly smart doctor visiting from Russia to take her to a movie, and then back to her apartment for a cup of hot chocolate. As he stood in the living room chatting amiably about the movie in rather poor English, she stood at the stove stirring cocoa into a saucepan of milk and looking at the icicles which hung like evil needles from the power lines outside her kitchen window. At that moment, Frances experienced a remarkable convergence. Recall that she was recently inspired by novels, it was the right time of the month, the icicles spoke of a grim and frozen future, the apartment had grown pleasantly warm, the doctor had salt-and-pepper sideburns, and he would be heading back to Russia within a couple of weeks—likely never to return. All these elements came together, so that yes, before she left the kitchen, she gently removed a shapeless sweater, adjusted her dress, and chose a smile.

More years passed, and soon eight billion visions lived in the hearts of human beings. But in Paris, Mickey had pretty much stopped drawing, and he again found himself just a guy who worked in someone else's deli. At the terrifying age of thirty-nine, lonely and defeated, he headed back to New York. On the plane home he was several times observed by the other passengers to hang his head and cry.

Meanwhile, in Cuyahoga Falls, Frances discovered that single motherhood bore little resemblance to the heroic image in her feminist novels. Her little girl, Elena, was beautiful, but had a strangely serious look, and at six she was more shy than spritely. Despite a mop of unruly hair, she did not much like jazz or tree-climbing, preferring to watch dumb children's videos and play with bright plastic toys. Because Frances had to work and found herself perpetually low on funds, she had to put Elena into traditional daycare and then into a school run with standard capitalist assumptions. The heroic Frances lost the look of cheerful wisdom she had achieved with her prematurely gray hair, and now merely looked about ten years older than her true years. Because of frequent absences and exhaustion, along with the loss of her charismatic appearance, her reputation at the hospital declined. When a cost-cutting wave swept the pale green hallways, she had no firm allies. In the taxi from LaGuardia back to her mother's apartment in Brooklyn, where she knew with horrifying certainty that the walls were hung with fake oils of mills, farmhouses, and inspirational sunsets, she too cried. When Elena noticed her tears, the child grew yet more serious.

Nearly another year passed before Mickey and Frances ran into each other at a laundromat on Atlantic Avenue, not far from the apartment that Mickey had re-occupied. It was a gritty July afternoon, and the air conditioning was busted. Sitting on grimy plastic chairs not five feet apart, they did not immediately recognize one other. After all, it had been nearly a decade. Mickey had not shaved the small beard he had grown in Paris, while Frances looked much older and had rather lost her figure. She sweated. Her hair hung lankly. Elena was playing with a remote-control electric car which was irritating just about everyone in the laundromat. Frances spoke in annoyance, and when Elena ran to get it out of the way of someone's feet, the car dropped out of her hands, and parts scattered. Mickey stood to help. As they spoke, he noticed a searching, even desperate look in the little girl's eyes.

Only when he was sixty-eight years old did the vision of the Tremendous Mountain finally return to Mickey Kohl—in the same year as I begin writing this story. Just months ago, actually. Thirty-seven years had passed since the vision in Central Park, and then in the tiny Greenwich Village bar where the young singer with the wild blond hair had been shouting "I gotta whole lotta love!" That young singer was now fifty-eight.

Mickey was walking down an especially crowded part of Lexington Avenue, mid-town on a sunny April afternoon. He was occupied by thoughts about health insurance, Frances's desire to get a dog, a pending worker's comp claim at the Amsterdam Avenue deli, and an email from Elena asking advice on getting a mortgage.

Even after all those years and concerns, Mickey recognized the great vision instantly. His legs grew weak and he sat on a bench inside a bus shelter so he would not lose his balance as the vision grew to occupy his entire sight. Lexington and Thirty-Fourth, the cars, the pedestrians, the noise, the confusion—all faded in pointillist splendor until nothing could be seen but a vast green meadow with a terrifying river, and beyond the river, separate but not so very far off, the Tremendous Mountain. Again it rose great and lofty, ridge after ridge covered with snow, a cloud blowing mightily off its topmost peak.

A great mountain.

Mickey himself stood in the meadow, right next to the worn circle where the last angry horse ran a final angry lap. When he turned to the horse, it came to stare him in the eye, snorting and stamping. It was tall and threatening.

Mickey spoke to God. He said:

"Surely, it has been enough. Surely enough. I tried, really I did. But I never had the least idea how to ride this horse across the river and up the Mountain. Not the least idea. Still, I tried, didn't I? Weren't the nine years in Paris enough? The wild nights with Nicole? The twenty-nine years with Frances and Elena? When I found Elena—that very afternoon I took out my charcoal and drew the oddly sad and beautiful expression on her face. That was the one true drawing of my life. You can see it framed above the piano in the den. Go, go look!"

The horse calmed a bit. The snorting and stamping ceased. Now it stood expressionlessly, only shifting heavily back and forth on its hind legs. Mickey knew that although the drawing of the girl had deep personal meaning, he had not created any great work of art which would survive himself into the future. No fame. No significance. No change in the world's understanding. No preservation of the brief flicker of his soul like the light from a distant star. In fact, he had little doubt that his pitiful efforts at art gave insufficient meaning to justify his life.

So he shifted focus.

"And when I loved Frances deep into the night, did that not count? That trip to the Florida Keys...the long drive in the sun, with all our joy? The dance at the wedding of Elena and Nicolas?"

Surely, he could come up with more.

"Often, over the years," he argued, "I stood at the window of our apartment and reveled in the thunderstorms crossing Brooklyn, booming along the avenues."

At last it was enough. In his left hand, Mickey found that he held a rough rope halter. The magnificent animal snorted and bowed its head slightly, allowing him to reach up and place the halter over the massive head. The horse skittered a little, shook its head with anxiety. But it let him cinch the halter into place.

"Easy boy," said Mickey, and reached down into his pocket, where he knew he'd find a few sugar cubes. "Come on, come on," he said gently. Then lo, he began to lead the horse away from the worn track and across the long grass of the meadow toward the river. At the water, they looked up at the Tremendous Mountain. And then they looked down at the deep and raging current, which was probably traffic along Lexington Avenue. The horse became extremely agitated, and made as if to leap, but Mickey held it back. He said, "No, don't die, not yet." It was the first time he had been down to the very edge of the river, and he saw now, to his surprise, that the width of it was not all the same. It was not all fierce current. In some places sand banks extended part way, and he could see bits of safe rock here and there. Perhaps if one stepped very carefully. Perhaps if one were on a tall horse, and guided it with deep attention. He tried to mount the horse and failed. He tried to mount again and failed. And because it was Lexington Avenue, no one looked twice at a crazy old man climbing up and down on a bus bench, up and down, scrabbling now and then at the shelter supports.

And then at last he saw a way, by putting his foot just so on a rock, to mount the horse. And then he was alight with the rope in his hand and the horse whinnying and dancing. But he himself, with the balance of his sixty-eight years, he sat straight.

Mickey urged the horse to the water: not to leap, but to step carefully, gently across the raging river, sandbank to stone to sandbank. Only at the very last did the horse feel the need to leap the final few feet onto the impossible shore.

Both man and horse were soaking wet when they emerged. But Mickey saw that he had been wrong. He saw that here on the other side of the river, threaded between the scattered rock and gorse, scree and driftwood, there had always been a path toward the Tremendous Mountain. In fact, he saw that millions had passed that way. Maybe billions.

END